The American

A Nathan Grant Thriller

Kenneth Rosenberg

Also by Kenneth Rosenberg

Chapter One

A cold wind blew across the frozen sheet of ice that was the Baltic Sea in winter as Nathan Grant walked with hands tucked deeply into the pockets of his wool coat. To his left were the weathered wooden buildings of the Kalamaja neighborhood, home to a mix of working-class Estonians, retirees and hipsters. To his right was an empty field, with piles of concrete rubble dusted in snow. Beyond that, the frozen sea stretched to a dark and dusky horizon. Nathan was here to meet a contact, though the meeting place itself left him feeling disconcerted. He'd have preferred the typical park bench, or maybe a table in the back of a quiet cafe. Nathan was a company man, however. He did what was required, though that didn't mean he had to like it.

When he arrived at the gate to Patarei Prison, he found that it was open just a crack, as he'd been told to expect. Patarei was infamous in the Soviet days, and remained in operation from 1920 until 2002. It was now an unlikely tourist destination in the summer months, though empty and abandoned in winter. As he slipped through the opening in the solid metal gate, Nathan had to admit that his contact possessed a wicked sense of humor, under the circumstances. The man was Yuri Kuznetsov, a member of the Russian opposition. This wouldn't be the first time they'd met. In fact, Nathan was the officer who first recruited Kuznetsov, several years earlier. They'd kept a low-profile relationship ever since, with Kuznetsov occasionally providing useful information when it suited his own cause. Both sides had similar objectives, which included the destabilization of the current regime, or at least the ability to know what they were up to. Kuznetsov had his own sources inside the government, who had thus far proven reliable. Now he had something new to share, and Nathan Grant was to be the courier for that information.

When he'd entered the grounds, Nathan checked his watch. It was 2:45 on a brutally cold winter afternoon. Nathan didn't like the setup from the start. This seemed to be the only entrance, and thus the only exit. If things went south, he could end up trapped in this place. As a former Army Ranger, he'd have preferred to be carrying, but that's not how things worked in the CIA. They didn't want him shooting up the place. That could create an international incident, and yet his adversaries didn't always play by those same rules. Nathan was early, by design. He wanted to take a look around, to make sure they didn't have any uninvited company. Instead of heading directly for the meeting point in the yard, he opened a door to a large brick building and ducked into what was one of several former cell blocks. The temperature wasn't any warmer inside. Indeed, a dampness hung in the air, seeping through to his bones. Nathan made his way down a long corridor, with cells lining either side. Behind the bars, peeling paint and filthy cots were covered in dust. Peering into one cell he saw a small, rusted toilet protruding from the floor in the back. The walls were plastered with pictures of women, cut from the pages of decades-old pop-culture magazines. It all conveyed a desperately sad existence, but a man would do what he could to stave off the loneliness and despair. Right now, Nathan couldn't afford to let his mind wander. He continued forward and then up a set of stairs. On the third floor, he came upon the prison surgery, still equipped with an operating table and a rusted array of overhead lights. On a counter nearby was a set of instruments, all set to slice into their next victim. Opening a drawer, he saw a collection of rusty scalpels. Lifting one, he wrapped it in a torn piece of rag and dropped it into a pocket. You never knew when something like this might come in handy. Flashing backwards, he couldn't help but see what must have happened here, decades earlier, with prisoners strapped to this table while being cut open by doctors unfit to practice anywhere else. Nathan continued on until he came to a window overlooking the empty prison yard down below, covered in snow and ringed by tall, rusty fences topped with razor wire. A pair of benches was set into concrete along the fence, beyond which was the vast expanse of the sea. In the distance, he saw the headlights of cars and trucks moving along an ice road across the frozen Baltic. From this view, Nathan didn't like the meeting place any better. This spot was far too exposed. He could simply walk away. He'd call his boss at Langley and tell him to renegotiate the arrangements. But then, he was here now. The chance might not present itself again anytime soon, if ever. He was due to fly out that very night.

Two minutes before the meeting time, a figure appeared in the yard below. The man stopped at the edge of the square and took in the scene, peering from right to left and back. He was tall and thin, with a winter coat, scarf around his neck, and a knit cap on the top of his head. Yuri Kuznetsov. Nathan plunged his gloved hands into his pockets as Kuznetsov ducked into the wind and walked forward, turning his back to the sea and taking a seat on one of the benches, hands on his knees. From Nathan's perch up above, he scanned the area, looking for any additional signs of movement. He saw none; just this solitary man, sitting alone on a bench and waiting.

Nathan moved back along the corridor and then down the stairs once more before emerging into the yard himself. He saw Kuznetsov stiffen, straightening his back as Nathan approached. The man was nervous, and he had every reason to be. This was someone who had enemies of the worst possible kind. If the Russian authorities found out that he was talking to the CIA, he wouldn't last the week. Hell, he probably wouldn't last the day. Nathan drew close and stopped a few feet away. "Hello Yuri. You couldn't have picked a warmer spot, could you? Indoors, maybe?"

"I wanted to make a point."

"Clearly." Taking a seat beside his contact, Nathan's eyes once again moved left to right, peering into the prison windows surrounding them. Still nothing. "What have you got for us?" Nathan was eager to get this meeting over and done with. His hotel had not only a Jacuzzi, but a sauna, too. Either one sounded awfully good right now. Maybe he could get an hour in, to defrost before he headed to the airport.

"I have a favor to ask."

"A favor, huh?" Nathan was skeptical, but it wasn't his job to make any judgments. "What is it?"

"We want to arrange for a prisoner swap."

Nathan scratched at his cheek with one hand. "What prisoners? You're going to have to spell it out."

"Yes, of course." Kuznetsov was an anxious man by nature. He didn't want to linger here any more than Nathan did. From his demeanor, he seemed to expect that his request would be denied, but still he took a deep breath and pressed forward. "As you undoubtedly know, the leader of our movement is behind bars. Reports are that she is seriously ill. We are afraid that she won't survive much longer in this condition. In the meantime, your government is holding the captured Russian spy, Sergei Federov. We request a swap, Federov for Anna Petrova."

More than anything else, Nathan now felt annoyed. Angry, even. This whole meeting was a colossal waste of his time. "Why on earth would my government agree to an exchange like that? If we give up Federov, it's going to be in exchange for one of our people, not one of yours. Not even Anna Petrova. Let me tell you, Yuri, you should know better than to bring something like this to me."

"Of course, we anticipated this response."

"So what the hell are we doing here? There's a sauna back at the hotel with my name on it."

"We have additional information to throw in the pot."

"This better be good."

"Oh, it is good. Yes, sir. This is information you'd do anything to get your hands on."

"Fine, spill it."

"No, no," Yuri managed a laugh. "It's not going to work that way."

"This is all a little bit too much for me. If you have something to share, go ahead, but if not, then I'll be on my way."

"Did you ever wonder why you've lost three officers in the last two years? Was it a concern for you that two of your colleagues merely vanished in Belarus and a third was found dead in Ukraine?"

"What do you know about that?" Alarm bells rang in Nathan's head. This conversation was taking a turn he hadn't expected.

"We know who blew their cover."

Nathan turned to better take Kuznetsov's measure. What he saw was a man with a narrow face, pale skin and a thin mustache. This was a pencil pusher, a desk jockey, not a man of action, and yet his demeanor was deadly serious. He did know something, apparently, or at least he believed that he did. Whatever the information, it would need to be verified. It was entirely possible that the FSB themselves had planted it, but that was for the analysts back at Langley to sort out. "You're telling me there's a mole?"

"That's precisely what I'm saying."

"Where? In the agency?"

"I'm not at liberty to disclose anything further at this stage. Not until we have an agreement."

"You understand, I can't make that kind of decision myself. All I can do is take your request back to my boss."

"Yes, I understand."

"If your information is valid, how do we know that this person won't be tipped off? It's a dangerous game you're playing. If the mole finds out what you're up to, the FSB finds out, end of story. I hate to be the bearer of bad news, but surely you've thought of that."

"I trust you will do what you can to protect me, to keep your source, as you say, 'close to the vest.'"

"You can't expect us to make a swap like this based solely on your word, Yuri. We'll need something more."

Kuznetsov reached into his pocket and pulled out a small flash drive. He handed it to Nathan. "Like I said, close to the vest."

Nathan took the drive. "When will we meet again?"

"Arrange for the prisoner swap. We will be in contact."

"I'll pass that along."

"Of course. Good day to you, then." Kuznetsov gave a slight bow of the head and then rose and began walking across the yard, back toward the cell blocks and the front gate beyond. Nathan watched him go, fingering the flash drive in his left hand before sliding it into his own pocket. If it was true that the Russians had a highly-placed mole, that would indeed explain a great deal. One of those officers lost in Belarus was a close friend of Nathan's. They'd joined the agency at the same time, and trained together. If his identity had been up for sale, then none of them were safe. Even now, Russian intelligence might be stalking Nathan's every move. He scanned the prison windows once again, one block at a time. From the shadows on the third floor, he thought he spotted movement. Nathan's adrenaline spiked as he sprang to his feet. "Yuri!" he shouted a warning, but it was too late. A single shot rang out and Kuznetsov collapsed to the ground.

Nathan bolted forward, straight toward the cell block until he was flat up against the bricks. With bars across the open windows up above, the shooter wouldn't be able to get an angle on him here. He couldn't reach out the window, nor see directly below. Kuznetsov's crumpled body was only a short distance away but Nathan saw blood streaming across the snowy ground, the man's eyes staring blankly toward the heavens. He was already gone.

Keeping close to the exterior of the building, Nathan scooted around toward the front gate, angry at himself for ever getting trapped here in the first place. When he reached a corner, Nathan peeked around and saw the gate ahead of him, some thirty meters away. If he made a break for it, he'd be exposed. According to CIA protocol, he was here to collect information, period. His bosses at Langley would tell him to get out, however he could: to protect himself if necessary, but avoid engagement if possible. But then there was his Army Ranger training. In the services, he'd learned hand-to-hand combat, and put it to use fighting terrorists in the urban environment of Mosul. It wasn't in his nature to simply run away from a fight. Instead of making a break for it, he took the scalpel out and unwrapped the cotton cloth before stuffing the rag back into his pocket. Clutching the surgical instrument in the fingers of his right hand, Nathan slid quietly through an open door and into the prison block's interior.

After moving to the stairwell, Nathan crept down toward a basement until he was out of sight, then listened carefully. At first all he heard was the sound of the frozen wind, whipping through the empty corridors. Where was the assassin? Had he taken another set of stairs? But then came the faint sound of boots on concrete. Somebody was coming down. Nathan waited. Closer and closer came the boots until they'd reached the ground level. The noise paused, but only for a moment, and then continued as the assailant made his way toward the exit. Nathan could easily just let him go. It was what his bosses would expect, but nobody was going to murder Nathan's contact and simply get away with it. He waited until the man had passed and then Nathan burst upwards from the stairwell. A man in black clothing spun around clutching a rifle in both hands, but he didn't have time to fire it. Instead, Nathan lunged forward with the scalpel, plunging it into the man's left shoulder. Their eyes met, and Nathan saw in his adversary, first shock at this unexpected development and then fury. The man pressed forward with his gun, trying to knock Nathan off his feet, but this was a fight to the death and Nathan Grant would not go down that easily. The two men grappled with the barrel of the gun, each trying to wrench it free. With his right foot, Nathan swept out the man's left leg and they both tumbled to the cold, hard tiles, still struggling for control of the weapon.

The assailant managed to get position, rolling on top of Nathan and placing the barrel of the gun across his neck, cutting off his breath. Nathan's eyes opened wide as he stared face-to-face with the man. If he lived through this moment, the man's face would be seared into his memory forever. His adversary was young, perhaps in his late 20s, with hair cut short in the style of a military recruit. As Nathan's air was quickly depleted, he summoned all of his strength to push the gun upwards and away. He'd nearly passed out when he managed to roll sideways, knocking the man off. Nathan released the gun with his right hand and grabbed the handle of the scalpel once more, pulling it out and then stabbing again, and again. Screaming in pain, the assailant dropped the gun himself and climbed to his feet before stumbling off down the hallway.

Nathan gasped for breath, filling his lungs before he scrambled up. The man had disappeared, but Nathan lifted the rifle and followed after. When he reached the doorway, he saw the man squeezing through the front gate and out. "Let him go," he heard a voice inside his head, but he wasn't about to listen. Instead, he rushed forward and moved through the gate in pursuit. On the other side he spotted the man sliding into the passenger seat of a silver Peugeot. The door slammed shut and the vehicle raced off down the road. Nathan ran a few steps after until he spotted an electrician standing beside a power pole, his work truck idling nearby. Wasting no time, Nathan tossed the rifle inside and then jumped into the driver's seat, popped the truck into drive and took off.

Traffic was light on this cold and icy afternoon, but Nathan weaved around a few other cars before he was on the Peugeot's tail. They wouldn't expect him in this work truck, though they'd figure it out soon enough. Nathan stepped on the gas and bashed into the Peugeot's rear bumper, sending it fishtailing down the road. He saw the passenger looking back at him. The man raised a pistol and began to fire. Nathan swerved, but he needn't have bothered. With multiple stab wounds already, the man could barely aim, other than to take out his own rear window. Nathan hit them again before the car picked up speed, then braked and took a hard right turn, nearly sliding into a drainage ditch. The chase continued as the Peugeot raced toward the frozen sea.

When he'd made the turn himself, Nathan saw the ice road up ahead, leading across the great expanse of the Baltic toward a distant offshore island. The Peugeot didn't slow as it left the mainland and raced onto the ice. Nathan was going to have a hard time keeping up in this bulky truck, but it wouldn't stop him from trying. He hit a small dip where the land met the sea, bounced in the air, and very nearly lost control. After swerving around an oncoming vehicle, he flew forward after the silver car moving ahead in the distance. Berms of snow hemmed in the road on either side. Nathan saw an accident coming before it even happened. Directly ahead of the Peugeot was a slow-moving plow. Further along the road, a tanker truck was headed their way. The Peugeot driver tried to pass the plow, but as he raced headlong into oncoming traffic, the tanker bore down on him, horn blaring. Nathan let off the gas of his own vehicle as he watched it play out. At first it looked as though the Peugeot might just make it. The vehicle cleared the front of the plow, but they were moving too fast. The car drifted slightly to the left, then corrected to the right, but their speed was too great and like a slow-motion video, the driver lost control until they were spinning straight down the center lane. The tanker driver hit the brakes, sending the truck skidding sideways. Nathan was two hundred meters away when the vehicles collided. An enormous fireball rose into the dusky afternoon, followed by a concussive blast that rippled out across the ice until it hit Nathan's truck, launching him into the air. When the shock wave passed, he pulled to a stop and then climbed from the cab. Ahead, he saw the wreckage of the Peugeot wedged beneath the flaming tanker. He heard a loud cracking sound as a gaping hole opened in the ice. The driver of the plow ran past on the way to shore as the tanker truck sank into the sea, pulling the Peugeot along with it.

Nathan took the piece of cotton rag from his pocket and walked back to the work truck. Very carefully, he wiped his prints off any surface he might have touched, including the door handle, shift knob and steering wheel. Next, he wiped down the rifle before using the rag to grasp it by the barrel, swinging it with one arm and tossing the gun far off across the snow-covered ice. Then, he turned and walked toward shore, wondering how he was ever going to explain this one to his bosses.

Chapter Two

The groom wore a freshly-pressed black tuxedo, with a matching bow tie. Nathan Grant was a handsome man, sturdy and strong, with an easy smile, dark hair and a twinkle in his eyes. His bride, the beautiful Jenna Taylor, wore all white, with a form-fitting modern gown and a thin veil. The church pastor conducted the ceremony in front of a small crowd of close friends and family. Until very recently, Nathan could hardly have imagined his path taking this turn. His chosen profession was not amenable to married life, to say the least. Settling down was not in his wheelhouse. His existence consisted of red-eye flights to Moscow, undercover missions in Beirut, and months at a time living out of a suitcase. Such was a career in covert operations for the CIA. The truth was, he lived for the thrill of it all, but after nearly a decade in the field, Nathan was beginning to feel that perhaps he'd pressed his luck far enough. From the moment he'd first laid eyes on Jenna, sitting at her desk at Langley, he'd known that this was a girl who could inspire him to hang it up.

Of course, to a large degree Nathan was surprised that he'd even had a choice. After things went so horribly wrong in Tallinn the previous winter, he'd very nearly been fired. Trying to explain how his contact had ended up dead, along with two foreign agents, was the low point of what had previously been a relatively bright career. This whole episode was a disaster of epic proportions. As it stood, America's connection to the Russian opposition movement was frayed near the breaking point, their leader Anna Petrova remained in prison, and the identity of the alleged CIA mole was still a mystery. They did know at least that a mole existed. This was confirmed by the flash drive Kuznetsov had provided, complete with a list of names of CIA operatives around the world. Everyone on that list was since recalled, their careers effectively over. Nathan Grant, it turned out, was not on the list, but with the mole still active, his identity could emerge at any time. These were perilous days for the entire organization.

In the end, what motivated Nathan to give up his position and take an early retirement from the profession was not his own personal danger. It was that he didn't want to put his new bride through the trauma of knowing that every time her husband went away, he might never return. That was no way to start a life together. In some sense, Nathan wanted it all. He wanted to lead that life of danger and excitement, traveling around the globe on secret missions, and yet he also wanted to raise a family and settle down. It was impossible to have both, and so he'd had to choose. This wasn't the first time he'd faced such a decision. He still sometimes thought back to the Moldovan girl, Natalia Nicolaeva, with whom he'd taken down a notorious arms dealer on a mega yacht in the Adriatic Sea. For a brief moment he'd thought they might have a future, and even made overtures to that effect, though she'd wisely turned him down. The problem as he saw it afterwards was that they were simply too much alike; two strong personalities unused to compromise. It never would have worked. Jenna, on the other hand, complimented Nathan perfectly. She was thoughtful and compassionate, as well as whip-smart. Jenna would keep him in line, but only because he would let her, because he knew she was nearly always right. For her, Nathan would do anything, and so here he was, standing at the altar and more terrified than he'd probably ever been in his life, but also more joyful. He'd had a good run at the agency overall, but from now on the CIA would have to make do without him.

"Do you, Jenna Taylor, take this man to be your lawfully wedded husband, in sickness and in health, 'till death do you part?" said the pastor.

"I do." Jenna's face radiated beneath her veil.

"And do you, Nathan Grant, take this woman to be your lawfully wedded wife, through good times and through bad, as long as you both shall live?"

Nathan's eyes locked onto his bride's and the calmness he saw there stilled his anxious heart. Nathan Grant was turning one page on his life and starting a whole new chapter. "I do."

"With the power vested in me by the Commonwealth of Virginia and our Holy Father, I now pronounce you husband and wife. You may kiss the bride."

Nathan reached forward and lifted Jenna's veil, meeting her gaze as a married couple for the first time. They were in this together, her eyes said to him, from now until eternity. Nathan Grant leaned forward and kissed her gently on the lips.

By the time the reception began to wind down, Nathan was ready to get going. He and Jenna had done their duty, making the rounds to all of the tables, and cutting the cake to smear some on each other's faces. They'd danced the first dance together and taken a spin with their parents, and each other's. Now they had a plane to catch. Nathan checked his watch as he stood near the dance floor with two colleagues, watching Jenna kick up her heels with a young niece.

"I'll tell you what, I never saw this coming," said Astrid Burns, an operations officer with the CIA's National Clandestine Service. "I mean, you're a beautiful couple, Nathan, don't get me wrong. It's just… marriage? I know I shouldn't be saying this."

"I don't see why you had to hang it up," added Drew Spinsky, paramilitary operations officer.

"Come on, guys, cut me some slack! At some point, a man's gotta put the fun and games behind him and move on."

"Is that what you call what we do?" said Spinsky.

"Don't tell me you're not addicted to the rush. We wouldn't be part of it otherwise."

"That's what I'm worried about. I mean, seriously, going from covert ops to changing diapers?" Spinsky shook his head.

"Let's not get too far ahead of things. Come on, we only tied the knot an hour ago. But, yeah, kids eventually. Why not?" From where he stood, Nathan saw the head of their division, Walter Peacock, dancing with his own wife. "I don't think I had much of a future after Tallinn anyway. Let's face it. I was going to be stuck in Botswana for the next ten years, if I was lucky. Anyway, I've made up my mind." He held up his left hand and pointed to the ring.

"More power to you, that's all I can say." Spinsky looked back to Jenna, twirling her niece. "She is a special woman, I'll give you that. You're a lucky bastard."

"I can't argue, there."

"What are you going to do with yourself next?" asked Burns. "I can't picture you as a desk jockey."

"He's going to be a greeter at one of those big box stores," said Spinsky. "Isn't that what you're supposed to do after retirement? *Excuse me, sir, can you point me toward the ladies undergarments?*"

"Very funny."

"Maybe he'll just hang out at the library all day, reading old magazines?" said Burns.

"If you have to know, I thought I'd try turning one of my hobbies into a profession."

"Let me guess," said Spinsky. "Video games. You're going to sit around in your underwear all day and play tournaments against a bunch of Chinese kids. Good luck with that."

"You have an awfully high opinion of me, don't you Spinsky?" Nathan shook his head.

"Just callin' it like I see it."

"Furniture. Hand-crafted wooden furniture. Ever since I made my first table in my dad's old barn I thought I might try making a living from it someday. I love working with my hands. I love the smell of sawdust in the air, the feel of a freshly sanded surface. I've got my eye on a studio space in old town. I think I'm gonna give it a go."

"Master craftsman, Nathan Grant," said Burns. "Do we get a discount?"

"We'll see about that. For a start, I'm going to take a little well-deserved time off, beginning with my honeymoon."

"Aren't you worried about loose ends?" Spinsky's tone turned serious.

"You're never going to get away from a job like this without loose ends, it's the nature of the business, but you've got to live your life."

"Just keep your eyes open, is all I'll say. Anyway, six months and you'll come crawling back to us," Spinsky predicted.

"Don't be so sure of yourself."

When the song ended, Jenna pulled away from her young dance partner and came over to Nathan, taking his hands in hers and leaning in for a quick kiss. A bead of sweat ran down her temple. "What do you say we blow this joint?"

"You must be reading my mind."

"The best couples always do."

"You two are making me ill," said Astrid. "Just go already, off to your happy, perfect lives!"

"Oh, come on Astrid, your turn will come." Jenna tweaked her on the nose. They'd been roommates for the past two years, but that ended today.

"Please, no! I couldn't take being that cute."

"We'd better say goodbye to our parents," Nathan turned to his bride.

"Absolutely."

The couple made their way to a table where Jenna's mother sat with Nathan's parents, while her father was off taking his turn on the dance floor with the niece and Jenna's sister, Melody. Nathan's mom was chatting with Kristin Simpson, the girl-next-door from Nathan's childhood. The Simpson's was the nearest home to the Grant's in the West Texas hill country, but it still was more than a mile away. Now Kristin lived in the DC area where she worked as an agent with the FBI. It had seemed only proper to invite her, though the "plus one" on her invitation had apparently gone unfilled. Nathan would have preferred if she'd brought a date. It shouldn't have felt awkward, they were nothing more than friends at this point, though some history did exist between them. Having Kristin here at his wedding, and single, only accentuated their failed romance. Nathan felt a flicker of guilt, that he'd found the love of his life while Kristin Simpson was still alone, relegated to the parents' table. There was nothing much he could do about that, though. She'd have to find her own way.

"How's it going, Kristin, having a good time?"

"Absolutely, it's been wonderful catching up with your mom and dad."

"I always thought you two might end up together," said Florence Grant.

Nathan looked to his bride, who appeared as if she'd swallowed a bitter pill. Jenna tried to hide the emotion as it flashed across her face and then dissipated.

"You two make an amazing couple. Thank you for including me in this special day," Kristin went for the save, her cheeks glowing red.

"I just came over to say that we're getting ready to pack it in," Nathan said.

"Already?" Florence checked the time.

"We've got a plane to catch, don't forget."

"Oh well, I don't blame you for wanting to get the honeymoon started," said Miriam Taylor.

"So long to all of you," said Jenna. "Thanks for everything, it's been the perfect wedding."

"Our pleasure," said Bill Taylor.

"It was nice to see you, Kristin," said Nathan. "Maybe we can catch up some time when we're back in town. Jenna and I could have you over for dinner."

"That would be terrific."

"Bye mom," Nathan kissed her on the cheek and then turned to Jenna. "Give me a minute, I'll talk to the DJ." He walked over to the table and had a few quick words with the man.

"Ladies and gentlemen!" the DJ announced. "It's time for everyone to gather on the steps out front to send our newlyweds off with a fond farewell!"

When the guests had arranged themselves outside, Nathan and Jenna made their way through the gantlet, showered by birdseed as they hurried to a white Bentley with tin cans tied to the back. A chauffeur opened the rear door and the couple ducked inside. When the door swung shut, they rolled down the window to wave. "So long, everybody!" Jenna cried out.

"Have fun!" came the response.

"Enjoy your honeymoon!"

"Don't do anything we wouldn't do!"

The driver pulled the car away and the couple leaned back in their seats, huddled closely together. "Well, Mrs. Grant, what do you think?"

"I think I'm the happiest girl on earth, Mr. Grant. How about you?"

"I'm the luckiest man alive."

"You just keep saying that, if you know what's good for you."

Nathan Grant gave her a laugh.

"I wish you'd told me where we're going. It would have been a whole lot easier to pack."

"But not nearly as much fun. Anyway, you'll have a pretty good idea once we check in at the airport."

Jenna let out a long sigh. "Anywhere with you will be lovely."

Nathan spotted a mini-bar, along with a row of glasses hanging in a rack. Atop the bar, a bottle of champagne was nestled inside an ice bucket. Nathan removed the bottle and quickly unwrapped the foil before popping the cork. Jenna took down two champagne flutes and held them out. When the glasses were full, Nathan put the bottle back on ice, took one glass in hand and offered a toast. "To the rest of our lives together."

"May each day be as blissful as this one."

The couple tapped their glasses and took a drink, the bubbles tickling at their noses. Nathan's life in covert operations was officially behind him now. It was time to embrace this new life that, on some level, he'd yearned for all along.

Chapter Three

The top was down on their Aston-Martin convertible as the newlywed couple wound through the foothills of the Italian Alps. Nathan Grant was behind the wheel, pressing on the accelerator to catapult through the turns. A thin scarf was wrapped around Jenna Grant's neck, fluttering in the breeze as she tilted her head to adjust her sunglasses and take in the view. Jagged mountain peaks tumbled steeply into the pristine blue waters of Lake Como down below. Ancient villas, covered in ivy, clung to the hillsides. As they approached the outskirts of the village of Bellagio, restaurants and small hotels began to appear. Nathan slowed, engine rumbling as they moved into the center of town past ancient, narrow alleys filled with picturesque shops. Just beyond the basilica, Nathan followed the directions of the navigation and turned left onto Via Roma. The road wound down to the lake, where he pulled into a parking space on the water's edge. "You have arrived at your destination," said the navigation.

"Not bad, Mr. Grant." Jenna craned her neck to see a row of stately Italian residences behind them, with lake-view balconies straight out of Romeo and Juliet. Directly in front of the car was a small dock, where a sleek wooden speedboat was tied up and waiting. "Is the boat ours, too?"

Nathan cracked a smile but didn't answer. Instead, he opened the driver's door and climbed out, walking around the car to open her door next. "Come on, let's check this place out."

"I don't know how you can afford all of this on your government salary, but I'm not complaining."

"What government salary? I resigned, if you recall."

"Don't remind me."

"It's your government salary, now!" Nathan smirked before popping the trunk. He lifted out their bags and began to roll them across the street, looking up at the address posted above the front door. "There's supposed to be a lock box."

"Here it is." Jenna found the box attached to a metal gate. "What's the combo?"

"I think it's 4-3-2-1."

"Ha! High security." After taking out the key, the pair went through the gate and then let themselves in the front door to the building.

"Second floor, apartment number four." Nathan led them up a small staircase, struggling with both bags.

"You want me to get one of those?"

"Never!"

On the second floor, Jenna unlocked the apartment door and Nathan moved past, dragging the bags inside. Jenna stood in the hallway, waiting. "Hey! Aren't you forgetting something?"

"What?" Nathan looked back, confused, but Jenna simply gave him that look he'd become used to. It was the one that reminded him what an idiot he was being, but then a light bulb flipped on in his brain. "Oh, yeah!" He let go of the bags and hurried back. Nathan put one arm under her legs and another behind her back before lifting her off her feet. "Is this better?"

"Much."

Nathan gave her a kiss on the lips before carrying Jenna across the threshold. Once inside, he kicked the door closed behind them with a heel and continued straight through and into the bedroom. Without stopping, Nathan dropped her onto the bed and then pounced, feeling her warm body under his as he held her hands, fingers interlocked. "Finally. Alone at last."

"Don't you want to check out the view?" A bright smile lit her face.

"This is the only view for me." He kissed her again, longer this time.

"Oh, Mr. Grant..." Jenna came up for air.

"Yes, Mrs. Grant?"

"I think you're right. I suppose the view will just have to wait."

An hour later, the couple stood on their balcony with Jenna at the rail in a white bathrobe and Nathan in a pair of shorts, his arms wrapped around her from behind. He squeezed her tightly, filled with a warm sense of well-being. On the lake before them, a boat cruised past with tourists snapping photos and merrily waving from the upper deck. Jenna waved back as Nathan surveyed the scene. A mother pushed a baby stroller along a waterfront path. An older gentleman in a straw hat sat on a bench, reading a book. This was the beginning of what would hopefully be a long and peaceful life as a civilian, but old habits died hard. Here he was with the love of his life in his arms, on the first day of their honeymoon, and yet he couldn't let down his guard. Drew Spinsky was right about that. His past could catch up with him at any moment. Nathan looked over the edge of the balcony for an escape route, just in case. A narrow ledge led from the balcony to the side of the building, where a drainpipe descended to the street below. Easy, he could slide down that in five seconds, but how about Jenna? Did she have it in her? Nathan pushed these thoughts from his mind. If he continued in this way, it would sap all of the joy out of living. The spy games were over. It was time to see what a normal life felt like. "How about we take a spin on the lake?" he said.

"I knew that boat had our name on it."

Nathan leaned forward and kissed her on the neck. "Let's get some clothes on."

"Do we have to?"

"I don't suppose we do," Nathan laughed. "But it might get a little chilly out there on the water."

"All right, fine," she relented.

"I thought we'd take the boat to dinner."

"Lovely, I'll put on something nice."

When they'd dressed, Nathan found the speedboat keys on a hook by the door on the way out. He locked up the apartment and they headed downstairs and across the street to the dock. The old man was gone. There was no sign of the woman with her stroller, or anybody else along this stretch of waterfront. The wooden speedboat was long and sleek, and Nathan undid a canvas cover before the two of them climbed into the cockpit. "She's a beauty, isn't she?" he said.

"I feel like a movie star!"

Nathan inserted the key and then fired up the engine. It coughed a few times and then roared to life. "I don't think they make them like this anymore."

"Who says you get to drive?"

"Be my guest." Nathan hopped back onto the dock, untied the lines fore and aft and then climbed back aboard. "You ready? Let 'er rip!"

Jenna eased the boat away slowly until they were clear and then pushed full forward on the throttle. They took off across the water, carving a path smooth as silk through the stillness of the lake. She weaved right and then left, getting a sense for the steering as the wind blew through their hair. "Where to?"

"Anywhere you'd like."

They spent the next hour cruising, first out to the center of the lake and then back along the shore, taking in the scenery and checking out the picturesque villages, farmlands and ancient villas on sprawling estates. When the sun was low on the horizon, Nathan took over and steered them back to the center of Bellagio, and a larger dock extending from a lakeside restaurant. When he shut off the engine, a valet stood waiting to take their lines. "Buonasera!" the valet called out as he secured their craft. "Do you have a reservation with us this evening?"

"Grant party, eight O'clock."

"Wonderful, right this way." The valet took Jenna's hand and helped her out of the boat before escorting them up a winding path, across a sloping lawn, through a colorful garden, past a patio filled with outdoor tables, and on inside where a maitre d' showed them to their table. The view was spectacular, at an open window overlooking the lake, with the sun setting behind mountain peaks. Everything was perfect. Down at the dock, another speedboat pulled in and the valet hurried back to tie it up as two men in casual clothing stepped out. They wore loose, short-sleeved shirts and tan pants. One was overweight, with a brown belt holding in his gut. The other was sturdy, with central Asian features and dark, curly hair. This second man eyed the villa, from table to table, briefly taking in Nathan and Jenna. Nathan kept an eye on them as they approached the restaurant and were shown to a table in the garden a short distance below, his internal alarm bells ringing. What were they doing here? Their serious expressions didn't match the demeanor of someone on vacation. They appeared to be more like businessmen, but Nathan was trained not to make assumptions. At least from where he sat, he could keep an eye on the two of them. In the back of his mind, he couldn't quite tamp down the lingering anxiety that he carried with him any time he left U.S. borders. That meant most of the time. If Nathan was willing to give up his career for Jenna, he'd have to give up his paranoia, too. Then again, it wasn't paranoia if they were really after him.

"What's up?" Jenna wore a curious expression.

"Huh? Nothing, sorry. Head in the clouds..." He looked to the menu in front of him. "This arugula salad with prosciutto and oyster mushrooms sounds like a nice starter."

"That does sound promising."

"What do you see?"

Jenna ran a finger down her own menu. "Ooo, look at this: Ricotta and roasted tomato bruschetta with pancetta."

"Done. Anything else?"

"Ummm, I think that and the salad will make a good start. One of each to share?"

"Perfect. How about wine?"

"I think a white would be in order. Maybe a Pinot Grigio?"

"So easy." Nathan scanned the wine list and they picked one out with a little assistance from their server, who took their starter order and hurried off toward the kitchen. He reappeared moments later with a bottle, placing an ice bucket in a stand beside the table and pouring Nathan a taste. "Excellent, thank you."

The server poured glasses for each and placed the bottle in the bucket. "Would you like a few more minutes with the menu?"

"Yes, thank you," said Jenna.

"Of course." The server bowed his head and hurried off once more.

Nathan raised a glass. "To the rest of our lives. Together."

Jenna smiled and tapped her glass to his. "I'd say we're off to a pretty good start."

"Not too shabby." They each took a drink and held one hand across the table as they turned to check out the view.

"Let's hope we can keep it up."

"What does that mean? Of course we can!" Down below, Nathan saw one of the two gentlemen of concern glance up at him with a flat stare. It set his alarm bells ringing once more. He put down his glass, let go of Jenna's hand, and took the phone out of his pocket. "Let me get a photo of you with the lake in the background."

"Don't you want us both?"

"I've got enough with me in them." Nathan opened his camera app and snapped her picture holding her glass of wine with the sun setting over the lake behind them. He scooted around in his chair a bit and took another, this time being sure to get the two men below in the photo. Finally, he held his camera out the window, zooming in on the men exclusively and snapping several shots. He managed a good, facing shot of the Asian man and a profile of the other. It seemed a little silly, but he couldn't help himself. Looking around at the rest of the place, he saw some other couples and a few families. These all seemed like typical tourists. Sitting at a table a bit closer was an attractive couple about the same age as Nathan and Jenna. The man was tall and thin, wearing a white sport coat. The woman had long blond hair and wore a loose, blue summer dress. They seemed happy and relaxed. It was all just a state of mind, Nathan realized. He could be happy and relaxed as well, if he merely let himself.

Jenna seemed confused. "Do you know someone down there?"

"No, just… Nothing. Never mind. Where were we?" He put his phone away.

"Is there something you're not telling me?"

"No."

Skepticism showed on Jenna's face. "How are you feeling about things?"

"What do you mean? I'm on my honeymoon with the most beautiful girl in the world. How do you think I feel?"

"I don't know. That's why I'm asking."

"I feel fantastic. Quite honestly, I've never felt better. Why?"

"I don't know. I'm picking up something."

"What kind of something?"

Jenna shrugged, trying to put a finger on it. "That you're not all in? It is an awfully big step we've taken. Isn't it?"

"Of course I'm all in! How could you even say that? I hope you're not projecting."

"Me? No, never."

"So, where is this coming from?"

Jenna looked him in the eye as she lifted her glass of wine and took a sip. "Maybe I'm just worried that you're going to end up resenting me."

"Why on earth would I do that?" Nathan took her hands across the table.

"Isn't it obvious?"

"No, it's not obvious. Resent you? How is that even possible?"

"I know what you're giving up for me. Your job is your life. It's your identity. It's who you are. Don't you think you're going to end up blaming me, just a little bit?"

"I made this choice. It's what I wanted. No regrets."

"You're sure?"

"Jenna… before I met you, I never even realized what was missing from my life. I was just going about my business, trying to pretend that nothing was wrong, unaware of what a huge hole existed in my heart. Then I met you and it was like the clouds parted and I saw clearly what was missing all along. For years that hole was there, and you were the one to fill it. It was the first time in my life I truly understood what love is."

"You're just flattering me."

"Baby, come on, what do I have to say?"

"Tell me that the minute you're bored with this new life, you'll come back to the agency and do what you love. Tell me that you won't let me stop you from living the life you really want?"

"Is that what you think I want?"

"I know, wooden furniture. I just… I have a hard time believing it. I'm sorry. You're a man of action. Sitting around in a furniture studio all day might be great for six months, but the rest of your life? Do you really think that will make you happy? At some point, you're going to look back and feel that your life was wasted, and it's going to be all my fault."

"Jenna, I don't know how else to say it, but jetting off around the world on assignment, alone, is torture for me now. I love you. I will never, ever resent you. Not for one moment. Every other relationship I've ever been in, I've always had one foot out the door. Commitment was never my thing, I admit that. Living up to another person's expectations has always been a challenge. That's why I love you so much, don't you see? I don't have to conform to whatever it is *you* want me to be. You let me be myself. You give me my freedom, and in return you have my devotion. I'm not hitching my wagon to your train because you're forcing me to. I'm doing it because I wouldn't have it any other way."

Jenna looked at their hands, clasped on the table between them. Nathan saw one tear cascade down her cheek. He raised a hand to her chin and lifted it up. Then, he stood, leaned across the table, and kissed her on the lips.

"You've made me a very happy man, Jenna Grant."

"And me a happy woman."

Nathan sat back down and they gazed into each other's eyes, feeling the warm bliss that only a newlywed couple can know.

Jenna's main was a heaping bowl of pasta primavera while Nathan chose a veal parmigiana. When they'd finished their meal, Jenna asked for the remains of her pasta to go, and the server brought it back to the table in a little paper carton. "Would you like anything else? Coffee? Dessert?"

"Yes, and yes," Nathan replied. The two of them each had a cup of decaf coffee and shared a tiramisu. Down in the garden, the two men had gone. The other couple was just finishing their dessert. A few remaining families sprawled out at their tables, the children becoming anxious. Nathan paid their bill and they stood to go.

"This has been a perfect evening, Mr. Grant."

"I'm happy that you enjoyed it, Mrs. Grant."

"Maybe I'll use the facilities, before we get back on the boat."

"Good thinking. That's what I like about you. So practical."

"Is that what you like?" Jenna laughed.

"Among other things."

They found their way to the restrooms, and when Nathan was finished, he waited for Jenna to emerge. It was dark outside when they left the restaurant, with electric lights reflecting off the stillness of the lake. They walked down a set of stairs toward their speedboat, still tied up on the dock. The valet was nowhere in sight as Nathan pulled the keys from his pocket.

"My pasta! I left it on the table!" said Jenna.

"I'll get it." Nathan handed her the keys and turned back to the restaurant. "Just don't go anywhere without me."

"I think I can wait, as long as I'm driving."

"I know better than to argue."

"Smart man."

Nathan reentered the restaurant, where a waiter met him halfway to the door and handed him the cardboard container. "Here you are, sir, have a nice evening."

"Grazie." Nathan headed back out, a sense of contentedness settling over him. As long as he was with Jenna, everything was going to be all right. She was the first woman he'd ever known who he could really talk to, about anything at any time. She understood him, and wasn't that what everyone on earth wanted? He liked to think that he understood her, too. When he stepped back out into the Italian night, a chill breeze blew up off the lake. Down on the dock, Jenna stood beside the boat beneath an overhead lamp. He held up her pasta to show that he had it, and Jenna waved and climbed aboard. He was moving along the lit pathway when he saw her take the key and insert it into the ignition. "Wait for me!" he shouted.

"You better hurry up," she laughed and then started the engine. The blast that followed lifted Nathan off his feet and threw him backwards onto the wet lawn, a wave of heat searing his skin. So sudden was the explosion, so unexpected, that it took a long moment for his brain to process what was happening. When he began to understand, Nathan rolled onto his side and saw the speedboat engulfed in towering flames. "Jenna?!" he tried calling out. "Jenna!!!" Nathan scrambled to his feet and stumbled forward, desperately trying to reach her. When he made it to the dock, the wall of fire emitted an impenetrable veil of heat, searing his skin and clothing. Next, the fuel tank ignited, rocking him once more. Nathan fell to his knees on the shoreline as the boat began to sink, his brain struggling to process what had happened. His beautiful bride, the love of his life, was gone.

Chapter Four

From a conference room at CIA headquarters, Nathan sat back in his chair and looked out on a small garden two floors below. It was just past noon, and a group of analysts were having their lunch at a picnic table underneath a sprawling maple tree. Some of them must have known Jenna, Nathan thought. Maybe she'd even had her lunches there, beneath the same stately tree. For years he'd learned to live with death. He'd lost comrades in battle and learned to compartmentalize it, but this was different. This was as if his own life was over, and indeed he deeply wished it had been him instead. Ever since they'd started dating, he could hardly stand to be apart from her. Now he faced the cold, dark reality that he'd never, ever see her again. Never hold her in his arms, or feel the brush of her lips against his. Never smell her soft scent, or feel the warmth of her body beside him in bed late at night. In the days since it happened, he'd walked around in a fog, half dead and half alive himself. There was no doubt that he was the target. Assassins didn't plot the deaths of analysts like Jenna, no matter how good she was at her job. No, it was Nathan they were after, whoever *they* were. He was a civilian now, but that hadn't stopped them, nor did it keep the CIA from sending a private jet to collect him and bring him back to Virginia for a debriefing. As soon as he'd walked into the building, he began to sense their pity. Those who had known her looked pale when they spotted him, mumbling a few words of condolence before turning away. Nathan didn't want to be here, he didn't want to be anywhere near this place, but while he didn't technically work for them anymore, his sense of loyalty remained. He owed it to Jenna to find out who was responsible, and to his fellow officers so that they might not be next. Nathan also understood that whoever had failed the first time might come after him again, and so here he was, waiting to pass on whatever information he could and hoping to learn what the agency might already know. He didn't have to wait long before Walter Peacock came through the door, looking slightly disheveled as usual. His hair was uncombed and a pair of glasses hung low on his nose. In his hands, he held a single manila folder. Following behind him was Astrid Burns who carried a laptop computer and looked grief-stricken as her eyes met Nathan's.

"I'm so sorry, Nathan. I'm so, so sorry."

Nathan was unable to respond with more than a brief nod before looking away.

"We all feel your loss," said Peacock. "She was a wonderful person and a fantastic analyst. It's devastating for the entire CIA family."

"Thank you," Nathan managed.

"I know how hard it must be for you to be here in this moment of grief. I sincerely thank you for coming."

"Let's just try to get on with it, shall we?"

"Of course." Peacock nodded to Burns and the pair sat down at the table opposite to Nathan.

"If you need anything, some water perhaps, or time to collect your thoughts, please just let us know," said Burns.

Nathan gave her a nod.

"Ok, we'll get started. As you are aware, our interview today will be recorded." Peacock nodded toward a camera mounted in a corner near the door.

"Yes."

"Good." From his folder, Peacock pulled out a yellow legal pad and a pen, to take some notes. "The first question we have is, how did they know where to find you? Who knew where you'd planned to take your honeymoon? Did you tell anybody?"

"No. Not a soul. Even Jenna didn't know."

"I see." Peacock seemed perplexed. "Perhaps one of your electronic devices was compromised."

Nathan shook his head. "You know how careful I am. I never click on a link unless I know what it is, never open suspicious emails, update my anti-virus software weekly, scan incessantly. I used an alternate identity for the accommodation booking and the payment."

"You were still with us at that point, when you made the arrangements?"

"Yes."

"And what passport did you travel under?"

"My own."

"I see, so the plane tickets were in your real name?"

"Both Jenna and I traveled under our real names."

"Perhaps they spotted you on a manifest, then."

"Perhaps *who* spotted me?"

"We don't know that."

"It was the Russians, wasn't it?"

"We can't be sure at this stage."

"But you think so." This wasn't a question so much as a statement, though in an extended career of international assignments, it could have been any one of their adversaries. Nathan had his fair share of run-ins with not only Russian agents, but also Iranians, Chinese, North Koreans and Saudis, as well as one particularly harrowing posting in Venezuela. An assassination attempt, however, was an entirely different level of conflict. It was true that the Russian authorities often targeted their opponents for execution. The list was long and distinguished. They didn't care where they carried out their deadly deeds, either. Some took place within Russia itself, such as the murders of the opposition leader Boris Nemtsov in Red Square, or the journalist Anna Politkovskaya in front of her Moscow apartment. Other victims were dispatched abroad, like the dissident former spy Alexander Litvinenko in London, or the Chechen leader Zelimkhan Khangoshvili in Berlin. And, of course, Yuri Kuznetsov in Estonia. The difference was that these were all internal opponents. Trying to murder a CIA officer, even a retired one, was a major escalation. Once they started down that road, there was no telling where it might lead. Tit for tat extra-judicial killings could wipe out the intelligence operations on both sides. That was why an unwritten truce of sorts had always existed between the agencies when it came to their officers. The CIA had a pretty good idea which "diplomats" posted in the Russian compounds were actually spies. The same went for the FSB on the other end. They watched each other, did their best to foil each other's operations, but rarely, if ever, deployed the use of lethal force.

From his folder, Peacock took out a single photo and placed it on the desk, spinning it around so that Nathan could get a good look. "Recognize this man?" said Peacock.

The photo showed a figure climbing out of a Lamborghini convertible. He was tall and muscular, and he wore dark trousers with a light-colored sport coat. He had dark, curly hair, and although sunglasses covered his eyes, the identity of the man was unmistakable. "The last time I saw him, he was in a flaming SUV, sinking into the icy depths of the Baltic Sea."

"He's the man who killed Kuznetsov?"

"That's right. What do you know about him?"

Peacock looked to Burns. "That's Lev Volkov. He handles special assignments for the GRU. At least he used to," said Burns. "Before that he was associated with the Steiner Group. He spent time in Syria, and a stint fomenting civil unrest in Ukraine. Pretty much wherever the action was for the last ten years when it comes to Russian aggression overseas, Lev Volkov had a hand in it."

"Is that what this is all about? Revenge?" asked Nathan. "This guy would have known the score. You push your luck long enough, it has a way of catching up to you. Why do you think I got out when I did?"

"Lev Volkov happens to be the son of Vasily Volkov. Colonel Vasily Volkov. Heard of him?"

The name rang a bell. "Sure. He was involved in the Skripal case if I'm not mistaken."

"Very good." Peacock pulled out another photo from his folder. This one showed the colonel, in uniform. He was tall and narrow, with a bald head and thin face that made him look ghoulish in appearance. "We don't think he ordered that one himself, it would have come from higher up, but the colonel certainly had a hand in the planning of the operation. It was a highly provocative maneuver."

"What's the story with the son? Was he involved with Skripal?"

"Not that we know of, no, but the colonel did seem to put a lot of trust in young Lev. He sent him on quite a few of the agency's most delicate missions."

"Including Kuznetsov."

"Yes. Including Kuznetsov."

"And now this colonel is after me, to avenge the death of his boy. Only instead of me, they killed my wife." Nathan leaned back in his chair, trying to collect himself as a wave of grief washed over him. "What about the men in the photo I sent you? They parked their speedboat right next to ours. I should have kept my eyes on them. I never should have let them out of my sight."

"We did a facial search on both men. They didn't show up in our database. I'm sorry, Nathan. If they were in any way related to the intelligence services, we'd have most likely picked them up."

"You know how they work. Look at Berlin. They took a convict with a life sentence and let him loose in the Tiergarten with a wig, a gun and a target. We wouldn't have ID'd *him* either. Just because we don't have a match on these other two doesn't mean they didn't plant the bomb."

"No," Peacock agreed. "We just don't know, but it's too soon to make assumptions."

"There must have been a camera on the dock. What about the valet? Did he see anything? Have you been in contact with the local police?"

"The valet's body was recovered at the scene," said Burns. "He was in his booth on the dock when the explosion occurred, but that's not what killed him. An autopsy found an entry and exit wound to the cranium, likely a 40 caliber pistol with a silencer. No cameras on the dock."

"You had your eyes on the boat, didn't you say? During dinner?" asked Peacock.

"Most of the time, sure, but we were talking, you know, about life. I might have been distracted."

"Was there any period of time when the boat was out of your field of vision?"

"We went to the restroom, right toward the end. After dinner."

Burns and Peacock looked to each other, as though this somehow made it Nathan's fault.

"The suspects were gone by that point," Nathan explained.

"If it's the two gentlemen you're referring to, they're not suspects. Not at this stage."

"Who, then?"

"I really am sorry for your loss, Nathan," said Peacock. "We all are. She was… a beautiful, beautiful soul."

"What about the mole? Kuznetsov said there was a mole."

Peacock's entire body tensed up. "I know this is hard for you, Nathan, but we didn't call you in here today to share information with you. We called you in to find out what happened to you over there. One of our analysts was killed, and you were an eyewitness."

"My security clearance is still active."

"That's true, but you understand how these things go. Whatever we may or may not have uncovered regarding the Kuznetsov information is on a need to know basis, and as a private citizen there is no need for you to know."

"I'm not just some ordinary citizen, Walter," Nathan snapped. "I worked with you for more than eight years. This is my wife we're talking about! You could at least have the common decency to tell me what you know. Otherwise, this whole meeting is a waste of my time. I don't even know why I'm here."

"Your life is still in danger, Nathan. They are very likely to come after you again, as I'm sure you understand. They will keep coming after you until they finish the job."

"So, what do you suggest? I go live in a bunker somewhere? I lead the rest of my life in fear? What am I supposed to do? With all due respect, I wouldn't mind if they did finish me off. In fact, I think I'd prefer it."

Peacock's face glowed red. "We're trying to help you. We're trying to get to the bottom of it."

"I loved her, too, Nathan, we all did," said Burns. "We have to carry on. That's the way she'd want it, for us to honor her and remember her and continue our lives as best we can."

Nathan looked once more to the photo of Colonel Vasily Volkov, lifting it off the table. This was the man responsible. Not only that, he was behind a string of death, destruction and mayhem worldwide. If there was any real justice in the world, it was this man who would be paying with his life, but that would never happen. They would never go after a Russian colonel, no matter what he was accused of. Perhaps they'd slap some sanctions on him, or maybe freeze his American bank accounts if he had any. It would all amount to a slap on the wrist. In the meantime, Nathan Grant would be forced to endure the rest of his life, however long it lasted, without the only woman he had ever truly loved.

"We can provide you with a new identity," said Peacock. "Choose any state in the country and you can live out the rest of your days in peace. We'll give you a new ID, a social security number, a background story. Think of it as a fresh start."

Nathan took the colonel's photo in both hands and tore it in half before dropping it onto the table. "He already took my wife from me. That's more than enough. Thank you for the offer, sir, but I'm going to live and die by the name of Nathan Grant." He stood to go, turning to Burns. "Take care of yourself Astrid."

"Thank you, Nathan, you too."

"Sir," Nathan nodded to Peacock and then walked out of the room. He took the elevator to the ground floor and made his way out through the lobby, past the memorial wall. He paused to look at the stars carved in marble, each representing the life of an officer lost in the line of service. Jenna Grant would never be among them, though she certainly deserved to be. Being blown up on your honeymoon most likely didn't qualify, though to Nathan, she'd given her life for her country. And what did they offer in return? Sweep it under the rug. Forget about it. Send Nathan into hiding. No, he wasn't going to play that game. Nathan continued through the lobby and on out to his white Jeep, then he drove off the compound, passing through the front gates for what would likely be the very last time.

Chapter Five

The only place on earth that Nathan Grant could hide from the world and retreat into himself was the family ranch, deep in the heart of the Texas Hill Country. It was like returning to the womb, coming to this place where everything in his life began and all of his formative memories were made. From the moment he pulled off the highway and passed under the arching sign, Horseshoe Ranch, he felt his blood pressure falling away. He rolled down the window to take in the blended aromas of dry grass and sage. This was where he could breathe. Nathan had no idea how long he would stay, only that for now there was nowhere else he could possibly be. He followed the dirt road up and over a ridge, down through a gully, and across the facing incline until he came to the ranch house itself, along with the barn, two corrals and a large garage. Out front was his father's pickup, and beside it, his mother's dusty SUV. Nathan parked his rental car and shut off the engine. Before he'd even stepped out, his mom and dad appeared on the front porch. Racing down to meet him was Rosie, their excited black lab, whose tail whipped back and forth as her whole body shook. "Hey baby," Nathan climbed out of the car and reached down to scratch her behind the ears. "You're a sight for sore eyes." He grabbed his single duffel bag from the back seat and then walked across the gravel with the dog by his side, up the porch steps until he faced his parents, whose anxiety and sorrow showed in their eyes.

"Welcome home, son," said his father.

Nathan dropped his bag on the wooden planks and embraced his mother, squeezing her tight. Next he offered a hand to his father, but the old man wrapped him in a bear hug. "You know you're welcome to stay as long as you need," he said.

"Thank you, dad."

"There's clean sheets on your bed, and clean towels in the bathroom," said his mom.

"What's for supper?"

"What do you think?" said his dad.

"Horseshoe Ranch tenderloins on the grill?"

"Did you even have to ask?"

"Let me wash up. I haven't had a shower in ages."

"You take your time," said his mom. "Settle in."

"It's good to be home."

"We're glad to have you." She didn't need to state the obvious, to face the circumstances that had brought him back here. There'd be time enough for that later, if Nathan felt like talking. For now, he simply needed this safe space, to hide out from the numbness of it all. Not that he could ever forget, or ever want to, but he needed a place where he could put one day after another and focus his attention squarely on the here and now as much as possible.

For the next four days, Nathan joined his father and a few trusted hands, working the ranch. They mended fences and set an irrigation line. They saddled up and moved the cattle from a scrub land plateau to a lush spring valley. Nathan didn't say much, other than asking a bit about his brother Blake, a lawyer in Dallas, and his sister Shelley, married into a ranching family in the next county over. He and his siblings had always gotten along just fine, but in the past few decades they'd grown apart. In fact, Nathan had grown apart from just about everybody he'd ever been close to. It was the nature of his business. With Jenna, he'd hoped to change that, settling down to raise a family of his own. Now, he didn't know what was possible.

On his fifth day at the ranch, Nathan decided to take some time off for himself. He woke early, before dawn, and packed a lunch. In his closet, he found a matching set of camo pants and a jacket he hadn't worn since college, though somehow they still fit. From his father's gun case downstairs, he took out a Weatherby Vanguard deluxe .30-06 rifle, with a Vortex Optics Viper scope. He knew the gun well. It was with this same rifle that he bagged his first buck, some twenty years earlier. After sliding a box of cartridges into his pocket, he locked the cabinet and dropped the key back into his father's desk.

"Heading out?" he heard his dad's voice from the top of the stairs in the entryway.

"Yeah, dad, I thought I'd take some time alone."

"Sure. You need anything?"

"No, thanks. I'm good." Nathan put his lunch and two bottles of water into a knapsack, then carried the rifle out to the garage, where he strapped it to the back of an ATV. Raising the garage door, he saw the first pale glow of light on the eastern horizon. He was getting a late start, but it would have to do. As he drove the four-wheeler up the rutted road and then off into the interior of the ranch, his headlights caught the occasional jackrabbit scrambling out of the way. Nathan could have driven blindfolded, he knew the way so well. Up over the hills, he weaved across the Edwards Plateau. When he neared his destination, Nathan pulled over and shut off the engine. He was met with the serenade of birds, waking from their slumber for a new day. He unstrapped the rifle from the rack, slung it over his shoulder, and proceeded on foot for the last half mile until he came to a small clearing, with a stand of Texas Red Oak on the far side. High up in one of the trees was a flat wooden platform he'd built with his brother, all the way back in high school. In front, they'd cleared away the branches, giving them an unobstructed view. On the trunk, they'd nailed wooden slats as a ladder, and though several were now missing, enough were left for Nathan to scramble up. He was a little bit surprised to find that the platform itself was in reasonably decent shape. A few boards were missing here, too, but when Nathan banged on those that remained, they mostly held tight. It would certainly do.

When he'd un-slung his rifle, Nathan positioned himself flat on the platform. If things hadn't changed too much, he wouldn't be waiting long. From directly behind him, the sun began to rise, illuminating the meadow below. Being back here gave Nathan time to put things in perspective. He remembered that first buck, taken from just this spot, and how proud he'd been at the time. Looking back now, it almost seemed like another life, lived by another person entirely. He thought of everything that had happened in between. He'd known death and loss during his time in the army, but this one felt like a cruel joke, like the ultimate punishment for his sins. He'd been shown what heaven looked like, allowed to try it on for size, and then had it snatched away. Mercy would have been letting Nathan switch places on that boat, so that Jenna might be the one who lived. Getting through the days now was an exercise in torment, but all that he could do was wake up every morning and carry that burden. He knew that he'd keep on carrying it, every day for the rest of his life.

Sitting on the platform, Nathan opened his backpack and pulled out the box of ammunition. He took five rounds and slid them into the chamber, one by one, then set the pack aside and positioned himself prone across the boards, propped up on his elbows. After pulling back the bolt and flipping the safety switch with his thumb, he settled in to wait. It was peaceful here, just as he'd remembered. Jenna would have liked it, even if she was no fan of hunting. She'd have been too busy pulling out a guidebook, looking up the scientific names of all the flowers, and the birds. He laughed at the thought. What had ever made them think things between them would work? And yet, they had.

It didn't take too long for the first animals to appear. A doe ambled into the clearing, ears twitching left, then right as she listened for danger. Close behind her was a young fawn, skipping with youthful energy. They continued on until they came to some small tufts of grass, the mother stretching her neck down to eat. Nathan eyed them through his scope, more curious than anything. Jenna would have loved to see the fawn. He smiled at the thought, lowering his rifle as he watched her play. After a time, they moved on, disappearing into the woods on the opposite side of the meadow. Nathan took out a water bottle and quietly unscrewed the cap before taking a long drink. He rolled back and forth, twisting his body and moving his legs to keep the circulation going. It was half an hour later that he saw a twelve-point whitetail buck appear. This animal was regal in the way he strode into the meadow as if he owned the place, which in a sense, perhaps he did. Nathan silently lifted his rifle once more. He focused the scope on his prey, aiming right for the heart. His finger rested on the trigger. All he had to do was squeeze. In the back of his mind, Jenna's voice berated him. "You're not going to shoot that beautiful creature, are you?" he heard her say. "You can't be serious!"

The buck seemed to hear this phantom voice as well. In a quick movement, his head swung around until he was staring at Nathan, right down the scope. Nathan laughed lightly to himself. "No, Jenna, I'm not going to shoot him," he said out loud. In a flash, the buck bounded away across the clearing and disappeared into the brush. Nathan flipped the safety switch back on. He sat up on the platform, took a peanut butter sandwich out of his backpack and unwrapped it. As he ate his lunch for breakfast, he thought about that buck. It was just minding its own business, going about its life. It didn't deserve to die. But there were others, certain others, who did. He understood that the CIA would never take out Colonel Volkov. They wouldn't hunt down the men who'd planted the explosives, either. His government wouldn't want to start a turf war, with both countries killing off each other's intelligence officers. But Nathan didn't work for the CIA. He was no longer bound to their rules. Sure, killing was still killing, and if he was caught he'd spend the rest of his life in jail, or worse. What he understood at this moment, however, was that he could never rest until he had his vengeance. Knowing that the colonel and his minions were still out there, after what they had done, would haunt Nathan until the day that he died. The only way to expunge that pain was to kill Colonel Vasily Volkov and his assassins, whoever they were. He understood that it wouldn't bring Jenna back. He understood that she wouldn't even want him to do this, but it couldn't be helped. From this moment on, Nathan Grant had only one goal in life. He would get his revenge or die trying.

After climbing down from his perch, Nathan strapped the gun back onto the rack and started the long drive back to the ranch house. When he pulled in past the corrals, he saw his father walking out of the barn.

"No luck, today, huh son?"

"No, dad. Not today."

"That's OK, there's always tomorrow."

"Sure, you bet." Nathan parked the ATV in the garage and took the gun back into the house, carefully unloading it and returning it to the case. Then he went upstairs to his room, where he found a notepad and a pen and sat down at his desk to think. This was going to be the biggest challenge of his life, by far. Nathan had some serious planning to do.

Chapter Six

How had the Russians known that Nathan and Jenna would be at Lake Como in the first place? That was the first question. The Russians, or whoever was actually behind it, would have needed some heads up. They would have had to get there with the explosives, and the tools to attach them to the speedboat's ignition switch, all within a few hours of Nathan and Jenna's arrival. Clearly they knew in advance. They knew where Nathan would be, when he would be there, and that the speedboat was included in the package. Nathan sat in his childhood room as he pondered these questions. The only explanation he could come up with was that they'd hacked his computer, however unlikely that seemed. He used encrypted apps, with a Virtual Private Network. As he'd explained to Walter Peacock, he ran the best anti-virus software and followed best practices, never clicking on an unknown link or attachment. Still, they must have managed to get inside somehow. If Russian intelligence could hack the Pentagon and the Treasury Department, they could certainly hack Nathan Grant. From his seat at his desk he saw a brown and white pennant from his high school football team hanging on the wall. He saw a photo of himself in pads and uniform, surrounded by teammates after a hard-fought victory. There was a model plane, hanging from the ceiling on fishing line, and a bookcase filled with novels, yearbooks, and bobblehead dolls of his favorite professional baseball players. Life was simpler back then, but he didn't have time for nostalgia.

Reaching for the duffel bag near his feet, Nathan pulled out his laptop computer and set it up on the desk. It was this computer that he'd used to book the honeymoon. If they had managed to get inside, they undoubtedly still were. Knowing so might present an advantage for him at this point. Nathan opened the laptop and powered it on. As long as they wanted him dead, nowhere on earth was really safe, not even his childhood home in the depths of the Texas Hill Country. But what if he decided to take a little trip somewhere? He opened his browser and pulled up the same travel site he'd used to book his honeymoon, then ran some options through his mind. It should be a country with solid Western alliances, in case things went poorly and he needed political connections to extricate himself. That ruled out some of the Eastern European countries. He wasn't sure he could count on the governments in Hungary, for example, or Poland. Nathan didn't think he could face Italy again so soon. France might work, or Spain. But then his mind came to Portugal. It was a solid American ally, and yet inconsequential enough on the world stage that the Russians wouldn't worry so much about upsetting them with unruly behavior. Portugal was always a little bit on the wild side. They had a history of British spies and Nazis intermingling during the Second World War. It was where Ian Fleming, an intelligence operative himself, first came up with his character James Bond, prowling the casino at Estoril. Yes, Portugal was perfect. Nathan booked a flight to Lisbon and then a second-floor room at a little bed and breakfast in one of the winding narrow streets of the Alfama neighborhood. Next, he closed his laptop and took it downstairs and then out to the driveway where he placed it on the ground behind the right rear tire of his rental car. He probably could have simply wiped clean the hard drive, but Nathan knew that he would still never trust this computer again. He climbed into the car, started it up, and drove first backwards and then forwards again, smashing the laptop to smithereens. He threw the pieces into a garbage bin and went back inside where he found his mother in the living room. "Hey mom, is it all right if I use your computer?"

"Sure, Nathan. Is something wrong with yours?"

"It's acting up a little bit."

"Mine's on my desk, help yourself."

"Is there a password?"

"Rosie."

Nathan laughed. "Thanks, mom. You should probably strengthen that." He went into his parents' study and turned on his mother's computer before navigating to a different travel site and booking another hotel room, this time directly across the street from the first. The trap was now set. All he had left to do was to show up and see what he might catch.

The trip over was mostly uneventful. With two empty seats beside him, Nathan was able to stretch out and sleep a bit. Having resigned from the CIA did leave him with certain deficiencies. For one thing, he'd had to turn in all of his alias documents. The only passport currently in his possession was the authentic American one that read Nathan Grant. The only other ID he had left was his actual Virginia driver's license. That said, he wanted them to know he was coming. He'd managed to put together a supply kit, of sorts, on his own. It included a series of disguises, from a green workman's coveralls and yellow hard hat, to several lifelike rubber masks, two wigs, and a set of fake rubber fingerprints. In addition, he'd packed a pair of binoculars, a night-vision monocular scope and a DSLR camera with a 28-300mm zoom lens. He had plenty of cash in the form of euros, dollars and pounds, so that he wouldn't leave an electronic trail if he had to beat a hasty retreat. Lastly, and perhaps most important of all, stowed away in his checked bag was a Glock 17, 9mm handgun with a silencer and four 17-round magazines. Of course, it was illegal to bring such a weapon into the country, but so was shooting somebody, and he planned to do that, too. The only challenge was in not getting caught. For his purposes, he'd rather have brought a sniper rifle, but on such short notice this was the best he could do.

When he landed, Nathan went through immigration control with no problems, as a bored-looking officer gave his passport a quick stamp. He collected his duffel bag and proceeded through customs, where he walked out through the "Nothing to Declare" lane without so much as a second look. He caught a taxi into town and was dropped off near the water, walking the last of the way through the narrow, winding pedestrian alleys of the old Arab quarter. His senses were already on high alert. He was the bait, after all, and his pursuers might easily have beaten him here. They could very well be staking out his accommodations already.

Nathan found the bed and breakfast on the left side but continued past along the alley, ducking up a set of stairs on the right. From here he could see the B&B. It was a thin building, three-stories high with one room on top of another. Large windows overlooked the alley. His room, on the second floor, had the curtains drawn. Directly across the street was the hotel where he'd booked his second room. This place was a bit larger, with three rooms on each floor, side-by-side, and thin balconies extending over the walkway below. So far, everything seemed all right. He wasn't being followed, as far as he could tell. The alley was completely deserted, except for an old woman in rough peasant clothing with a mop and bucket, washing down the cobblestone walkway in front of her home. Nathan peered at the buildings up and down the block. He saw no signs of life other than laundry hanging out to dry on lines stretched across the passageway. He returned toward the bed and breakfast and moved inside where there was a small sitting area, and on the far side a counter with a bell on top. From a kitchen in the back, he smelled garlic and oil along with the associated aromas of fish and potatoes being fried on a hot stove. Nathan rang the bell and then waited until a middle-aged woman appeared, wiping her hands on a wash towel.

"Boa noite," said the woman.

"I'm checking in. Nathan Grant."

"Welcome, Mr. Grant." The woman looked him up on her computer. "Five nights?"

"That's right."

"Excellent." She printed a document and slid it onto the counter, along with a pen. "Please sign here. I just need to see your passport."

Nathan jotted down his signature and then took his passport from his pocket and put it beside the document. When she'd copied the passport, she handed it back, along with a key. "Breakfast is in the dining room from seven to ten in the morning. Do you require any assistance with your luggage, Mr. Grant?"

"No, thank you."

"My name is Maria. My husband is Jordy. If there is anything we can do to make your stay more pleasant, please don't hesitate to ask. Your room is on the second floor, number 203."

"Thank you, Maria." Nathan hoisted his bag. He felt a little bad for her, knowing that if all went according to plan, he was likely to be leaving a very big mess in the room, but there was not much to be done about that. He'd have preferred not to use his real name, but then, he was the bait. It was Nathan Grant that the Russians were apparently after, and he wanted to make it as easy for them to find him as possible.

Up in the room, he dropped his bag on the bed and then opened the curtains. From here he had a view up the winding alley to the left, toward the Castelo de São Jorge, and down to the right toward the river Tagus. Almost directly across the street, the hotel rooms were only fifteen feet away. A sniper rifle was definitely not warranted. Nathan took some extra blankets from a wardrobe and arranged them under the comforter in the shape of a sleeping body. It was highly unlikely to fool a professional for more than a split second, but maybe in the dark... Next, he took his bag into the bathroom and placed it on the counter. Unzipping it, he pulled out three life-like rubber masks. He chose one and slid it over his head, adjusted it, and then tucked the rubber edges along the bottom under his shirt. Staring back at him from the mirror was a man with gray hair and wrinkles, roughly 70 years of age. To help disguise the eyes, he put on a pair of tinted glasses. All-in-all it was a remarkable transformation, but one that Nathan had used before several times. He knew that nobody was bound to identify him as anything but an elderly pensioner. To complete the effect, he threw on a worn, loose-fitting tweed jacket with a patch on one elbow. Lastly, he affixed his false prints to the tips of his fingers. Looking himself over one more time, he was satisfied. This would do. Nathan zipped his bag back up and carried it downstairs, slipping out the door without being spotted by Maria.

Across the street, he checked in once again. This time, he used a false identity, and instead of a passport, he provided the clerk with a crisp 100 euro note. For that low price, the man was content not to ask any questions. After receiving the key, Nathan climbed the stairs, let himself into to his room and dropped his bag on the bed. From here he could practically take out his pursuers with a rock, it really was that close. In the early evening light, his sleeping dummy didn't look particularly convincing, but

Nathan wasn't about to go back to adjust it. Instead, he would settle in and wait.

Nathan took out his gun, loaded a magazine, and attached the silencer. Next, he arranged a chair just far enough from the window that he could still see the entrance to the B&B across the street, but not so close that he was likely to be spotted himself. Beside the chair he placed a small table. On the table, he put his binoculars, his night-vision scope and his camera. The last thing he needed was something to eat. This might be a while. It could be days, in fact. Or perhaps his adversaries would never come at all. There was no way of knowing, but Nathan was already starving.

Instead of ordering online, which would require an electronic record, Nathan opted to duck out of the room and do some in-person shopping. Down the alley toward the river he found a small market where he was able to pick up some bread, cheese and salami. He also picked up some containers of yogurt, granola, a six-pack of cola and two large bottles of water. Across from the market was a cafe, where he ducked in to find a row of sandwiches behind a glass counter. Nathan pointed to a Portuguese tortilla sandwich, with eggs and potatoes and sausage on a roll. He held up two fingers, "Dois," he said to an attendant, who placed two sandwiches into paper bags and then rang him up.

Back in the hotel room, Nathan took off his mask and then sat in the chair, ravenously attacking one sandwich and then the next, washing them down with a soda. When he was done, he put the rest of the groceries in a small mini-fridge. Across the street he saw a few guests coming and going from the B&B, but no signs of the two Russian thugs or anyone else who looked particularly suspicious. It was getting dark by this point, and the lights in the windows were beginning to come on. Satiated now, Nathan settled into his chair.

Thinking back about what brought him here, Nathan understood how foolhardy he was being. In fact, if Jenna could speak to him from beyond the grave, she'd tell him to go home. There was no way she would want this. Killing in her name brought no honor to her memory, and besides, he was potentially going to make a catastrophic situation even worse. If he even succeeded at this mission, it was an extra-judicial killing that his former bosses at the CIA would never approve of. He was running the risk of upending a delicate balance. But then again, the Russians had started it... Succeed or fail, if he went through with this, there was every chance that not only would Moscow redouble their efforts to kill him, but the CIA would be after him as well. All of these reasons told him that he should simply pack it up and go home. Maybe he should listen to the advice of Walter Peacock and adopt a new identity to live out the rest of his life in a small American town somewhere. The Rocky Mountains might be nice, or maybe one of the ranges in Idaho or Montana. That was beautiful country up there, no doubt. He could spend his days hunting and fishing. He could buy a ranch of his own. But then, it wouldn't be his own life. If he gave up his identity for a new one, he'd never be able to spend time at his parents' ranch, or visit his friends in Virginia, or travel abroad at all. The Mountain West was beautiful country indeed, but it would be his prison. Maybe killing whatever thugs came after him here in Lisbon wouldn't solve those problems, but Nathan was not about to be cowed. The bottom line was that he didn't care what the CIA might think, or what the risks were. He didn't care about upending international balances, or the fact that he could spend the rest of his life in a Portuguese prison. Nathan was consumed by an all-powerful, overwhelming desire for revenge. It burned white-hot inside of him. He needed vengeance, passionately, desperately. For what they had done, these people needed to pay with their lives, to die the cold, hard deaths that they deserved. For Nathan, it was an instinctual, visceral reaction. He was willing to risk everything to make it happen. In the process, he would show the Russians back in Moscow that Nathan Grant would not go quietly into the night. If they wanted to come after him, they would pay a heavy price.

When darkness settled upon the city, Nathan was still in his chair with the room lights off. Streetlamps illuminated the building across the way. The motionless lump he'd arranged in the bed looked a little more convincing in these conditions, as he'd hoped. It could pass as a human body. He lifted the night-vision scope to his eyes. The room across the way glowed a phosphorescent green. He put the scope back down and tried the binoculars. He could see just fine with these. In the room above his, he saw a middle-aged couple preparing to go out for dinner, with the husband standing at a mirror to adjust his tie and the wife walking in and out of the bathroom. Nathan yawned, jet lag catching up to him. He did the math. It was only 1:30 in the afternoon in Texas but he hadn't slept in a day and a half. Staying up all night to keep an eye on the room was going to be a challenge. He took out his phone and opened a music streaming app, listening to that for a while, then switching to news radio, and finally a podcast interview of an author he admired. All the while, the minutes bled into hours. A few times, Nathan nearly nodded off, but then jumped up in his seat. He stood to stretch his legs and made himself a cup of instant coffee with a kettle that sat on top of the mini-fridge. He had a salami sandwich and a carton of yogurt. Then he checked the time again as he settled back down in the chair. It was going on two-thirty in the morning. He could do this, he told himself, all while wondering if anybody was even coming at all. Amphetamines might have helped. Unfortunately, he didn't have any. Leaning back in the chair with his head slumped to one side, consciousness slowly drained away.

Nathan woke to bright sunlight streaming through the window of his room. He checked the time again and saw that it was nine-thirty in the morning. Rubbing the two-day stubble on his chin, he lifted the binoculars. Nothing in the room across the way had changed. The same inert lump lay bunched beneath the bed covers. In the room above he saw the husband standing in the window, talking to his wife. She put on a straw sunhat and the pair of them headed out, off to take in the sights for the day. In his own hotel, he heard a door open, and the muffled voices of a different couple chatting. Across the hall, a maid was knocking on another door. "Housekeeping!" came her voice.

Nathan took a deep breath. The whole thing might end up being an enormous waste of time and energy. He took another container of yogurt from the mini-fridge, ate it for breakfast, and drank down another instant coffee. He gave himself the luxury of a hot shower and a shave. When he was finished, he put on clean clothes. Still hungry, he decided to go back to the small cafe for a few more tortilla sandwiches. His adversaries might still be coming for him across the way, but Nathan was running this as a one-man show. He couldn't simply sit in his chair, waiting in place, for the next five days. If any time was least likely for them to attack, it was now, in full daylight, with the streets as busy as they got around here. He took his rubber mask and fitted it back over his head once again, tucking in the flaps before he put the glasses back on. It would be good to get out, to stretch his legs and take in some fresh air. If he had to wait up again tonight, he would do a better job at staying awake.

After a last look in the mirror, Nathan put on his jacket. He slid his wallet in one pocket, then unscrewed the silencer from his Glock and put them both in the other. He checked to make sure that he had his room key and then took a "Do Not Disturb" sign off the inside of the door handle. Upon emerging into the hallway, he put the sign on the outside handle and closed the door behind him. At the end of the hall was an elevator on the left side and a stairway on the right. He'd taken a few steps forward when the elevator opened and a woman in a blue dress walked out, with blond hair in a ponytail, looped over her right shoulder. She had sunglasses perched on top of her head and carried a grocery bag in one hand. Nathan slowed his stride as she passed him in the hallway. One thing Nathan had learned in his years in the field was that an old man was virtually invisible. The woman paid him no attention as she stopped at the room next to his and knocked twice on the door.

"Da?" came a male voice from inside.

"Eto ya," the woman answered in Russian. "It's me." The door opened and she disappeared inside before it quickly swung closed behind her. Nathan recognized this woman. He'd seen her once before. She and a man were having dinner on the patio at Lake Como, just before the speedboat blew up. It wasn't the two businessmen after all. He should have known not to make assumptions. Very quietly he padded back to his room, opened the door and went inside. He had set a trap, and they'd fallen right into it. Maybe it wasn't going down quite as he'd planned, but there was still time to improvise. One thing he knew was that there was no turning back.

Chapter Seven

They were right there in the room next door, two Russian operatives sent to finish the job they'd attempted in Italy. How long would it take for them to suspect that the inert figure in the bed across the street was a ploy? They might have already. Nathan had to think fast. His adrenaline spiked as he ran the options through his mind. The time to act was upon him. He could exit the building, hide out in a doorway up the block, and then stalk them when they appeared on the street themselves. Maybe he'd catch one of them in a quiet alley the next time they went out for food. But then, how did he know an opportunity would present itself? No, it was better to take care of this right away, with no delay. In a perfect world, they'd have entered his room in the B&B across the street, giving him a clear shot from here, but operations like this rarely went according to plan. It was time to improvise.

Still in his disguise, Nathan took out the gun and silencer and screwed them back together. He removed the eyeglasses and put them in his pocket before easing himself into the hallway and closing his door quietly behind him. Standing beside his neighbors' door, he held the gun in both hands and took three deep breaths in a row, psyching himself up for what he was about to do. He could knock, to draw one close and then shoot them through the door, but that would only alert the other. He could charge in, gun blazing, and hope to catch them both off guard. Further up the hall another door opened and a middle-aged gentleman stepped out from his own room. Nathan tucked the gun under his jacket and nodded to the man as he went past. "Bom dia," said Nathan.

"Bom dia." The man walked on to the opposite end of the hall before taking the stairs down. Now there was a witness, but all he'd seen was an old man loitering in the hallway. Standing here wasting time was getting Nathan nowhere. He pulled his gun back out and took another step away before pointing it at the lock. Here went nothing. Once he pulled the trigger, hesitation would be fatal. Speed was of the essence.

Nathan fired off two quick rounds, splintering the wood around the mechanism, and then kicked hard at the lock with the back of his heel. The door swung open. Inside he saw the same woman, standing behind a mounted sniper's rifle in the center of the room. She held a pastry in one hand, with a thin line of powdered sugar etched across her upper lip. In her eyes, Nathan saw a momentary flicker of disbelief before he pulled the trigger once more and she collapsed to the floor, taking out the rifle and stand as she went. Nathan rushed forward, two steps. The bathroom door to his left swung open violently, knocking him backwards against the wall. A man's hands pulled the door back and swung it again, like a battering ram. In the next instant, the man himself appeared and was on Nathan, grasping his right wrist as they fought for control of the gun.

In the heat of battle, Nathan knew this was the same man, too, from Lake Como. This couple killed Jenna, and now the man was trying to kill him, too. It was a fight to the death and they both knew that only one of them would make it out alive, but Nathan had pure, bitter fury on his side. He pressed a foot against the wall to use as leverage and then shoved the man backwards, slamming him against the bathroom door frame. For a fraction of a second, the advantage was Nathan's, but the man twisted sideways and the pair of them crashed to the floor, with the Russian on top.

Training and desperation drove Nathan as he wrestled to survive, summoning reserves of strength that only appear when one's life is on the line. He was pinned to the floor with the full weight of the Russian on top of him. The man's left hand held tight to Nathan's wrist while his right forearm was pressed across Nathan's neck and as he leaned hard into it, he cut off the airway entirely. Their faces were inches apart as Nathan's adversary gritted his teeth, the veins pulsing in his forehead. Everything in the periphery faded as all Nathan saw was this face, this Russian's face. It was perhaps the last thing he would ever see, as oxygen deprivation blurred his vision. Images from throughout his life flashed through his mind. He saw himself in high school, wrestling an opponent on the mat. The next moment, he was in Ranger training, with an instructor barking commands. He pictured Jenna, laughing at a dumb joke he'd just shared. Determination swelled within him. This was not how he was going to die. Twisting his right wrist, he forced the barrel of the gun upwards. With his finger still on the trigger, he managed to get off one shot, then another. It was enough to send the Russian sprawling to his left, letting up on Nathan's air passage as all focus shifted to the pistol. The man slammed Nathan's wrist against the ground hard, once, then twice. The Glock fell from his fingers, but before the other man could grab it, Nathan connected a blow with the underside of his hand, crushing his palm upwards into the man's chin. Instead of continuing the fight, the Russian scrambled to his feet and ran across the room to the open balcony, launching himself over the rail with his right arm and dropping out of sight.

Grabbing for the gun once again, Nathan hurried after the man. When he reached the balcony, he saw the Russian running up the alley toward the castle, holding his left bicep with his right hand. Nathan hopped over the rail and landed on the roof of a delivery truck parked below, then slid to the street and rushed forward in pursuit, following a trail of blood on the cobblestones. He rounded a corner and saw the man pressing past a group of tourists and sprinting up a narrow stone stairway. Nathan was hot on his heels. From the onlookers' perspective, he was a sprightly old man with a large gun in one hand. He moved past the tourists and on up the stairs, winding through more narrow alleys, like an ancient maze. When he neared the top, he saw the man again, looking back over his shoulder. Before Nathan could get off a shot, the man bounded around a corner. Next came a scream, and a thud, and he saw a white and yellow electric tram appear, screeching to a halt as it dragged the Russian's body underneath across the pavement.

Nathan stood where he was for a beat as a small crowd followed the driver off the tram and gathered around the body in horror. Mothers shielded the eyes of their children. Nathan unscrewed the silencer once again and put the gun back in his pocket, taking out his glasses and putting them back on before he approached the scene. The tram driver knelt down over the Russian, examined the body and then looked up to the others. "Morto," he said. "Dead." Nathan had to get a good look for himself, just to be sure. He worked his way through the spectators.

"He must have tripped," said a tourist.

"We weren't even going that fast," came a response.

"He slipped on the cobblestones," said another. "But why was he running like that?"

"I feel so bad for the poor driver."

"Forget the driver. What about the dead guy? That's one hell of a vacation."

"How do you know he was on vacation? Maybe he lives here."

"I'm a doctor," Nathan said as he leaned down over what he could clearly see now was a corpse, crushed by the weight of the tram. He could also see why the man had given up the fight back in the hotel room. His left shirt sleeve was torn and soaked in blood, and a gaping wound peeked through. Nathan quickly rifled the man's pockets. He found a wallet and a passport. "I'm afraid he's dead, all right." Nathan raised his left hand in the air to distract the crowd while dropping the wallet and passport into his jacket pocket with his right. "Somebody call the police!" He stood back up as the crowd continued to murmur their collective horror.

Walking away, Nathan continued up the hill, away from the scene and from his hotel. He wound all the way up to a castle garden overlooking the sprawling city of Lisbon. Nathan's duffel bag with clothes and extra masks was back in his room, along with a night-vision scope, camera, binoculars and the equivalent of $10,000 in cash, divided in various currencies. He could leave it all there. Nothing in the room, or the hotel in general, was tied to Nathan Grant. He could hop on a train with the clothes on his back. That would be the wisest option, though curiosity enticed him to swing back past to take a look at the very least, to see if the coast was still clear. Maybe nobody had noticed yet that the girl in room 203 had been shot in the head. If he could just duck back inside to get his things, the cash in particular would make it a whole lot easier to flee.

Taking a different route down the hill, Nathan wound his way back to the hotel. From across the street, all seemed quiet. He spotted the clerk, sitting at the front desk reading something on his phone. Upstairs in room 203, the balcony door was open, but there were no signs of anything out of the ordinary. Just as he took a step toward the front door, however, Nathan heard a scream. If he wanted his things, he'd have to move fast. When he entered the small lobby, he saw the clerk looking up toward the ceiling, wondering what the noise was about. Nathan moved past and into the stairwell, quickly hurrying up to the second floor. When he emerged into the hallway, he saw a maid, backing out of room 203 with a hand held to her mouth. The woman turned to Nathan and then pointed into the room. "Ela está morta!" she said.

Nathan moved toward her, pausing by her side. In the room, the woman's body was sprawled on the ground, with blood soaking the carpet from a mortal wound to the head. Yes indeed, she was dead. The clerk emerged from the stairs next and started down the hallway toward them. Nathan ducked into the Russian's room where he found the woman's passport sitting on a table. He quickly pocketed it. A phone was there as well, but he decided to leave that, lest they use it to track his location. He also spotted a set of luggage in one corner. Sitting on a chair was an MP-433 Yarygin pistol, a standard sidearm of the Russian armed forces. Nathan didn't have much time. He hurried back out of the room just as the clerk reached the doorway, frozen in horror as he took in the scene.

"Somebody phone the police." Nathan didn't wait for a response. He entered his own room next door, retrieved the cash from the safe and threw all of his things into his duffel. When he exited back into the hallway, the front desk clerk and cleaning woman were busy shouting at each other in Portuguese. Nathan passed them and went on down the stairs, through the lobby and out into the street, turning left toward the river. After several blocks, he reached the water's edge and then walked a further half mile until he came to a quiet stretch of docks. After looking left, then right, he was confident that nobody was watching. He saw no security cameras. Nathan took the pistol from his pocket and tossed it far out into the river. He hated to get rid of it, but ballistics tests would tie the gun directly to a murder. Two, actually, if you counted the man who'd been crushed by a tram. Unzipping the duffel, he pulled out the extra magazines and threw them after, followed by his phone. Then he moved around to the back of a dockside warehouse and squeezed behind a dumpster before removing his rubber mask. Next, he peeled away the false rubber fingerprints. Lastly, he took off the jacket. Placing the mask and the prints into the center of the jacket, he folded it up into a bundle. Climbing inside the dumpster, he buried his bundle beneath bags of waste and then hopped out. Nathan dusted himself off, picked up his duffel, and walked back along the river toward the center of town. He'd accomplished his mission. The two people directly responsible for killing his wife were now dead.

Nathan hadn't mentally prepared himself for how he might feel at this point. He'd approached this as a job that needed to be done. Now that he'd accomplished the first part, he was amped up on adrenaline, though not so much that he didn't feel some satisfaction. Of course, these two hadn't ordered the assassination. That was on the colonel, as far as Nathan knew, but he couldn't just march into Russia and kill a high-ranking military officer. Could he? It would be a suicide mission, and very likely to fail. Nathan Grant against the world. At this point, though, he wasn't going to rule it out.

Chapter Eight

An overhead television in the waiting area of Lisbon's Oriente train station showed a news anchor announcing a diplomatic breakthrough between the governments of Russia and the United States. The volume was turned down, but from the Portuguese subtitles, Nathan Grant made out that a prisoner swap was underway. Video images showed a leader of the Russian opposition, Anna Petrova, being traded for Sergei Federov, a Russian spy who'd been arrested two years earlier in Washington, DC. To Nathan, it made little sense. Of course that was the plan that Kuznetsov had lobbied for, but Nathan still didn't get it. Why would the American government give up one Russian for another? Something fishy was going on. Nathan took the two Russian passports out of his pocket and looked them over one at a time. The first was the woman, listed as Svetlana Federova. Her passport was only six months old, but it held entry stamps for Portugal, Spain, the United States, Syria and Libya. She had interesting travel habits indeed. Most interesting of all was both an entry and exit stamp from Italy, the day before and the day after Jenna's murder. The man's passport, with the name of Igor Bagrov, was issued on the same day as the woman's, with consecutive numbers. His stamps matched hers, with the addition of two extra trips to Libya. Apparently there was something of interest to them there. Looking inside the man's wallet, Nathan found nothing but a room key card and three hundred euros in cash.

Checking the time on the departure board, Nathan saw that he still had twenty minutes before his train left for Madrid. He had no particular reason for going to that city, but then he had no particular reason to go anywhere else. He wanted to put some distance between himself and these two dead Russians. Being caught with their passports wouldn't do him any good, so he walked to the nearest garbage bin and dropped them and the man's wallet inside. Next, he stepped into a kiosk in the middle of the station where he used some of Igor's cash to buy a new mobile phone and sim card.

After settling into his seat on the train, Nathan used his new phone to continue reading the latest news. Details on the prisoner transfer were scant. He sat back and thought things over as the train pulled out of the station, trying to make sense of it all. The deal, as presented to him in Estonia, was a three-way trade where the benefit to the American government was the identity of a purported mole within the intelligence services. Who, then, was the mole? If the deal actually did go through, which apparently it had, then the CIA must have this person in their custody, or at the very least know their name. There was one person Nathan knew who might be able to provide him with some information about it. He did still have his connections, after all. He checked the time and did a quick calculation to determine that it was currently 6:28 a.m. in Washington, DC. Astrid Burns ought to be just waking up. Nathan downloaded an encrypted app onto his new phone and then looked up Astrid before firing off a text.

Hey Astrid, you up? It's Nathan. Can we talk?

The train entered a long, dark tunnel, cutting off Nathan's signal, but when they emerged on the other side there was still no response. Perhaps she was sleeping in. As the train continued through the outskirts of Lisbon, the scenery slowly shifted from a dense urban environment, with bridges and tunnels covered in graffiti, to suburban sprawl, and ultimately to rolling grasslands, punctuated by groves of cork trees, their bark peeled off around the trunk. The seat to Nathan's right was vacant, but across the aisle sat a businessman in a gray suit, reading a local paper. The rest of the train car was a mix of solo travelers, youthful backpackers and retirees. Even if Astrid did call him back, he'd have to be careful about their conversation. You never knew who might be listening, electronically or otherwise. It was thirty minutes later when his phone finally rang, and Nathan picked it up.

"Astrid," he said. "What's going on?"

"Nathan? What do you mean what's going on? Where are you?"

"I'm traveling. I saw the news. I thought you might fill me in on some of the details."

"You know I can't do that. You don't work here anymore, Nathan. I could get fired, or worse."

There was something about Astrid's voice that set Nathan's alarm bells ringing. She sounded stilted and afraid. For somebody he'd grown close to, as the roommate of his former fiancee, the distance that he heard from her now struck him as peculiar.

"You know I still have my security clearance," Nathan replied. "They haven't taken that away from me."

"I understand." Astrid paused, as though she were communicating with somebody else on the side. "I'd love to tell you what I know in person. Are you anywhere near Virginia? Maybe we could have lunch?"

"I'm afraid that would be a little difficult at the moment."

"That's too bad. Where are you traveling? Stateside? I heard you might go visit your parents."

"I saw them, yes, but I've left there now. Look, Astrid, did the Russian opposition give up the name of the mole? They made the trade, but otherwise I don't see what we got out of it."

"I can't, Nathan, really. I'd love to see you, though."

"I'd love to see you, too, Astrid. Maybe another time. Take care." Nathan hung up the phone. The whole conversation had been puzzling. Astrid Burns was always easy-going and relaxed around him. He'd never once spoken to her when she sounded uncomfortable. Somebody else was there in the room, it seemed to him, maybe jotting notes on a pad, coaching her on what to say. Was it Walter Peacock? She'd been so insistent on meeting Nathan in person. For some reason, it seemed that they wanted to get their hands on him.

The train to Madrid took nearly nine hours, which gave Nathan plenty of time to think. This whole thing seemed to be betrayal on top of betrayal on top of betrayal, and his mind spun in circles of speculation as he tried to work it out. It was best to stick to what he knew to be true, or at the very least what he had strong evidence for. What were the *facts*? Number one, the Russians had come after him and in the process killed his wife. Number two, he'd managed to exact his revenge on the assassins, though the person who sent them was still at large. Number three, that person was most likely Colonel Volkov, who had direct ties to the infamous Steiner Group of mercenaries. Nathan knew from public reporting that the Steiner Group was deeply involved in operations in Libya. He also knew that the two assassins had recently traveled there.

Whatever was going on, it was much larger than Nathan Grant and his desire for revenge. At this point, he was sinking deeper by the day into something he could not entirely understand. What he did realize, however, was that he would see this through, wherever it led him. His first target had been whoever blew up the speedboat on Lake Como. Having crossed that pair off his list, he now had two more targets. First was the colonel himself. That would certainly prove tricky if the man stayed on Russian soil. In fact, for a lone operator like Nathan, it was likely to be next to impossible. Nathan's other target was the actual mole, if one did indeed exist. Perhaps the CIA knew who that person was at this point, and perhaps they didn't, but Nathan wouldn't rest until he'd uncovered that identity as well. He was drifting into an abyss from which there seemed to be no way out. The only direction he could travel, though, was forward. He would continue on until he reached whatever inevitable conclusion awaited him.

Nathan's next step was to obtain a new passport, with his photo and an alias. Now that he was no longer with the agency, he'd have to do this the illegal way. Money could buy anything, if one knew where to look. The problem was that Nathan Grant did not. His connections were more political than underworld. He knew foreign officials and well-placed individuals who might provide the American government with intelligence. As long as Nathan stayed within the Schengen zone he could manage crossing borders, but eventually he'd need to leave it. Surely there must be somebody he knew within this European bloc who could assist him. He wracked his brain until it came to him. The perfect man was just one country away, in France. From Madrid, Nathan would catch another train to Marseille. He would go pay a visit to his old friend Amal Khalil.

Chapter Nine

The Lebanese consulate was in the south of the city, just a few blocks from the beach. When the weather permitted, Amal Khalil used his lunch break to take a relaxing dip in the Mediterranean Sea. It was here at the Parc Balnéaire du Prado that Nathan Grant awaited him, seated at an outdoor table at a small brasserie across the street. While he waited, Nathan sipped an espresso and read the latest news on his phone. Anna Petrova, the opposition leader, was recovering at a hospital in Geneva. Looking frail in a photo from her hospital bed, she nonetheless vowed to continue her fight to expose corruption at the highest levels. Any return to Russia, however, was in question.

Nathan thought again about the prisoner swap. The Russians got their spy back, but it didn't seem like an even trade to give up Petrova. Of course, they could always turn around and drop some poison into her tea if she caused them too much trouble in the future. It would follow a well-worn pattern. But why was this spy, Sergei Federov, worth so much to them? Nathan might never know, but first things first. If he wanted to do anything, he needed a travel document. He spotted Amal Khalil ambling down the sidewalk in his bathing suit and flip-flops, with a towel around his neck. Nathan finished his espresso and put the phone into his pocket before leaving his table and exiting the cafe. He followed Khalil through the park and watched as the man walked out onto the sand, dropped his towel and began his daily stretches. Amal Khalil was small in stature and exceptionally skinny. He had curly dark hair and a thin mustache, and hummed to himself as he put his hands on his hips and leaned from one side to the other and back. Nathan walked up silently from behind.

"I'm glad to see you're keeping yourself in good shape."

Khalil jumped at the sound of the voice, turning to face Nathan with deep apprehension. "Oh, no," he said. "Not you people. I'm done with you! No more!"

"Don't worry, Amal, I'm not with the agency anymore."

Amal looked around in an attempt to see if anybody else was watching them. They were alone on the beach, with the nearest bathers far out of earshot. "What are you here for, then?"

"I need a favor."

Amal's eyes narrowed. "No. No favors. I'm finished doing favors."

"A passport. I'd like you to issue one for me." Nathan opened his wallet and took out two passport photos in a small plastic bag, along with a folded piece of paper. "All of the details are listed here."

Amal looked at Nathan's outstretched hand. "What, you don't understand me? Beat it! You've never caused me anything but grief."

"I know we had some difficult times, but think of it this way: you never got caught, you earned some money, and now we've cut you loose. All's well that ends well, right?"

"I'd take it all back if I could." Amal shook his head in disgust. "Leave me alone. I'm finished." The man took off his shirt, dropped it beside the towel, and then walked toward the water. Nathan watched him go and then sat down on the sand to wait. Amal eased into the sea to his waist and then dove headfirst before swimming straight out toward the horizon. When he reached a yellow buoy he rounded it and turned right, joining a string of swimmers, kicking up a parade of white water in the turquoise blue Med. Khalil would change his mind, Nathan had no doubt. He just had to be a little bit more persuasive.

Thirty minutes later, Amal Khalil emerged from the water and walked back onto the sand, smacking his head on the side of his palm to drain the water from his ears. When he made it back to his towel, he picked it up and began to dry himself. "Don't you have anything better to do?" he said.

Nathan stood and brushed the sand from his pants. "I don't want to have to force the issue, Amal, but I know things. Lots of things."

Khalil straightened his back, tilting his chin up. "You wouldn't dare."

"I'm a desperate man, Amal. I won't go into details, but there are people after me, you see. It would be quite inadvisable for me to travel on my own passport. I need a new one."

"What did you do?"

"That's not important. What's important is that you did some great work for us, but if anybody in the upper levels of the Lebanese government were to find out, it would not go well for you. I would say, there is a certain organization in your country that would be very interested to learn what you got up to."

The blood drained from Amal's face. "Do I need to remind you, your government made certain promises, to protect me."

"But I don't work for the government. Not anymore."

"Perhaps I should tell them about *you*."

"Do you really want to risk that? Come on, Amal, it's not hard. I don't want to threaten you, that was never my intention. I'd just as soon let sleeping dogs lie, as we say, but I do need your help. Just think of it as a favor, from one friend to another." Nathan held out the photos and the slip of paper.

Amal stood stock still. "What do I get in return?"

"I'll owe you one."

Khalil had the expression of a man who has just eaten something extremely distasteful, but all he could do at this point was to swallow it. He reached forward and took the note and photos from Nathan's hand.

"That's more like it. How long do you think it will take?"

"Two days. After that, I never want to see you again for as long as I live."

"Another thing. I'll need a Schengen visa, with an entry stamp."

"You ask too much."

"Only because I know you can deliver. I'll be back here, same time in two days."

"You'd better make it three to be sure."

Nathan nodded. "Fine." He turned and walked off the beach. Three days waiting in the south of France wouldn't be so bad. Perhaps he'd catch a train down to the Riviera, to wile away the hours in Nice, or maybe Saint Tropez. The problem, as he knew, was that Jenna wasn't with him. What good were three days on the French Riviera if he couldn't spend it with the woman he loved? The pain was still just as fierce as it had been that night on Lake Como, but for Nathan the only way to manage it was to move forward, doing whatever he could to make sense of the machinations he'd found himself caught up in.

In the end, Nathan didn't leave the city. For the next three days, he stayed in a small hotel beside the old port, the spiritual heart of Marseille. This was a rough and tumble town, worthy of its dark reputation, yet this central patch of real estate maintained its old-world charm. Nathan knew it well. He'd been posted in this place for two years, working under diplomatic cover out of the American consulate where he monitored the North African gangs that were ensconced here, constantly looking for new assets to recruit. That was when he'd managed to turn Amal Khalil a few years earlier. Every asset had their own reason for betraying their country, or their organization, or their criminal gang. Sometimes it was for personal reasons. Maybe they'd been overlooked for a promotion one too many times, or perhaps they despised their boss. Perhaps they were subjected to harassment of some form. Sometimes, people fed Nathan information based on their ideology, or else they just thrilled at the excitement of being recruited as a spy, having seen too many James Bond movies. Far and away the most common motivation, however, was also the basest. Most people who became assets for the CIA did it for the money. This was the case with Amal Khalil. He was a man with a family to support, who struggled to get by on a Lebanese diplomat's salary. As such, he was an easy mark. At first it was standard information that he passed, nothing particularly useful. He gave Nathan the names and the job titles of anyone working at the consulate, either officially or otherwise. Later, he set listening devices in various rooms within the building, including the consul general's private office. Pay dirt came, however, when a colleague and his wife held a birthday party for their two-year-old son. Guests included fellow diplomats as well as some members of the security staff and various friends and relatives. Amal Khalil happened to overhear a particularly useful bit of information at this party. The Hamas organization, which enjoyed a power-sharing agreement with the Lebanese government, was planning an incursion into Israel to kidnap Israeli soldiers for use as bargaining chips. Khalil passed the info along. Nathan informed his superiors. His bosses made a call to Tel Aviv, and the operation was taken out by two F-16 fighter jets armed with air-to-ground missiles. Khalil was never suspected as the leak, but just the idea that he might be uncovered caused him such terror that he never spoke a word to Nathan Grant again. Not until now, anyway. Nathan knew that there was a possibility that Khalil might betray him, but it was highly unlikely. All Nathan had to do was make Khalil's complicity public and that would be the end of him. Of course, Nathan would never stoop as low as that. Honor among spies was probably too strong a phrase for it, but they'd been on the same side. He wouldn't rat Khalil out, but it wasn't beyond him to imply as much. Sometimes a man had to do what a man had to do. In the meantime, while Nathan waited for the passport, he spent most of his time in his hotel room. When he did venture out, he made sure to wear one of the masks that he was still carrying. It wouldn't do very well to be spotted by somebody he'd known while he lived here. One person might mention it to another, and then another, and before long the CIA would know exactly where to find him. Or worse yet, the Russians might, too.

When Nathan did take a stroll in the evening, he headed along the water, past rows of boats safely tied up in their slips. Near the harbor entrance, on the south side, he climbed a hill and made his way through a park, where families gathered with their children playing on the grass. Vendors sold balloons and hot dogs and cotton candy. Nathan bought a soda and continued past the stately Palais du Pharo until he found a bench with an expansive view of the sea on one side, the port on the other, and the sprawl of Marseille beyond. It was one of his favorite spots from the years he'd spent in this city, and he was surprised to find himself missing the life. He'd given it up of his own accord, sure, but that didn't preclude him from feeling a sense of nostalgia. His years with the agency had their ups and downs, as could be said about any job, but by and large they'd been among the best in his life. He'd thrilled at the excitement of it, and the sense of purpose it gave him. Just like the army, working for the CIA came with the understanding that he was part of something larger than himself. The realization that this was all behind him at this stage struck a painful blow. Instead of being one in a vast team, he was simply one. Never in his life had he felt so isolated. Nathan sipped his soda as he watched a young couple playing with their toddler nearby. That was the life he'd thought he was headed toward. It was what he gave everything else up for. Now that Jenna was gone, he was adrift without an anchor. It was these quiet times when the grief nearly consumed him. He pictured her beside him in bed on a Sunday morning as he used one finger to gently sweep the hair from her eyes. He saw her before him on the altar, beaming behind her thin veil. And then, he flashed forward to Jenna in the speedboat, waving to him before she turned the key. That last vision was like a stab in the heart that he replayed over and over again. He was the one meant to die, not her. It should never have been this way. The guilt was a burden that he couldn't seem to lift. Nathan had no idea where his life was headed from here, or what he even wanted out of it anymore, yet the one thing that was clear was the yearning for justice that still burned within him even after Lisbon. Going back to work for the CIA was not an option. He'd burned that bridge as soon as he went rogue and dispatched two Russian operatives. Langley wanted to meet with him, that much he knew from his conversation with Astrid, but to what purpose? Nathan wasn't ready to find that out. What he needed to do was to pull on the strings and try to unravel whatever it was that had started him down this path. That meant talking to the group of people who had initiated this whole thing. He had to meet with the leaders of the Russian opposition. Ideally, he'd meet with Anna Petrova herself, though this would be a challenge. Russian intelligence would be keeping a very close eye on Ms. Petrova's hospital. The CIA would likely be watching her, too. It was the last place that Nathan Grant should ever show up, but with no other leads, it would be his most logical next stop. With some luck, he'd manage to come away with a bit of information. That was his currency, after all. Nathan needed to understand what was going on here, who was involved, and why his wife had died because of it. He took a last drink of his soda and tossed the bottle into a bin beside the bench. Those were some good years that he'd spent here working for the agency, but all of that was past. The only direction a person could go was forward, and Nathan Grant would make the most of whatever days he had left.

Chapter Ten

He'd estimated there was perhaps a twenty percent chance that Amal Khalil might turn on him, that Lebanese security services, or French police, or Russian agents would be waiting for him near the beach. It crossed his mind that Khalil might even have alerted the CIA, but in the end Nathan's original instincts proved correct. Khalil was too frightened to do anything but quietly put through the paperwork. When they met on the beach the second time, he handed over the document and turned to leave as quickly as he could.

"Hey, Amal!" Nathan called out as he held the Lebanese passport in his hand.

Khalil turned back without a word, anxiety on his face as creases spread across his forehead.

"Thank you."

"Don't ever come back. I never want to see you again."

"Understood." Nathan flipped open the cover to see his own picture staring back, along with the name Elias Mansour. An entry stamp showed that he'd arrived in France one day before on a 90-day tourist visa. A Lebanese passport didn't come with the same travel privileges as an American, or European, but beggars couldn't be choosers. Nathan had an official travel document and nobody, not the Russians or the Americans or anybody else, would be looking for Elias Mansour.

From the beach, Nathan went straight to the St. Charles train station and bought a ticket to Geneva, keeping a close eye out for any old acquaintances. Seeing none, he boarded just after 1:00 in the afternoon. He'd be in Geneva by that evening. What he might uncover there, he had no idea, but the only way to find out was to start digging.

Anna Petrova was being treated at the Hopitaux Universitaires in the center of the city. Nathan knew that she would be very closely monitored and protected by both local police and hospital security guards, and probably a few federal officers thrown in the mix. Indeed, when he arrived at the hospital, two cruisers from the Cantonal Police of Geneva were parked out front. There was no way he'd ever get in to speak to her. Of course, this was not unexpected. She may have been released from Russian custody, but that didn't mean she wasn't still a target. Most likely, there was a Russian operative or two poking around to keep an eye on the situation. At the very least, they'd want to know what she was planning and whether they should expect her back in Russia any time soon. To these ends, they might have already recruited an asset inside the hospital. Perhaps there was a member of the staff, willing to report back for a bit of extra money. Nathan would have to follow his own plan. After working this beat for the past few years, he knew all of the players in the opposition movement, at least by their photos. A few of them would recognize him as well. Yuri Kuznetsov wasn't the first contact he'd met with personally. After what had happened to Kuznetsov, though, garnering the cooperation of any others was going to be a hard sell. It was still his best shot at prying out a bit of information.

Disguised once again as yet another older gentleman, Nathan entered the hospital lobby. Directly ahead was a check-in desk. Behind the desk sat a hospital staffer, and beside her stood a uniformed officer of the cantonal police. To the right was a waiting area, with upholstered chairs and small tables strewn with magazines. Beside that was a children's play area, where a mother was helping her young daughter put wooden blocks through matching holes. Closer to the door was an automatic coffee machine and a few other vending machines selling sandwiches and snacks. Nathan looked over the drink options, plugged in two euros, and pushed the button for a cafe creme. The machine whirred and hissed. Steam shot out of a metal tube above a paper cup, followed by hot milk and then dark coffee. When it was ready, Nathan lifted the cup and carried it to a seat in the waiting area, where he made himself comfortable and placed his coffee on a table before lifting one of the magazines. From here, he could see everybody, coming and going. No doubt, Anna Petrova would have visitors. As long as Nathan could recognize them, it would be game on. One thing he'd learned during his years of surveillance missions, however, was that it might take some time. You had to be patient. In the meantime, he'd read the room.

For the next few hours Nathan watched as patients and visitors came and went, checking in at the desk and then moving on to a block of elevators. Occasionally, a family member would join him in the sitting area to wait while their loved one was brought down. Over time, Nathan developed two concerns. The first was that he was getting hungry. It was possible to drink from a cup with his rubber mask on and not garner any suspicious looks, as long as he sipped lightly. Eating something was another matter entirely. It simply couldn't be done without giving himself away. If he wanted to feed himself, he'd have to do it in private. Nathan's second concern was that the police officer near the check-in desk had started to notice him. The man repeatedly glanced in Nathan's direction, with his head tilted slightly sideways and a quizzical expression on his face. At any moment, he was going to walk over to talk to Nathan, and at that point, the jig would be up. His mask might fool a casual observer from some distance, but up close in conversation, the officer would see right through it. This was not going to work. When he saw the officer say a few words into his radio, Nathan put the magazine he was reading down on the table, stood, and slowly walked toward the front door, hobbling a bit in his best approximation of an elderly gait.

"Excusez-moi, monsieur!" the police officer called out.

Nathan continued out the door just as an ambulance pulled up, lights flashing.

"Monsieur!" the officer repeated, but Nathan kept moving. The ambulance doors swung open and two paramedics jumped out. They quickly unloaded a patient on a gurney, wheeling him inside. Amid the commotion, Nathan made an easy getaway, ambling casually down the sidewalk. He passed the glass side of a bus stop shelter and in the reflection he saw the officer walk out the door and peer after him briefly before the man's attention turned back to the drama at hand.

When Nathan had gone a few more blocks, he entered a parking garage. Surveillance cameras covered every angle, but when he moved into a bathroom, he found there were none. If anybody was watching, they might notice that an old man had walked in, yet a younger man walked out. What were the chances that somebody was actually paying that close attention? Under normal circumstances, it would likely not be a problem, but these were not normal circumstances. The hospital happened to be treating a political figure that the Russian government would be more than happy to dispose of at any opportunity. After availing himself of the facilities, Nathan washed his hands and exited the restroom, still in his mask.

Leaving the garage, Nathan continued further down the sidewalk, his stomach grumbling. He kept his eye out for a better opportunity to ditch the disguise. Clearly, he couldn't use this mask again. That one officer in particular would have an eye out for him. Several blocks away, he found a small bistro with outdoor tables along a broad sidewalk. Continuing past, he turned into a quiet alley. Nathan crouched beside a dumpster, pulled off the mask and then tossed it into the garbage. His face was wet with perspiration and he took off his jacket and used it to dry himself with the inner lining. He donned the jacket once more, walked out of the alley, and found a seat in the cafe. So far, his surveillance had not gone as he'd hoped, but then these things rarely did. One might have the clearest of intentions, but other people didn't often behave as expected. He'd spotted nobody that he recognized from his experience with the opposition movement. He'd heard nobody speaking Russian, or with a Russian accent. If Anna Petrova was receiving visitors, they didn't seem to be straying from her side.

A waiter approached the table to drop off a menu and Nathan perused the options, eventually settling on a classic hamburger with melted Gruyère cheese on an artisan French roll, side salad, frites, and a glass of Stella Artois. The cafe was only lightly occupied with the lunch rush having already come and gone. A retired couple sat at one table, and nearby was a mother and her teenage daughter having an afternoon dessert. When Nathan's lunch arrived, he devoured it, perhaps a bit too quickly, and then ordered a second glass of beer. He needed a new plan. Hanging out all day in the waiting area at the hospital entrance was not going to work. Posing as a journalist to request an interview with Petrova crossed his mind, but her team would do their homework. Unless he had an extensive body of work matching his name, they'd never grant him an audience. If he used the name of an existing reporter, they might find the real person's photo online. He might try to don a janitor's uniform and make his way into her room, but clearly she was being too closely guarded for that. Even if he did somehow get to her bedside, what would she tell him? Most likely, she'd never trust him at all.

Nathan was feeling discouraged as he finished off the last of his fries, but then just like that, his luck turned. Coming toward the cafe was a familiar face. He'd met Paulina Sokolova during a brief assignment to Ukraine some years prior. Sokolova was a Russian ex-pat who had fled the country after her punk rock band briefly became the government's enemy number one. After one particularly heated musical protest, she and her bandmates were arrested and thrown into prison. Her boyfriend was poisoned and barely survived. When she was released after three years behind bars, the pair of them fled the country and settled in Stockholm where they continued their outspoken criticism of the regime. Nathan had met them both at a meeting of activists in Kyiv, where they mapped out a strategy and the U.S. government sent a few representatives as a show of support. He'd always been an admirer of Sokolova's, and they'd hit it off well, though now he quickly grabbed a menu from an adjoining table and held it in front of his face.

Sokolova walked past Nathan's table and entered the cafe, where she went to the bar to pick up a takeaway order. Nathan studied her with one eye from around the side of his menu. She hadn't changed so much from the girl he remembered. Paulina still had that punk-rock aura about her. She wore torn jeans with black leather boots laced up the front. Her shirt was a loose gray tank top that showed off the tattoos on both arms. She was tall and thin with dark hair, long at the back but shaved on the sides. There was an undeniable charisma about her. This was the kind of girl that people watched, and paid attention to. She might have had a successful career in acting, or in music, but instead it was activism that caught her interest. She supported the opposition movement from afar, by giving interviews and writing articles and organizing. Nathan had found himself feeling for her when they'd met, in that she loved her country so much but was legitimately fearful of returning.

When Sokolova picked up her order and walked back out of the cafe, Nathan waited until she'd gone around the corner before he put his menu down and quickly fished forty euros out of his wallet. He dropped the bills on the table and stood to go, lifting his glass to swallow the last of his beer before hurrying after. Rounding the corner himself, he saw her a block ahead, weaving through pedestrians on the sidewalk with her brown paper lunch bag in hand. She wasn't going to the hospital. In fact, she was walking in the opposite direction. A few times she looked over her shoulder, but Nathan was far enough back that she didn't pick him out of the crowd as they moved along. It was a little trickier after she left the main road, but he managed to tail her through a residential neighborhood until she entered a narrow, three-story apartment building. After she'd gone in, Nathan approached the front door. A series of six doorbells listed the names of the residents, two apartments for each floor. None of the names were Russian. Nathan crossed the street and looked up. On the third floor, he saw Paulina open a set of blinds in the apartment on the right and then walk out onto a small balcony, food order still in hand. Nathan moved back across into the building's doorway and then peered up and down the street. If the Russians were monitoring her, they were being careful about it. As for his own approach, Nathan decided that sometimes it was best to simply be direct. He looked at the two top buttons on the panel and pressed the one on the right, waited ten seconds and then pressed it again.

"Oui?" The voice was male, speaking French with a strong Russian accent. "Qu'est-ce?"

"I'd like to speak with Paulina Sokolova."

There was a long pause before the man replied, this time in English. "Who are you?"

"It's an old American friend. We met in Kyiv a few years ago."

"Which American friend?"

"I'd rather not say. You never know who might be listening."

"What do you want?"

"I'd just like to talk, that's all. Please, it's important."

Again there was a long pause before Paulina's voice came on. "Who is this?"

"Hi Paulina, we met in Kyiv some years ago. I was the American representative. Perhaps you remember my voice? I'd like to ask you some questions, that's all."

"Ah yes, the American. I remember you. Come on up, third floor." Nathan heard the buzz of an electric lock. He pushed open the front door and moved through a small foyer to a stairwell in the back. Up he went, around and around, until he emerged on the third floor, where Paulina stood waiting in an open doorway. "Nathan… right? What was your last name?"

"Grant," he admitted.

"Yes, of course. Nathan Grant." Paulina held up an electronic bug detector. "Nobody is listening. We sweep the entire apartment twice per day."

"That's very proactive of you."

"We do what we can. What do you want?"

"Can I come in?"

Paulina was skeptical, but curiosity got the best of her and she moved aside to let him pass. When Nathan entered the apartment, he was struck by how antiquated the place felt. The furniture was old and outdated. Lace doilies decorated the shelves on a glass case filled with ceramic figurines of birds and angels. The cabinets and light fixtures hadn't been updated since the 1970s. Luggage was piled along one wall. At a kitchen table, a pale, thin man in his 20s sat in front of a laptop computer. Strewn across the table were bags of chips, an empty pizza box and several plastic bottles of soda.

"This is Ivan," said Paulina. "He's our technical specialist."

"Nice to meet you," said Nathan.

Ivan looked him over without a word, took a drink from his soda, and turned back to his computer screen.

"The style of this place isn't what I'd expect from you," Nathan said to Paulina.

"It's not like I'm actually living here." Paulina opened the refrigerator. "We've got a few beers if you'd like one."

"I don't know if I should. I just had two with lunch."

"Come on, live a little." She pulled out two cans of beer, handing one to Nathan. "I hope you don't mind if I eat while we talk. How the hell did you find us anyway?"

"Lucky break. We seem to like the same cafe."

Paulina opened a drawer and pulled out a knife and fork before cocking her head to one side. "It's nicer on the balcony."

Nathan followed her out, where they each sat on opposite sides of a small table. Paulina put her beer down and then opened her takeaway bag, pulling out a chicken Cesar salad in a cardboard container with a clear plastic lid. "So much packaging."

"At least the salad looks good."

After taking the lid off her container, Paulina cracked her beer open and took a drink. "What are you doing in Geneva, Nathan, or need I ask?"

"Just looking for some information."

"You're not trying to recruit me again, are you? Because if that's the case, I think I made myself clear the last time." Pauline dug into her salad.

"No, no, it's nothing like that. In fact, I'm not working for them anymore."

"What do you mean?" Pauline's eyes narrowed with suspicion. "Who are you working for?"

"Nobody. I'm retired."

"So, what then, you're here on a holiday? Is that it?"

"Not exactly."

"You're married now. That's new."

Nathan followed her gaze and realized that he was twirling his wedding band with the thumb and forefinger on his right hand. It was becoming an unconscious habit. He hadn't taken the band off since his wedding day and didn't think that he ever would. Somehow, feeling that smooth, round band brought him a small measure of peace. "I did get married, yes. How about you? What's the latest with..." Nathan couldn't quite remember the man's name.

"Yevgeny," she reminded him. "Unfortunately, that didn't turn out so well. Two years together in Stockholm and he ran off with a buxom blond Swede."

"I'm sorry."

Pauline waved a hand in the air as she ate, then took another drink of beer. "I'm over it. Of course, I didn't feel that way at the time, but he wasn't committed enough to the cause. That's what really drove us apart."

"Maybe you should have gone a little bit easier on him."

"What are you, now, my therapist?"

"All I'm saying is that I can see things from both sides."

"I'm a little too intense? Is that it?"

Nathan laughed. "For Yevgeny, apparently yes."

"And what about your wife? I'll bet she's completely supportive, huh?"

"I quit for her. She was the reason I hung it up. I didn't want her to feel that pressure, never knowing if I'd make it home."

"How noble. And how does she feel about that?"

"Unfortunately, she's dead."

Paulina froze momentarily and then slowly lowered her fork to her plate. "I'm sorry."

"Which brings me to the point of why I'm here. It was the GRU who killed her."

Paulina leaned back in her seat as she took it all in. "Poison?"

"No, not poison. They used a bomb."

"That's not like them. Are you sure?"

"I'm sure. Apparently they were trying to make a point."

"I think we need something a little bit stronger than beer." Paulina rose from her seat and went back into the apartment. Through the window, Nathan could see her open a cabinet and pull out two glasses, followed by a clear glass bottle. She came back out and placed one glass at each setting, then unscrewed what could only be a bottle of vodka and poured them each a healthy serving.

"What on earth are you doing in this old woman's apartment anyway?"

"It was the best place we could find on short notice. We're here supporting Anna, of course, and she'll need somewhere to live while she continues her recovery."

"What's her condition?"

"Na zdorov'ye!" Paulina lifted her vodka.

"Cheers." Nathan tapped his glass to hers, then threw it back. Paulina quickly refilled them. "You're going to be the death of me," said Nathan.

"There are worse ways to go."

"No doubt."

"I'm sorry about..."

"Forget it. What about Anna? How is she?"

"She'll survive." Paulina took a deep breath. "It was mostly malnutrition. She was on a hunger strike at the end, you know."

"I wasn't aware of that."

"The hospital plans to release her in another few days. They're just running a few more tests, and getting her strength up."

"I'm glad to hear it."

"She is the one you really want to speak with, yes?"

"I want to speak with anybody who can help me understand what's going on."

Paulina looked to her vodka glass and spun it backwards and forwards on the table. "I don't think I am in a position to make such a determination. I will speak to Anna."

"I'd rather you didn't."

Paulina's eyes shot up, meeting Nathan's. "You distrust her?"

"The problem is not with Anna, it's with the hospital and who might be listening in there. The GRU is already trying to kill me. If they find out I'm here in Geneva..."

"She'll be here in the apartment in a few days."

"I would prefer not to wait."

"What do you want from me, Nathan?"

"I just want to understand. Why was the Russian government so eager to trade Anna for this agent, Sergei Federov? Why is he so important to them? I want to know why Yuri Kuznetsov met with me in Tallinn. How did he know we had a mole, and who was this person? Was the identity revealed as part of the exchange?"

"That was you with Kuznetsov?"

"Yes. That was me."

Paulina looked away. "What the hell happened there?"

"He told me there was a mole inside the agency. And then they shot him."

"Why not you, too?"

"I don't know, Paulina. I guess I wasn't a priority at that point. Is there anything you can tell me? Anything at all?"

"Maybe you should ask your former bosses that question."

Nathan's frustration was building. This was so far getting him nowhere. "I'm afraid they wouldn't approve of my current methods."

"What methods are those?"

"Paulina, look… They killed my wife, in front of my very own eyes. I want to know what's going on. Do you know who the mole is? Can you tell me that much?"

Paulina drank down another slug of vodka, this time on her own. "No, I don't know. Ivan might."

Nathan peered through the window at the man behind the computer, still staring intently at his screen as he tapped away at the keyboard. "Can we ask him?"

"Let me talk to him first."

"Thank you, Paulina."

"Don't thank me yet." Paulina rose from her chair and moved inside. From his position on the balcony, Nathan could see them in a heated discussion. Ivan looked from Paulina, through the glass to Nathan, and back. He waved a hand in the air and shook his head. Nathan could hear them arguing in Russian, but couldn't understand. This didn't seem to be going well. Finally, Ivan fell silent. Paulina waited a moment longer, said a few last words, and then came back to the balcony. "He's agreed."

"Agreed to what?"

"He has a photo of the mole, meeting with a GRU handler last year. It's the same photo we provided to your bosses as part of the exchange."

"Did the Russians know this was part of the deal?"

"No. They never would have gone along with it."

"They thought the U.S. government was willing to give up Federov for Petrova, just like that?"

"I don't know what they thought. Do you want to see the photo or not?"

"Yes, of course."

Nathan followed Paulina back inside. Ivan spun his laptop around. "This is your mole." There on the screen was a photo of Colonel Vasily Volkov at an outdoor cafe. Beside him was a young woman, leaning close in conversation. Nathan's knees went weak. The entire room seemed to close in on him as he reached for a chair to steady himself. "No. No, no, no. It can't be." He looked to Paulina, pleadingly.

"You know her?"

Nathan turned back to the computer, as if to make sure that his eyes had not deceived him. The girl in the photo was his wife.

Chapter Eleven

"I don't believe it. Where did you get this?" Nathan leaned closer to the image, looking for signs that it might have been photo-shopped. It simply wasn't possible that this was real.

"You expect us to give up our sources?" Ivan replied.

Nathan grabbed him by the shirt with both hands and pulled him close. "Where the *fuck* did you get that photograph?!"

"Easy, Nathan, easy," Paulina leaned in to separate them, pushing the two men apart. "We're only trying to help you."

"Help me? You're telling me that my wife worked for Russian intelligence! My wife was not a spy, not for Russia or anybody else. Jenna was an analyst. She wrote reports."

"Apparently, she was thorough with her research," said Ivan.

Nathan made fists with both of his hands. Anger surged through him. He wanted to punch this Ivan character in the face, to slam him against the wall. The man was so smug and condescending. Beating him to a pulp might make Nathan feel better in the short term, but in the long term it would provide him with no answers, and so he pushed that anger down inside himself and fought to contain it. He unclenched his fists and took a few deep breaths, trying to calm himself. "This was the information you traded for the release of Anna Petrova?"

Paulina and Ivan looked at each other. "Yes," said Paulina. "This was the information."

"Nobody on the American side questioned it? You gave them one photo? That was all? And the Americans gave up this Russian spy, Sergei Federov, for that?"

"We had more than one photo." Ivan proceeded to scroll through several more. A wider angle showed a sign in the background. The place appeared to be a pub called the Red Wagon, written in English.

"Where was this? When?!" Nathan demanded.

Ivan abruptly closed the lid of his laptop. "We have told you enough."

"You've told me lies. Fictions!"

"You saw for yourself, she was meeting with Volkov."

"I'm sorry, Nathan," said Paulina. "I really am."

Nathan stood straight and tall, still flushing with fury. He wasn't sure what to do next. He didn't know whether to plead for more information, or simply throw Ivan's laptop out the window.

"I probably shouldn't tell you this but..." Paulina seemed to pity him. "There is a journalist you might speak with. Perhaps you've heard of her. Irina Baranova lives in St. Petersburg."

"Baranova," Nathan repeated the last name. "Is that where the photo came from?"

"Honestly, Nathan, I don't know. They don't share that much with me. I know that she's been working on some things, that's all. Maybe you can persuade her to give you something, though you know what the state would do if they find out you've contacted her."

Of course, Nathan knew that only too well, but he needed answers and he would follow these threads wherever they led him. "Thank you for seeing me." He walked out the door and raced down the stairway and into the street. He needed to walk, to think, to clear his mind. What *was* Jenna doing in those photos? It made no sense at all. He let his feet guide him, walking with his head down, trying to get away from the entire world, but still he couldn't escape from himself. When he reached the edge of the lake, he turned right and continued on, past the giant water fountain, and marinas filled with boats, and a small beach where parents played with their children. Nathan tried not to look. The sight of happy young families was an unendurable pain. He dropped his head once more and kept moving.

After an hour, he'd left the city behind. Nathan stopped in a small park and stood beside the water. He wanted to scream, to pound his chest. He wanted to face Colonel Vasily Volkov and strangle the life out of the man with his bare hands. Nathan collapsed onto a bench and held his head in his hands. How had everything gone so horribly wrong? His future had shown such promise just a few weeks earlier, and now he was left to wonder if he'd ever really known the real Jenna Taylor at all. Nathan no longer knew who to trust, or what to believe. She was the one person on earth who would never deceive him under any circumstances, and yet there she was with Volkov. Why? He pulled out his phone and typed "Red Wagon Pub" into the search bar. The result came back with a listing by that name in Dublin, Ireland. He clicked on the photos and saw an outdoor patio in front. There were the same tables that Jenna and Volkov sat at, and the same sign in the background. As far as Nathan knew, Jenna hadn't been to Dublin since the summer after her college graduation, when she'd gone on a European trip with friends. But there she was in the photos, sitting in a Temple Bar pub with a high-ranking officer in Russian military intelligence. He struggled to come up with an explanation. It was certainly possible that the photos were faked. Jenna was not a foreign operative. If the agency had sent anyone to meet with Volkov undercover, it would have been somebody else. She simply wasn't trained for this kind of mission. But what if it was true? What if Jenna was the mole all along? Nathan wasn't ready to accept that she would betray her country. The bottom line was that he simply didn't have any answers. What had started as a quest for vengeance was now a search for the truth. He lifted his phone once again and did a quick search. A ferry was leaving for St. Petersburg from Helsinki the following afternoon. As a ferry passenger, he could visit the city visa-free for seventy-two hours. He quickly made the arrangements and then booked a flight to Finland. It would give him three days to track down the journalist Irina Baranova and ask her some difficult questions.

Two days later, Nathan's ferry cruised along the docklands of St. Petersburg's inner harbor, past oil refineries and storage yards and giant cranes loading multi-colored containers onto cargo ships. When the ferry tied up at the pier, Nathan joined a crowd of passengers moving through the ship and across the gangway until they entered long lines for immigration control. He was used to traveling incognito under false passports, and his paperwork was in order, though he couldn't say for sure if this Lebanese passport he was carrying would pass muster. Using his real one was not an option. The name Nathan Grant would set off an instant alarm amongst the intelligence services. They knew who he was, and wouldn't take kindly to an unannounced visit. He'd end up first in an immigration cell and then in an unmarked grave. Instead, when he reached the front of the line, Nathan slid across his documents with the name Elias Mansour. It was time to find out how much his trust in Amal Khalil was warranted. Nathan smiled at the immigration officer and did his best to give off the appearance of an eager tourist. The officer was not much more than a boy, maybe twenty years old and wearing a loose blue uniform with a matching cap. He looked at Nathan's papers; a form from the ferry company with proof of a return ticket and another slip with the name of his hotel. Next the officer flipped through the passport, checking Nathan's name and photo before saying a few words in Russian.

"I'm sorry, do you speak English?" Nathan smiled.

Frustration clouded the man's face. "Military?" he said.

"Me? No. Not military. Tourist."

The man held the power over Nathan's life or death in his hands, and while Nathan continued to exude confidence, the officer glowered for another few seconds before he stamped the passport. He slid the papers through a Plexiglas slot without another word.

"Thank you." Nathan continued past the booth, trying to maintain his calm demeanor. He carried his duffel over one shoulder. Inside were a few sets of clothes, toiletries, and nothing more. He knew better than to try smuggling in any guns, or night vision scopes, or even disguises. One tap on the shoulder from customs officials would have meant the end of him. Instead, he walked through the Nothing to Declare line and out. Murphy's Law, he told himself. If he'd had a gun, they probably would have checked him. His apprehension would have given him away. Instead, unarmed and unprepared, he walked out of the terminal and climbed onto a shuttle bus for the center of town. When he reached his stop, he got off and walked the last few blocks.

Nathan's hotel faced the dimly-lit interior courtyard of an ancient residential building off the Moika Canal, not far from the famous Hermitage Museum. If he had been a tourist, this would certainly be an ideal location. He checked in with a receptionist in a cramped lobby on the ground floor and then climbed two flights of stairs to his room, where he found two single beds, one on either side, and a small wooden desk pushed up against the window in the middle. He dropped his bag on one of the beds and took out a folded paper map of the city. The fewer digital footprints he left behind, the better. He planned to keep his phone turned off entirely unless he absolutely needed it. He unfolded the map and laid it out on the desk before taking a seat, using a pen to sketch a line between the hotel and the last known address he had for Irina Baranova. He also put an X on the location for the offices of Russia Free Press, the largely independent news organization that published her work. Even if he did manage to track her down, Nathan wasn't sure what he would say, but as it was, he had just under seventy-two hours to find her and sort that out. If the next ferry left without him, it would be Elias Mansour who would be the wanted man.

Chapter Twelve

Irina Baranova would certainly understand that if she were spotted talking with a former CIA officer, she would likely end up poisoned to death, or shot, or convicted in court and sent off to rot in prison for the rest of her life. Such was the state of independent journalism in Russia. Baranova put her life on the line every single day. In this case, the state might actually be justified in their fears, based on what she could potentially pass along. Nathan wanted secrets. He wanted to know as much as possible about what the Kremlin was up to when it came to Jenna's murder and everything attached to it. In making contact with Baranova, he'd have to be stealthy both for her sake and for his own.

Before Nathan even arrived in the city, he'd done his homework. Baranova had been locked up twice already on trumped-up charges, fined, and released after serving short sentences. He knew how this would work. They would threaten her with a twenty-year term, let her see what life was like behind bars, and then offer her an out. If she agreed to cooperate, she could walk out the door a free woman. All she'd have to do was give them a little bit of information once in a while, on her colleagues and their publications, and anything else of interest she might come across along the way. If she sold her soul to the devil, she could breathe fresh air. That sort of incentive would be hard to resist. Did Baranova have it in her? It was a question that Nathan could only speculate about. In his experience, she didn't seem the type to cave in to such pressure. On the surface anyway, Irina Baranova was deeply idealistic. This was a woman who spent the first twenty years of her life under Soviet rule and when that empire began to crumble, she was on the front lines, helping lead protests up and down the bustling Nevsky Prospekt. She was on the radar of the KGB very early on, and though much had changed during the intervening years, much remained the same. The KGB may have been renamed, but their people still kept a close eye on Baranova. She longed for freedom, not only for herself but for her country. Tantalizing signs of progress showed up in the early days, but now the darkness had returned. It was hard to believe that anything could turn Irina Baranova into an informant, not even the prospect of a life behind bars, but Nathan couldn't make any assumptions. To mitigate this problem, he would need to make contact in a public space. He couldn't show up at her home. Even if she wasn't being watched there, she was likely being listened to. The same went for her place of work. In fact, there even more so. Instead, he would need to surveille her until he was confident that nobody else was following, to protect them both. Fortunately, Nathan had some experience in this business. He'd recruited countless agents all around the world, though this time was different. This time it was personal.

The publication where Baranova worked was located in a nondescript building that was a mix of residential units and small offices. Nathan stood out front, reading a list of names on the intercom. Aside from a dozen or so residents, he saw the listings for an advertising agency, a few non-profit organizations, and the office of the Internet daily, Russia Free Press, on the third floor. He didn't dare buzz it. Instead, he lingered nearby until a woman walked out and he was able to catch the door and slide inside. After walking through a corridor, he emerged into a central courtyard. The building was four floors high, with exterior walkways on each level behind iron railings and blue sky poking through from above. He ducked into a stairwell and made his way up. When he got to the third floor, he emerged onto the walkway. On the opposite side, across the courtyard, he saw the door to Russia Free Press. Through a pair of windows, he spotted a small news room, with six desks topped by computers, books, loose printouts and a few lonely houseplants. Two of the desks were empty, with the others occupied by staff members hard at work. None of them were Irina Baranova. Nathan knew what she looked like. Finding photos of her online was easy enough. She was middle-aged, with a round face, and preferred to wear her hair in a brown bob, speckled with gray. Apparently, she was working in the field today, or perhaps from home. He descended the stairs and exited to the street. Directly opposite was a small Mediterranean restaurant. Nathan made his way across, where he took a seat by a window with a view to the street and ordered a falafel plate, hoping that she'd make an appearance. After waiting for over an hour, he had no such luck.

Nathan paid his bill and moved on. Next stop was Baranova's apartment building, or at least the address he had for her. It was a twenty-minute walk, but that gave Nathan the opportunity to clear his mind and consider what he might actually say if he eventually tracked her down. Chances were he'd only get one shot, if that. He'd come an awfully long way for answers, and if she refused to speak he had no backup plan. He couldn't afford to frighten her away.

When he reached the address, Nathan eyed the building. It was five-stories high, old and gray, and covered in layers of soot and grime. Opposition journalism didn't pay very well, clearly, but that wasn't why Irina Baranova did what she did. Nathan crossed the street and scanned the names on the intercom until he spotted hers. Apparently, this was the place. He retreated back across the street and continued up the block until he came to a bus stop, where a few weary pensioners stood waiting. Nathan read the bus schedules, simultaneously eyeing the door to Baranova's building. A bus pulled up and the pensioners climbed on. Nathan took a seat on a bench. This was a reasonable place to wait without calling too much attention on himself.

As the minutes ticked past, Nathan's thoughts turned back to Jenna. Nearly everything, it seemed, reminded him of her. When he passed a gelato shop, he pictured her happily licking a scoop on a summer day at the beach. When he heard a song she liked, he remembered her turning up the volume to sing along in the car. No matter what Nathan did or where he went, she was always there with him in spirit, yet the swirling questions drove him nearly mad. Why was she sitting at a table with the colonel? Only two possibilities made any sense to him. The first was that she was working undercover for the agency herself. The second was that the Russians had actually recruited her. Nathan thought of himself as a good judge of character, yet how much did anybody really know about another person? Even a spouse? Everybody had their secrets. Nathan wondered if he was somehow partially at fault. He wasn't always entirely honest with her, either. There were plenty of things that he kept to himself, afraid to share. Most glaring in his mind was how terrified he really was of marriage, even with Jenna. He'd always done his best to put a good face on it, to pretend those insecurities did not exist, but they were there, lurking below the surface. Part of him wanted these things, sure, but another part wrestled with doubts. He'd always been so independent minded, settling down was going to be quite possibly his biggest challenge to date. That last night, at dinner, she'd worried that he might grow to resent her for upending his career. Nathan had assured her that would never be the case, but in truth, he wasn't entirely convinced. He wished now that he'd had the courage to admit his fears. He wished he'd allowed himself to be more honest with her. Of course, she seemed to know how he really felt about it all and was willing to take the chance on him anyway. Now he felt an odd sense of guilt, that maybe if he'd found a way to be more forthright with her, she'd have returned the favor. Clearly, though, her secrets were more extreme. Was it hard for her, deceiving him in this way, or did it come easily? He imagined that she was tormented by all of it. Unraveling this mystery was to uncover her true nature. Nathan pictured her the very first time they'd ever really talked at length, at a backyard BBQ thrown by a colleague in the District. She'd come off as brash and outgoing, eminently comfortable in her own skin. At first, it had put him off just a little bit. She wasn't holding back, or trying to impress him. It made him think that he didn't really have much of a chance with her, though it was only much later that she admitted how nervous she'd been around him at first. He flashed to another memory, strolling through Georgetown together on an autumn afternoon several months later, as they were beginning to settle into a rhythm, both of them understanding by this point that it was something serious. Nathan spent a lot of mental energy during those early days trying to figure out what was going on in her mind on a personal level. Did she love him? Was she all in? Was he? By the time he proposed, he thought he had her pretty well figured out. If indeed she had betrayed her country, and her husband, she was awfully good at hiding it.

Nathan was looking back toward Baranova's building when another bus pulled up. The rear doors opened and another pensioner ambled down the stairs, wheeling a grocery trolley from one step to the next. Nathan stood to help her lift it to the sidewalk, but she brushed his hand aside and managed on her own. Behind the woman was a young man in a business suit, with a headset covering his ears. Next came a woman whose eyes met Nathan's briefly. He tried not to stare. She was middle-aged, with a round face and a brown bob haircut, with specks of gray. Apprehension showed in the creases of her eyes as the two of them quickly sized each other up. The woman was Irina Baranova. There was no reason for her to recognize him. Nathan took a step back to let her pass, and she quickly moved around him and on up the sidewalk. He watched her go until she crossed the street and entered her building, disappearing through the front door.

It was all just a flash of a moment. Normally, Nathan would take his time in such a situation, to build up the target's confidence more slowly, but in this case the clock was ticking. Yet if he'd simply blurted something out to Baranova on the street, she'd have surely fled and never given him another chance. Nathan left the bus stop and moved up the street, crossing past the apartment building and on along the block until he came to a small convenience store. Continuing inside, he stood near a front window, perusing the snack selections as he bought himself some time. At least he knew that he had the right spot, and that Baranova was here in St. Petersburg and not out of town. He couldn't stalk her on the street like this for long. He'd have to initiate conversation at some point. Nathan was thinking over what he might say when he saw her reappear, this time with a shopping trolley of her own. She exited her building and turned right up the sidewalk, wheeling the trolley along behind her. He let her get halfway up the block before he exited the convenience store and fell in behind.

Baranova turned right at the next intersection and walked two more blocks before entering a supermarket. She was just going about her life, buying groceries after a day at work. Nathan paused momentarily outside the shop, looking over his shoulder to see if he could spot any potential FSB agents on her tail. He saw nobody that raised an alarm. It was all just local residents going about their own shopping or on their way home at the end of the day. Nathan ducked inside the store and picked up a small hand basket. Moving through a turnstile, he continued past a bakery section and then on to the produce department. Irina Baranova stood near a bin, examining a batch of bell peppers. She chose two and placed them into a bag before moving on to the tomatoes. This time, Nathan didn't hesitate. He'd take his chance. He walked up to a bin of cucumbers directly opposite Baranova, watching as she picked out a pair of plump red tomatoes.

"Irina Baranova?" Nathan said.

Baranova's head shot up. When their eyes met, the color drained from her cheeks, but she said not a word.

"My name is Nathan Grant. I'd like to talk to you."

Irina Baranova turned her gaze toward the store entrance, to see who else might be watching, or perhaps to plan her escape. "Leave me alone." She wheeled her cart away.

"Please." Nathan followed after. "It's important."

"You're American?" she shot back at him.

"Yes."

"I have nothing to say to you."

"It's not what you think."

"I don't care what it is, I don't want to talk to you."

"You're afraid. I understand."

Baranova stopped and stared him in the eye, defiant now. "Do you?"

"Yes."

Baranova looked around again and then entered the pasta aisle, taking a box of rigatoni off the shelf, and then a bottle of sauce.

"Ms. Baranova, they killed my wife. Your government. I want to know what happened."

"And so you came all this way, to track down a reporter in the grocery store?" Baranova was incredulous. "Why on earth do you think that I can possibly help you?"

"Because you took a photo of my wife, sitting in a cafe with Colonel Vasily Volkov."

A hint of recognition crossed Baranova's face. "I didn't take that photo."

"But you know it?"

"I know nothing."

"Please. I *have* come a long way, you're right. Is there anything at all you can tell me?"

"Nathan Grant is your name?"

"That's right." Nathan was putting himself at risk. If she'd gone over to the government side, they'd know who he was and where he was before he even set foot outside the store. If he wanted her to level with him, though, he'd have to be honest in return.

"You are either very brave or very foolish to have come here."

"Maybe both."

"Yes. Maybe both."

"Will you help me?"

"Why should I?"

Nathan didn't have a good answer. He should have, after days of thinking about what he was going to say at this moment, but he didn't. Perhaps he'd been hoping that inspiration would strike, once he saw Baranova face to face. Now he knew that his precious seconds with her were slipping away. "This isn't political. It's not ideological. It's not about intelligence. This is personal. They killed my wife. Can you understand how that feels? Have you been married, Ms. Baranova? Do you have a daughter, or a son? Can you imagine..." Nathan's eyes took on a far-off cast as he pictured Jenna waving to him from that speedboat, and then… "If it was your daughter, can you imagine?" he pleaded.

"Why me, Mr. Grant? Why bother me? If somebody killed your wife, go to the police. File a report with Interpol. Ask your government for an extradition. I'm a reporter, not a law enforcement officer."

"No, but you understand how things work. You don't go to the police when the GRU is involved."

"No, you keep your head down and do your best to stay alive. That's what I recommend for you, Mr. Grant. This is a dangerous game you are playing at."

"It's no game."

"I'm sorry, Mr. Grant," Baranova began to move away once again.

"Wait!" Nathan grabbed her wrist. "You have a daughter, don't you? What's her name?"

Baranova pulled her wrist away. "That's none of your business!"

"If it was her, you'd do whatever you could, wouldn't you? To find out the truth?"

Baranova didn't answer, but didn't hurry off either. Perhaps Nathan was getting somewhere.

"Please. All I want is some information. Can't you help me?"

"I don't even know who you are!"

"Look me up, take your time. I know you have your sources."

"You work for your government. Tell me the truth."

"I did, yes, but no longer. I'm retired."

"Retired? You must be all of thirty-five years old?"

"I quit the agency. I'm here on my own, as a private citizen. As a husband."

Baranova was still deeply skeptical, but she seemed to be softening. "I'd need to do some digging, to make sure you are who you say you are."

"Fine, that's fine."

Baranova paused a few seconds longer. "Meet me on Sunday."

"My ferry leaves Sunday evening."

"What time?"

"Six p.m."

"Fine. Be at the Alexander Column in the Palace Square at 4 p.m. If I decide to help you, I will be there."

"And if not?"

"Then you will catch your ferry and good luck to you."

Nathan nodded. It was the best he could hope for. At least she wasn't turning him away outright. "Thank you."

As Irina Baranova wheeled her cart away down the aisle, Nathan watched her go for a moment and then headed toward the exit. He had roughly forty-five hours to kill, but with some luck, after that she'd be waiting with the next chapter in this sad and dismal saga.

Chapter Thirteen

Palace Square was an enormous open space, facing the Winter Palace on one side and the Hermitage Museum on the other. In the center of it all rose the towering Alexander Column, topped with an angel holding a cross. Nathan arrived early, with his duffel slung over one shoulder, and wandered around the square eyeing tour groups who followed leaders holding small flags in the air. Buses disgorged more tourists on one side, while horse-drawn carriages picked up honeymooning couples at the palace entrance. Nathan had spent the past day and a half pretending to be a tourist in the city, trying not to attract any undue attention to himself. He'd seen no signs of anybody following him, but one could never be entirely sure. These days, surveillance cameras did most of the work. It was possible that somebody in a dark office somewhere was keeping track of him even now. The question was, were the security services concerned enough about a single man from Lebanon to expend the resources on him? Or had their facial recognition software already pegged him for who he really was? Of course they would have had a file on Nathan Grant, and a thick one. That knowledge only drove home the risk that Irina Baranova was taking in speaking with him, if she showed up at all. He checked his watch. Five minutes to go, and there was still no sign of her. Nathan wandered slowly toward the column, pausing to snap a few photos on the way.

Standing directly in front of the monument itself, Nathan didn't have to wait much longer. He saw Baranova approaching from across the square, moving quickly and with purpose. "Let's walk," she said when she'd reached him.

"I didn't think you'd come." Nathan matched her stride as they headed across the square toward Alexander Park.

"Neither did I."

"Why did you change your mind?"

"Don't make me think about that. I might change it back."

Nathan kept his mouth shut, asking no more questions as they crossed a busy avenue and entered the park. Gravel pathways wound through a broad garden, past beds of colorful flowers. A pair of lovers snuggled together on one bench while an elderly man in a threadbare coat fed pigeons from another. It seemed clear to Nathan that Baranova was both anxious and angry, and yet she was here despite her apprehensions. One look at her career, taking on the all-powerful apparatus of the state for a very small salary told him all he needed to know about her motivations. This was a woman with a steady moral compass. She did what she thought was right. In this case, that meant giving aid to a grieving husband. Nathan still knew better than to press her too hard. Instead, he was here to listen.

When they reached the center of the park, they came to a large round fountain, encircled by yet more benches, half of them unoccupied. Baranova led him to one that was some distance from any potential eavesdroppers. "Shall we sit?" she said.

"Of course." Nathan joined her on the bench, placing his duffel on the ground by his feet. Still, she was quiet for some time as thoughts ran through her head, as though she wasn't sure where to begin or whether she should at all.

"I did some research on you," she said. "You're CIA, aren't you? Don't lie to me."

"I told you, I'm not with them anymore."

Baranova eyed him as she tried to figure out his game.

"I have no reason to hide anything from you," said Nathan.

"Hiding things is your profession."

"No, finding things out *was* my profession."

"Why did you quit?"

Nathan's eyes glassed over. "For my wife. I wanted to be there for her. I didn't want her worrying every time I went away that I might not make it home."

"I see. Maybe you were the one who should have been worried."

"Where did that photo come from?"

"First, you can tell me how you came across it. Who showed you?"

"I met with Paulina Sokolova, in Geneva."

"Ah. Ms. Sokolova. I should have guessed."

"She was trying to help me."

"And what did she tell you?"

Nathan was quiet. He thought he'd already explained that.

"She gave you the photo. She told you that your wife was a traitor."

"Yes."

"Well, I'm sorry but I don't have any good news regarding that."

"All I want is the truth. Paulina suggested that I speak with you, and so here I am." As they sat together on their bench, Nathan maintained his situational awareness. Surrounding them were the usual families, and couples, and a few homeless men, the likes of which could be found in any park. Loitering on the far side of the fountain was a single woman in her 30s, typing on her mobile phone.

"I'm working on a story at the moment that is quite likely to get me killed."

"It seems to me that everything you write could get you killed. No offense, but I'm surprised that they haven't gotten to you yet."

Baranova blinked twice. It was a reality that she clearly lived with on a daily basis, though she didn't like being reminded. "I can't let my fear get in the way. I owe it to my country. To my people."

"I understand."

"My heart is here, my life is here, but if this one is published… I will likely be forced to flee. Even then they'll probably still come for me. I know how they operate. I don't think anything will stop them." Baranova looked at him sideways, trying once more to size him up. "I'll tell you what I know, but you have to make a vow."

"I'm not one for making promises that I don't know I can keep."

"Lives are at risk. American lives. If events unfold as I foresee them, I would never be able to live with myself. I need to do what I can to stop it, and I'm counting on you to help me."

"So now you want *my* help?"

"Tell me you'll try."

"Of course, whatever I can do for you."

Baranova nodded, though she wasn't entirely satisfied. "I'm sorry about your wife. Even if she was on the wrong side."

"I knew my wife. I knew her heart and her soul. She would never betray me, and she would never betray her country."

"Yes, well, let me start with a bit of history. In the year 2010, your government conducted an operation known as Ghost Stories. I assume you are familiar?"

"Ten Russian sleeper agents were uncovered and arrested. They were exchanged in a prisoner swap one month later."

"Ten were arrested on U.S. soil, two more escaped, and a third was picked up in Cyprus."

"I am deeply familiar with that episode."

"What would you say if I told you that not all of the Russian agents were uncovered? What would you think if I had evidence that several more are still in the U.S., deep undercover?"

"It wouldn't surprise me in the least."

Now it was Baranova's turn to peer around the park. The woman with the mobile phone was still directly across on the opposite side of the fountain. A homeless man was on the lawn, wrapped in a thin blanket. Two uniformed police officers strolled along another path a bit further away but paid them no attention. "The goal of the Russian state is to sow chaos and instability in your country," Baranova kept her voice down, to keep from being overheard. "I'm sure this isn't news to you. Over the years they've used social media to court extremist groups on both sides. One GRU officer, sitting in a basement on the outskirts of this very city will, with a few keystrokes, create opposing protests on opposite sides of the street in Chicago, or Cleveland, or Baltimore. They'll feed the rhetoric until white supremacists and anti-fascists are at each other's throats, quite literally. My government, you see, views this as a zero-sum game. When one country wins, another loses. If they can tear down America, it will only make the Russian homeland stronger. In fact, it's more than that. It's pride. It's ego. It's a yearning to regain the glory and the influence of a bygone era."

Nathan wanted to comment, but knew better than to interrupt. Baranova seemed to be on a roll. Sometimes it was best to keep quiet and let the information flow.

"The problem is that the results they are craving have taken too long to fully manifest," Baranova continued. "Leadership is looking for full-scale unrest. They'd like nothing more than to foment a second civil war. Let the Americans tear themselves to shreds. Simply pitting protesters against each other is no longer enough. They feel the need to instigate, directly."

The pair sat quietly as Baranova let that information sink in. Nathan allowed himself to speak. "Define instigate."

Baranova cleared her throat. "Directly engage in acts of violence. The protest shootings you've seen earlier this year, those that went unsolved, they weren't perpetrated by extremist Americans. Not all of them, anyway. I'm talking about operations conducted by Russian agents directly."

"Russian agents are shooting civilians on the streets of America?"

"That's exactly what I'm saying, yes. Why do you think the Russian government was so eager to get back their spy, Sergei Federov? Look at his record. He's a former Russian Army sniper: the perfect candidate to take out a protester or two from a safe distance and not get caught."

"But he did get caught."

"Not for shooting anybody. He was picked up because one of your FBI agents was doing his job and uncovered him communicating with a handler."

"But it wasn't Moscow that came up with this idea to swap him, it was the opposition. It was Yuri Kuznetsov who broached the idea to me personally at a meeting in Tallinn."

"What do you Americans say, 'I've got a bridge to sell you, in Brooklyn?'"

Nathan let the details of what she was telling him spin around in his brain, trying to make sense of it all.

"They turned the opposition?"

"At the very least, they found a way to plant the idea."

"And all the Americans got out of the deal was some phony picture of Jenna with this colonel?"

"That photo was real, Mr. Grant. I'm sorry to confirm that. I can also tell you that as we speak, Russian sleeper agents are still infiltrating extremist groups on either side of your American political divide. The next time they strike, it might not be guns any longer. It might be explosives. Nobody will know it's the Russians. The protest groups will blame each other. Revenge will be demanded. Well-armed militias will overwhelm law enforcement. The worst social chaos in generations will engulf your country in a wave of violence, and the Russian government will sit back and admire their handiwork."

"Why should I believe you? Why believe any of this?"

"You asked me what I know and I'm telling you. Believe me or not, but I can say, I trust my sources."

"What involvement does Vasily Volkov have with this?"

"Colonel Volkov is behind the entire operation, though the GRU prefers to create a sheen of deniability. They outsource their most sensitive endeavors and Volkov is the go-between, providing support to the mercenaries in Ukraine, and in Libya, and Syria. He's pulling the strings now in America as well."

"How am I supposed to stop it? You haven't told me who the sleeper agents are, or when they will strike, or where."

Baranova reached into her pocket and pulled out a tiny micro-SD card. "Everything I know is on this." She placed it into Nathan's palm before looking around the park once more. "You know better than to be caught with it."

Nathan closed his fist around the card.

"Be very careful who you trust," said Baranova. "Even your closest contacts. We don't know who else might be involved."

"I've got to pass this on up the chain."

"Please don't mention my name. I only hope that we can save some lives." With that, Baranova stood and walked back in the direction from which they had come, leaving Nathan alone on the bench. The woman on the cell phone stood and followed after the journalist.

"Ms. Baranova!" Nathan shouted after her, but he knew it was too late. They'd been watched this entire time. When Baranova turned back, she saw the other woman tailing her, but the reporter just turned and moved away, head down. Nathan switched his attention to the homeless man, who stood now and dropped his thin blanket. He was sturdy and young, too fit to be living on the streets. From the far side of the park, Nathan saw two more men approaching. He shoved the SD card deep into his pocket, lifted his duffel, and started off briskly in the opposite direction. Along the park's edge, he spotted a black sedan with tinted windows easing slowly along the road to cut him off. He couldn't risk being caught with the SD card, that was clear. It wasn't too late to simply drop it into a garbage bin or down a sewer grate. They might never find it, if he was surreptitious enough, but that would defeat the whole point of his coming here. No, he wasn't going to give up that easily. Instead, he took off running, toward the Admiralty building and then left along a frontage road as the sedan tore through the park behind him. Nathan looked back to see the car blocked by a gate, but with two men jumping out to give chase on foot.

When Nathan reached the next corner, with the Admiralty on his right and the park still on the left, he spotted a young man on a motorcycle, idling on the side of the road as he chatted with two young women. Nathan dropped his shoulder and channeled his high school football days as he rammed into the young man, knocking both him and the bike to the ground. As the young man crawled a few feet away in shock, Nathan lifted the bike and hopped on. His pursuers were only a few yards away when he popped the motorcycle into gear and took off, heading straight toward the Neva River. By the time he reached the embankment, the sedan was on his tail once more and barreling toward him. Nathan turned right and zipped around traffic as he moved along the river and then left across a bridge. Two more cars joined the chase, another sedan as well as a marked police car, lights flashing and siren blaring. His situation was getting dicier by the minute.

On the other side of the river, Nathan weaved through more traffic and then hopped a curb and left the road entirely, hurtling along a sidewalk and then down a narrow lane between two buildings. One of the sedans managed to follow, bumping and scraping against the walls as it went and sending pedestrians scrambling into doorways and out of the way in the nick of time. Nathan emerged into the courtyard of a hospital complex, gunning the throttle as he churned up a set of stairs and then continued through an open door and into the main hospital itself. Shouts rang out as he raced down the main corridor, past doctors in scrubs and patients on gurneys. At the far end of the hall, he slowed to let the automatic door swing open and then roared on out, jumping a set of concrete stairs to land in a central courtyard. Flying across to the opposite side, he shot down another path until he joined another roadway. When he emerged from the hospital complex, the police car was on his tail, but in city traffic, the driver couldn't keep up. Nathan opened the throttle and flew down the road, turning left, then right, then left again. Emerging again along the river, he passed a city bus headed in the direction of the port. Half a block ahead, he skidded to a stop behind a thick green hedge and ditched the bike, hustling back out just in time to climb on board the bus. Through the window, he saw the police vehicle race past. Next, he saw one of the black sedans and then the other rush by. Nathan found a seat at the back. As the bus pulled away from the curb, a conductor in an orange vest approached. Nathan paid the 50 ruble fare and then leaned back, trying to control his breathing. He checked his watch. The ferry would already be boarding. The question was, did the intelligence agents know who Nathan was? Did they realize he'd come on the boat? Or was a Lebanese tourist named Elias Mansour completely off their radar? Nathan had to hope so, because if he didn't manage to make this departure, he might never get out at all.

The bus continued along the river until Nathan saw the hulking white ferry looming before them, as large as a cruise ship with a long line of cars and trucks loading from a ramp at the stern. He exited the bus and joined a small group of passengers headed toward the terminal, keeping his eyes peeled for his pursuers while attempting to maintain his calm. He saw no further signs of trouble, and so he pulled his ticket from his bag as he entered the building and then joined a line at the immigration desk. His heartbeat pounded in his chest when he heard the wail of sirens, muted at first but growing ever louder. Instinct told Nathan to bolt, to get out of line and run as fast as he could, but where would he go? This ferry was his best shot at escape. If he ran, he would only call attention to himself, and so he stayed put. Through a window, he saw two police vehicles race past the terminal and continue on in the opposite direction without slowing down. He tried to tell himself that he was just a tourist, heading home after a relaxing weekend taking in the sights. He knew that any sign of distress would set off the immigration agent. When his turn came, he wiped his brow and approached the booth with a light smile, handing over his Lebanese passport. The agent looked at Nathan, and then the passport, and then back. Ultimately, he stamped it without a word and Nathan continued past, his blood pressure still off the charts.

After boarding across a gangway amidships, Nathan moved with a crowd through a lobby that resembled a dated hotel, with a brown and orange carpet in a swirling pattern, and a front desk where uniformed clerks directed passengers toward their cabins. A grand circular stairway wound downwards, with a glass chandelier hanging in the middle. Nathan checked the cabin number on his ticket and followed signs two decks below. Continuing down his hallway, a stale aroma hung in the air. It was a mix of cigarette smoke, beer and sweat that had soaked in over thirty-odd years of voyages. Overhead neon lights cast a harsh glare. Winding his way around travelers with roller bags, and eager children, Nathan found his own cabin, opened the door and then locked himself inside. There was a bed on one side, a table with a small fridge on the other, and his own private head. A porthole gave him a view of the terminal below and the avenue beyond. Nathan checked his watch. It was an hour until departure. He slid a chair near to the porthole and sat down to wait. The minutes ticked by. He thought of Irina Baranova, wondering what fate was in store for her. Maybe they didn't know who she'd met with, or what information she'd passed, but in the long run it wouldn't matter. Either now or sometime in the future, a bad end was likely. You didn't cross the state in Russia and expect to live a long and healthy life. Nathan admired her. She did what she thought was right, for her country and her people, as well as his own. She put her life on the line, to protect the lives of innocents, and for that he was grateful. The fruits of her resistance were on a small card in his pocket, and with some luck and good timing, he'd be able to pass this information along to those who could make the best use of it.

As the hour of departure drew near, Nathan spotted another pair of police vehicles hurtling toward the dock. These two pulled up just outside the terminal, along with another black sedan. A group of men jumped out of the vehicles; two uniformed officers and a couple of plainclothes agents in dark suits who were quite likely FSB. As they rushed into the terminal, Nathan felt a vibration and sensed movement in the ferry itself. He looked straight down and saw a gap between the ship and the dock beginning to spread, the sliver of water expanding as they pulled away. He expected the ship to reverse, to tie up snugly to the dock at any moment as the FSB men ordered it back ashore, but instead, the two men appeared at the gangway, running to take a flying leap across the chasm. They were on board, and they would be coming for him, whether they'd discovered his alias yet or not. Somewhere, officers were going through the scanned passport photos of all passengers. When they put his face together with the name on his passport, they'd look up his room number and come knocking. They had fourteen hours to find him before the ship docked in Helsinki. Nathan picked up his bag and moved out of the cabin, heading quickly down the hallway. It was a big ship and there were plenty of places to hide.

Chapter Fourteen

Surveillance cameras would be monitoring every public space on the ship besides the restrooms. Nathan spotted one along the ceiling in the hallway as soon as he exited his cabin. Once the FSB agents put a name to his face, and looked up the corresponding room number, all they'd need to do was go to the security office and check the video to follow along and see wherever Nathan went. Picking him up would be easy. That didn't apply to the sections of the ship reserved for crew, where surveillance cameras were less likely. This would include the engine room and all of the various mechanical spaces: the steering mechanism, water purification system, drive train and thruster compartments. There would be storage rooms and lockers, crew quarters and crew restrooms, but with a full compliment working on board, he'd need to be stealthy. If all else failed, once they reached international waters, he could find a life preserver and jump overboard, but floating alone in the middle of the Baltic Sea didn't sound like a good option.

At the main stairway, Nathan headed down, down, down. He passed families and couples, off to explore the restaurants and the casino and whatever entertainment was available during their crossing. Reaching the lowest public deck, he moved further toward the stern until he found another stairway, this one with narrow steel steps and a chain across the passage. A sign read "Crew Only" in both English and Russian. As he stepped over the chain and continued, Nathan heard the thrum of the engines growing louder. He realized a major drawback to this plan. It was likely the only entrance or exit from the engine room, which meant that if they knew he was down there, they could seal it off and search every square inch until they found him. Still, he had to stay one step ahead of them and at the very least this detour would buy him some time. When he pushed open a soundproof door and moved through, the noise became nearly unbearable. A row of headsets hung from hooks on the wall, and he took one set and put it over his ears before moving forward. To his right was another door, glass from the waist up, and inside he saw a control room where one engineer sat monitoring a panel while another stood drinking a cup of coffee with his back to the door. Nathan crouched low and scooted past. On the other side, a grated steel stairway continued even further down into a cavernous space, with rows of enormous diesel engines lined up along the bottom. He could feel the heat rising off them. Nathan saw a crew member, busily wiping one of the engines down with a rag. A large window inside the control room overlooked the entire scene. To his right, directly below the window, a metal pipe descended three decks straight down into the very bowels of the ship. He waited until the crew member below moved out of sight, then looped his duffel over one arm, climbed over a railing, and grasped the pipe. He was now hanging forty feet in the air, just below the window. The engineers couldn't see him from here unless they approached the glass, but the crewman below would reappear in a moment as he worked his way around from one engine to the next. Nathan slid quickly down the pipe. When he got to the bottom, his feet landed on another steel grating and he saw a passageway leading forward. He hurried along and ducked to his right into the first compartment he came to. Two more crewmen moved past along the walkway just outside, but they hadn't spotted him.

In his small space, Nathan slid backwards into a gap between two sets of shelves. It was a janitor's closet, with mops and buckets, commercial-sized bottles of cleaning compounds, sponges, rags and a large sink. On the shelves were several boxes, and Nathan peered into them one at a time. The first few held more cleaning supplies. Another box, from the top shelf, contained folded pairs of dark blue cotton coveralls. He checked the sizes and pulled out a large, then set it aside while he unzipped his duffel and extracted a change of clothes, taking off his blue jeans and exchanging them for a pair of brown slacks. He swapped a tan checkered shirt for a solid blue one, tucking it in and then putting on a black leather belt. Next, he unzipped his toiletry case and pulled out a compact pair of electric clippers. Moving to the sink, he leaned over it and flipped the clippers on. They buzzed in his hand as he ran them over his head, shaving off all of his hair, one row after another until he was totally bald. He ran one hand over his smooth pate to make sure he hadn't missed any spots. When he was satisfied, he put the clippers back in the bag and took out his two passports, American and Lebanese, and put them both in a pocket. From his jeans, he retrieved his wallet, and most importantly, the mini-SD card. He slid the SD card behind his driver's license and put the wallet and his phone in his other pocket. He stuffed the duffel and his extra clothes into the cardboard box, then scooped all of the hair out of the sink and put it into the box as well before running the faucet to rinse any extra hair down the drain. After turning the faucet back off, Nathan put the cardboard box with his things in it onto the top shelf and pushed it to the very back, sliding another box of supplies in front of it. Finally, he took the blue coveralls and put them on over his new set of clothing.

Exiting the storage room, Nathan continued further along the corridor. The next compartment he came upon was filled with painting supplies, including shelves stacked with cans of gray and white paint, brushes, rollers, and trays. Large metal scraping rods lined a rack along one wall. They were roughly four-foot tall octagonal steel bars with a sharpened edge on one end. Beside these was another shelf with cans of spray paint and a row of respirator masks. Nathan slid one of the masks over his face. He lifted a can of gray spray paint, and then took one of the heavy steel scraping rods from its holder. Walking back out of the compartment, he could have been any other member of the crew, in his coveralls and hidden by his mask, off to do some maintenance.

Further up the corridor, Nathan passed the crewman he'd seen wiping the engines, but the man merely nodded as he went by. When Nathan came to the enormous engine space, he began moving up the stairs, steadily and with deliberation. He reached the top and continued past the control room, where only one engineer remained, still seated at his panel. Nathan waved through the window. The engineer waved back. After passing through the soundproof door, he closed it behind him and then took off his headset, placing it back on the proper hook. One more flight up, Nathan exited onto the lower passenger deck and made his way along the corridor. He'd reached the next public stairway when he saw the two FSB men in their dark suits hurrying down. They ran past him without stopping and headed straight for the engine room, where they unhooked the chain and disappeared down the stairs.

Nathan continued up, then forward until he reached the stairs for the vehicle decks. A chain across this stairway contained a sign announcing that vehicle decks were off-limits to unauthorized personnel during the voyage. To Nathan, that meant no prying eyes. At least not in person. After unclipping this chain, he moved past and re-fastened it behind him before heading down once more. At the entrance for vehicle deck number one, he saw a single surveillance camera in the stairwell. He held up his spray can and pushed the button, covering the camera lens in gray paint. On the other side of the door, he saw another camera, and sprayed that one as well. Nathan continued up and down the deck, this one filled with passenger cars, spraying every camera he could find. If one was too high to reach, he lifted the scraping tool and used it to pry the camera from the ceiling. The next level down held the commercial trucks, and RVs, and SUVs towing boats and trailers. Nathan sprayed or destroyed all of the cameras on this level as well. When he was satisfied that he was no longer being watched, he found an 18-wheel truck with a trailer that was secured with a single padlock. Using the metal bar, he pried the lock free and then swung open the trailer doors. Inside, it was filled with pallets of canned food. Along the top was a three-foot gap between the pallets and the ceiling. Nathan took off his respirator and then peeled out of the coveralls. He slid the crowbar and the broken lock underneath one of the pallets, then climbed to the top of the stack with the coveralls and the mask. These he tossed as far back across the cans of baked beans as he could manage, then climbed back down and closed the truck once more. This ought to keep them busy, he thought. Once they suspected that he was hiding on the vehicle decks, it would take them hours to search all of the cars and trucks. The whole thing was a cat and mouse game, and Nathan didn't plan on getting caught.

The bald Nathan, with different clothes than they were looking for, moved to the stairwell and headed up, this time going all the way to deck number 2, where he emerged amid crowds of passengers, who strolled the promenade, enjoyed a leisurely dinner, or explored the duty-free shop. Nathan made his way to an Italian-themed restaurant and asked a bow-tie clad maitre d' for a table near the back. He was quickly accommodated.

"Please," the man gestured toward a seat. Nathan took a chair with his back to the wall that gave him an unobstructed view of the entire restaurant and the promenade beyond. Through a row of floor-to-ceiling windows, he saw the vast Baltic Sea all the way to the horizon with no land in sight. He checked his watch. It was less than thirty minutes since departure, but they'd be approaching international waters by this point. Once they left official Russian territory, the FSB agents would have no authority over him. Technically they couldn't arrest him, or hold him. That wouldn't stop them from coming after him, if they somehow figured out where he was. The maitre d' handed him a menu. "A waiter will be with you momentarily."

"Thank you." Nathan took the menu and read it over. It was the usual fare, greatly overpriced, including various pizzas and pastas and a few different salads. When his waiter did arrive, Nathan chose a spaghetti carbonara with a glass of white wine. Two security officers hurried past along the promenade, but Nathan wasn't particularly worried. Were they headed for the engine room or the vehicle decks? Either way, they'd likely be busy there all night.

After he'd finished his meal, Nathan paid the bill and then took a stroll on the outside deck, catching a bit of fresh air. It was summer in the far north, where 7 p.m. meant the sun wouldn't set for another four hours, and come up just a few later. The evening was a pleasant one, and passengers sat in pairs or small groups on benches facing the rail. Nathan heard Russian being spoken, as well as Finnish, Swedish and English. He'd realized already from the trip over that many of the people took this voyage as a sort of poor-man's cruise, traveling from Helsinki to St. Petersburg, then Tallinn to Stockholm and back. He also knew that there was a disco in the stern, which would be a good place to hide out overnight. It was dark, and crowded, and loud. It would be very hard for anybody to spot him there. In the meantime, though, he did feel a somewhat exposed. The change in clothes and lack of hair might only fool them for so long. He was a single man, in his 30s and all alone. Eventually they might suspect him, though if he was part of a group it would look better.

Nathan spotted three women sitting on one of the benches nearby. They appeared to be in their late 20s, two blondes and a brunette, with bottles of vodka and mixers lined up by their feet. They lifted plastic cups in the air. "Na zdorov'ye!" they said, before tossing their vodka back and then quickly refilling the cups.

"Cheers," Nathan said to them.

The women turned toward him in surprise. His comment had burst through their intimate bubble, as though the outside world were intruding on their fun. Two of them appeared to be annoyed, but one seemed curious. "America?" she said.

"Yes. American," he admitted.

"You like drink vodka?"

"Yes, I like vodka very much."

"You drink with us." She took another plastic cup from a small stack and held it out. Nathan could tell that she'd already had quite a few, from the slightly glazed look in her eyes, the perspiration on her forehead and crooked smile. He took the cup and his new friend quickly filled it with vodka and then some juice from a separate bottle. She slid herself down the bench to make some room for him. "Sit, America!"

Nathan did as he was told and held up his cup. "What shall we drink to?"

"What your name, America?" said the brunette.

"Alex."

"Alex," she repeated.

"We drink to Alex," said the first woman.

"Fair enough," Nathan replied. "Na zdorov'ye."

"Na zdorov'ye!" they sang out in unison, tapping their cups to his.

Nathan downed his cocktail in one go. It wasn't so bad. The vodka was lemon-flavored and the juice was apple, which made for a sweet combo. "What's your name?" he asked the blonde sitting next to him. Her hair was cut short in a bob and she had a sultry, playful air about her. She exuded elation, joyful over the freedom represented by two friends and a bottle. Perhaps she was escaping from something for a few days, and the wedding ring on her finger gave Nathan an idea of what that might be; an unhappy marriage, or the kids, or her ordinary life in general. She also happened to be stunningly attractive, which only fed the loneliness that gnawed at Nathan from inside. He missed Jenna at this moment with a deep and overwhelming desperation. The one thing he wanted in life was to hold her again in a warm embrace, to smell the sweet scent of her hair and feel the soft caress of her lips across his neck. The knowledge that none of this was to be left him bereft, and yet at the same time determined to carry on in her name. If he wanted to avenge her murder, and reveal those responsible for ordering it, he would first need to get off this ship in one piece. If that meant it was better to make a few friends along the way, then so be it.

"I am Tanya," said the woman with the bob.

"It is a pleasure to meet you."

Tanya took her bottles and refilled the cups, though the vodka was nearly empty. "This is my friend, Svetlana." She nodded to the brunette.

"Hellooo." Svetlana drew out the word.

"The little one, she is Nastya."

Nathan nodded to the last one at the far end of the bench, a mousy girl all of five-two. "Nice to meet you all," he said. The only one of the three without a wedding ring was Nastya and she also seemed the nervous type, afraid to look in Nathan's eyes for more than a moment. Svetlana wasn't afraid of him at all, but he could tell that she was bored. Nathan guessed that her command of English was limited.

"What you do in Russia, American?" said Tanya.

"Just traveling."

Tanya tilted her head sideways as she looked him over. Her eyes paused on *his* wedding band. "Where is your wife?"

"She couldn't come, unfortunately."

"She is with the children?"

"No, no children."

"No children? Why not?"

"We only married this year."

"So? I married last year. My daughter, she is seven."

Nathan laughed. "You're a step ahead of me. Where is your husband?"

Svetlana scoffed. Clearly she understood this much. "Home," she said.

"We have girls' trip. You say that? Girls' trip?" said Tanya.

"Sure."

"No husbands!" said Svetlana.

"No, no husbands," Tanya agreed.

"You seem to be happy about that," said Nathan.

"Russian men, they don't know how to treat the woman."

"I'm sorry to hear that."

Tanya shook her head. "My husband, no, we don't talk about him."

"All right."

"We drink."

Nathan smiled. He seemed to have latched onto some live wires. Tanya lifted her plastic cup once again and this time, when Nathan lifted his, she looped her arm around his and they both downed their shots together. "Nado tselovat'sya," she called out.

"What is that?" said Nathan.

"It means, 'We must kiss,'" said Nastya. "Russian tradition. Now you must kiss."

Tanya didn't wait for Nathan. Instead she leaned forward to kiss him on the lips. "Russian tradition," she repeated.

Svetlana held up the nearly empty vodka bottle. "No more."

"We go back to cabin. Come." Tanya stood and held out a hand for Nathan. He wasn't about to argue. Their cabin would be the perfect place to hide. He took her hand and rose to his feet. The four of them headed along the deck and through a pair of doors, passing across the lobby on the way to the grand staircase, with Tanya leaning her shoulder into Nathan's as they went, her fingers wrapped in his. If Jenna was watching them from heaven, Nathan could only hope that she understood. The cabin was one deck down and aft along another corridor. Nastya pulled a key card from her pocket, waved it over the lock and pushed the door open, entering first and followed by the others. Inside were two sets of bunk beds, one on each side, with a desk at the far end, just beneath the porthole. On the desk were more bottles, along with a pack of cigarettes, a lighter, and speaker playing techno music. Sitting on one of the lower bunks with their backs to the wall was another skinny dark-haired woman and a man of the same age. Neither said a word, though they both eyed Nathan with curiosity. When the cabin door closed behind them, he felt a glimmer of relief pass through him. No

FSB officer was likely to find him in here. "She's Katya," Tanya told him, nodding toward the other woman.

"Hello," Katya said.

"Alex is America," said Tanya.

"American. Yes. Hello."

Katya nodded impassively. The man reached out a hand. "My name is Boris."

"Hello, Boris." Nathan shook his hand.

"Boris is Ukraine," said Tanya. "He work on the ship."

"Are you hiding?" Nathan was aware of the irony in his question.

"No, not hiding. Today, it is my day off."

"We meet Boris on the tram," said Svetlana. "From the center. To the port."

"Just today?"

"Yes, today, we meet today."

"I work in the bar," said Boris. "Bartender."

"I see, having a bit of a busman's holiday, eh?" This question was met with blank stares all around. "Never mind."

"Come, sit!" Tanya took a spot on the empty bottom bunk and tapped the mattress beside her. Nathan did as requested and Tanya scooted those last few inches closer until their thighs were touching. Svetlana went for another bottle of flavored vodka, this one strawberry, and filled another round of plastic cups.

"No, no, not for me," said Nastya. "Too much!"

"Oh, come on, drink with us," said Boris.

"Nyet!"

Svetlana shook her head in disapproval and then passed out shots to everyone else. "Na zdorov'ye."

Tanya once more looped her arm around Nathan's and they tipped their cups back, down the hatch. "Nado tselovat'sya," she said, and kissed Nathan on the lips. He felt the alcohol now, swirling through his system, beginning to cloud his mind. It would complicate things if he crossed paths with the FSB men, but he'd still rather be here, hidden away in a cabin with strangers than wandering around in the open. They continued to drink, while Boris smoked a cigarette and chatted with Nathan about life in America. His English was the best of the group, and he had a slow, easy air about him. Meeting up with a clutch of Russian women to get drunk in their cabin was just another day in the life for Boris. Nathan checked his watch. Ten hours to go.

"You're boring!" Tanya said to Nathan.

"Bored, not boring," said Boris.

"What you say?" Tanya continued.

"She thinks you're bored, looking at your watch," Boris said to Nathan.

"No, no, not bored."

"We call you Sasha," said Katya. "Alexander, in Russia that means Sasha."

"Yes, Sasha." Tanya rose to her feet and offered Nathan both hands. "Come, we dance! I want to see nightclub."

"You're sure?"

"You'd better keep her happy," said Boris.

Nathan wasn't in a position to refuse, and so he took her hands and stood.

"Who else will come?" Tanya asked her friends but was met with blank stares. "Fine. We go." She led Nathan to the door and then out into the hall. They walked hand-in-hand, up the staircase and back toward the stern. When they entered the disco, a small crowd was already spread throughout the space. To the right was a horseshoe-shaped bar. In front was a series of plush couches and chairs arranged around small tables. Beyond that was a parquet floor, where half a dozen couples kicked up their heels to a pulsing beat. "Buy me drink!" said Tanya.

"You bet." Nathan bellied up to the bar and ordered two greyhounds. The room was plenty dark, with colored lights flashing across the dance floor. It was a decent place to lay low, just as he'd expected. When the drinks came, he led Tanya to the darkest table he could find, on the opposite side of the room. They sat side-by-side on a couch, sipping their drinks as they watched the dancers shaking their stuff. It didn't take long before one of the dark-suited FSB men walked alone into the club. Nathan played it cool, pretending not to notice. The men had split up, presumably to cover more ground on their own, dividing the ship between them. Apparently, they'd already gone through the vehicle decks and the engine room. Their frustration had to be growing. Nathan held up his half-empty glass. "Cheers," he said to Tanya.

"Cheers." Tanya looped her arm around his once more and they drank.

"And now we kiss."

She smiled and gave him a peck on the lips. The FSB man stopped beside the table, staring at Nathan without saying a word. When Tanya noticed, she snapped at him in Russian. He gave a reply, but she was having none of it, telling him off in a fit of anger. The man stood stock still. Nathan stared him in the eye with deep malice. Tanya stood and took Nathan's hand. She led him to the dance floor where they began to bump and sway to the music, with Nathan's partner grinding up against him. The FSB man paused for a moment longer and then continued around the room, scoping out the rest of the patrons before exiting out the double doors. Nathan's heart pounded, but he didn't know how much of it was from the close call and how much from the stirrings in his heart caused by this woman. It was wrong, all of it. She was married, unhappily or not. He was only weeks from losing the love of his life. At the core of it, they were simply two lost souls providing each other solace on a midnight voyage across the sea. He put his hands on her hips, his mind drifting off until it was Jenna after all; one last dance together. It was all he could do to hold himself together. When he couldn't take it any longer, they drank some more and shortly after midnight Nathan walked her back to her cabin, with Tanya stumbling along the way and grasping his hand extra tight. When they reached the door, she tried to find her key but struggled to empty her pocket. Nathan gave a light knock. A moment later, Nastya swung the door open. Tanya stepped halfway in. "Sashaaaa," she said.

"Good night, Tanya. Sleep well."

"Good night America." She stretched up and gave him one last kiss, and then she was gone, disappearing into the cabin with the door swinging closed behind her.

Nathan had to get as far away from these girls and the haunted memories they brought back as he could, to clear his mind. He made his way back up to the promenade deck and on outside. It was dark now, for those few hours on a far-northern summer night. He moved forward until he came to a lifeboat just along the rail. A cover was attached with metal snaps. Nathan unsnapped four of them and then took a quick look up and down the deck. With nobody in sight, he slid over the gunwale and into the boat, snapping the cover closed behind him. This was as good a place as any to get a little shut-eye. He pulled out his phone and turned on the light to take a quick look around. Between the cover and rows of benches was a three-foot gap. He took a life preserver from under the nearest bench and placed it on top as a pillow, then stretched out on his back. It wasn't the most comfortable bed he'd ever slept on, but it would do.

Chapter Fifteen

Nathan peeked out from under the lifeboat cover. It was early morning and the ship was just docking in Helsinki. An announcement over the intercom requested that all vehicle passengers make their way to their cars. He waited until the deck was clear and then slid out of the boat and then stood up tall, stretching his limbs. The FSB couldn't touch him here, officially. He was back in the European Union. The two agents who were tracking him probably didn't have visas themselves, which meant they'd be riding the ship straight back where they came from. Another announcement directed all pedestrian passengers to assemble in the main lobby. Nathan stretched once more and then made his way inside.

The lobby itself was packed with people, all eager to disembark as soon as possible. The crowd had an impatient air, with passengers using their luggage and their bodies to box each other out, doing what they could to protect their places in the line, though the gangway door was still closed tight. Nathan found a spot along one wall, near the reception desk, and settled in. While he waited, he looked over the gathered masses, expecting that he might see Tanya and the girls from the night before. They were nowhere in sight: probably still sleeping it off was his best guess. After ten minutes and a few more announcements, he saw the two dark-suited FSB men weaving their way through the crowd toward the front. Some of the other passengers pushed the men back, arguing with them. One of the agents spotted Nathan and paused, saying a few words to his partner. There was nowhere for Nathan to go at this point. It was better to be in a crowded room than to let these guys get him alone somewhere. He crossed his arms and stared straight at them. The two men began to make their way across. Grumbles continued from the crowd, along with complaints in Russian and in Finnish. The men kept coming.

"There is a line here!" said a passenger in English. He was a large man, all of six-foot-three and two-fifty, with a round, fleshy face. He stood in the men's way, pointing back in the direction from which they'd come. One of the FSB men shoved the passenger in the chest, but he didn't budge. Two other passengers came to his assistance, forming a virtual wall.

"You're gonna have to wait your turn, mates," said one of the others.

The FSB agents were frustrated and confused. They looked at Nathan, and at the wall of bodies in front of them, and around at the other passengers who stared at them with menace. The agents said a few words to each other in Russian and then begrudgingly turned and moved back to the far side of the room. Clapping and cheers erupted. An older woman jeered at the agents, pointing a finger as she spoke in a language Nathan couldn't identify. He smiled. They weren't going to get to him today. A few minutes later, the gangway door opened and the crowd began moving through it. Nathan joined along, disembarking from the ship, down a set of stairs and then lining up in the terminal for immigration control. When it was his turn, he handed over his Lebanese passport. The immigration officer took a look, flipped through to the visa page, and then gave it a stamp. Nathan moved on through and then out of the terminal. Looking back at the ship, he saw the FSB agents standing by the rail several decks up. Nathan raised a hand in the air and waved before turning his back on them and walking to a nearby tram stop. It only took a minute for the next tram to arrive, and he squeezed aboard, heading toward the city center.

Nathan's first order of business was to get some breakfast. His second was to find a quiet, out-of-the-way place to examine the contents of the SD card. After exiting the tram, he walked through the sprawling Senate Square, with the Helsinki cathedral to the north and the inner harbor a few blocks down on the south side. The square was quiet on a Monday morning, with the usual tourists only just beginning to show. On the west side, a few narrow side streets passed between three-story neoclassical buildings. Nathan chose a street at random and moved up the block until he came to a promising cafe. It was nearly empty, so he entered and found an isolated table in the back. A server offered him a menu and after a quick look, he ordered two eggs over easy with potatoes, sausages, toast and a large Americano.

After an anxious twenty-four hours, Nathan finally had a moment to himself where he wasn't working overtime to evade capture. Nobody had followed him from the ferry terminal, of that he was fairly sure. From where he sat now, he could see through a window to the street outside. There was no sign of trouble, just a few locals going about their business. From one pocket, he pulled out his phone. He'd kept it switched off for the past three days, but he pressed the button and turned it on now. He knew full well what intelligence operatives could do if they linked the device to him. Most likely they had no idea that this burner phone was his, but he wasn't about to take the chance. He'd already disabled location tracking and switched it to airplane mode. Now he took the backing off the phone and found an empty SD storage slot. He pulled out Baranova's card from his other pocket, slid it into the slot, and closed the phone back up. The server came back with his Americano, a teaspoon and a small container of cream, placing them in front of him. A small bowl of sugar was already on the table.

"Your breakfast will be right out," said the server.

"Thank you."

When she'd gone, Nathan opened a file folder on the SD card. A part of him was skeptical. Trust was not something that came easily for a former CIA officer. Every piece of information had to be carefully weighed. He couldn't say, for instance, how reliable the source was. He didn't know if the Russians had somehow gotten to Irina Baranova. There was always the chance that she'd flipped. Living your life under the constant threat of assassination had a way of reorganizing a person's priorities. Even if she was on the up-and-up, the files could still be filled with disinformation. How was Nathan to know that the FSB or the GRU weren't feeding Baranova what they wanted her to see? He would have to weigh the evidence she'd provided and make his best determination.

The folder contained ten documents. They were all PDF files, but their names were written in Cyrillic characters. He clicked to open the first document. It looked to be a personnel file, twelve pages long. On the top left of the first page was the insignia of the GRU, Russian military intelligence. On the right was a passport-type photo of a man in his late-20s. He had very short hair and a round face, with pudgy cheeks. The man had a far-away look in his eyes. No smile. From what Nathan did know about Cyrillic characters, he was able to make out a name below the picture. Ivan Shustov, if Nathan was correct. What followed was a resume. Nathan understood the years listed, but not much else. He scrolled through the rest of the pages. In between the text, he came to a few more photos, including one of Shustov on his wedding day, posing with his happy bride. Behind them gleamed the golden domes of a Russian Orthodox church.

Another photo showed the front of a quaint two-story house with columns supporting a front porch. An address listed beneath it in Roman characters was in White Plains, New York.

Nathan opened the next file. This one had no photos, but the resume listed a man named Vladimir, along with several references to the CIA. Ordinarily, Nathan would simply pass these documents along to his superiors, but he didn't work for the CIA anymore and was therefore under no obligation to share the information. Not legally anyway. He'd see what else there was before making a determination. He opened the next file but it was similar to the previous one, with no picture and a lot of text he couldn't read. He was scrolling through the pages when his breakfast came. The waitress put the plates down on the table in front of him.

"Can I bring you anything else?" she asked.

Looking at the food, Nathan was hit with deep pangs of hunger. "I'd like an order of the Belgian waffles, please. With strawberries and maple syrup."

The server nodded. "Anything else?"

"No, thank you." When she'd left, he dug into his eggs and potatoes. He buttered his toast, spread on some jam, and wolfed it down. He was halfway finished with his first breakfast when he opened the next document. Like the first one, this was a standard personnel file with a photo at the top. He scrolled in close. Staring back at him from the screen was a young woman. Nathan slowly put down his fork. The woman was roughly seventeen years old. Her sandy blond hair was tied back and she wore a flower-print cotton dress. She had a serious expression on her face. The name listed beneath the photo was written in Roman characters: Jenna Taylor.

Nathan looked around the room. It felt as though it must all be a practical joke. He must be on some hidden-camera television show, where a gregarious host was about to jump out and yell "Surprise!" At the same time, the shock of it was intensely personal. It was bad enough to have seen the photo of Jenna having lunch with the colonel, but this was like a dagger to the heart. Every other person in the cafe must have recognized from Nathan's expression the gravity of what he'd just uncovered. No wonder Irina Baranova had looked upon him with such pity in her eyes. She'd already known. Yet, here in the cafe, nobody gave him a second look. At one table, two women chatted enthusiastically, in their own world. At another, an older woman with her daughter ate quietly. Nathan looked back to his phone. He had to go on, drawn by a mix of curiosity and dread.

The next few pages had a few more photos, including one of Jenna when she was perhaps nine years old, posing with her parents in Red Square with the bulbous domes of St. Basil's Cathedral looming behind them. Nathan did the math. It must have been around the year 2003. What could they have possibly been doing there? The realization that Mr. and Mrs. Taylor might have been spies as well left Nathan feeling physically ill. When the server returned to place the waffles on his table, Nathan pushed them away without looking up. She must have realized that something was wrong, but she didn't say another word, just left the food and walked away. Nathan continued scrolling through the document, trying to glean what else he could. The last photo showed her at a firing range, again in her teens, holding a Kalashnikov AK-74 assault rifle and wearing a green infantry combat uniform. The Cyrillic name badge read Jelena Tokara. "Why???" Nathan said out loud to himself. "How could you not have told me?"

Chapter Sixteen

The next flight back to the U.S. was Helsinki to Dulles, leaving that night at 6:30 p.m. Nathan was able to book a seat in coach, last minute, for an arm and a leg. He had no luggage. His duffel was still probably stuffed in a box in the engine room of a St. Peter Line ferry, somewhere in the middle of the Baltic Sea. When Nathan boarded his flight, he used his American passport. If the CIA was paying attention, they might have officers waiting to intercept him as soon as he landed, but were they looking for him? He couldn't know. What he did know was that he had to go back, first to continue unraveling the mystery behind Jenna's secret life. She was certainly mixed up in something highly unfortunate, but Nathan still needed the full details, or whatever he could manage to glean. Did the Russians have something on her? Were they forcing her hand? Or was it the Russians she was betraying in the end? Nathan clung to this last possibility, but that didn't mitigate his second reason for coming home. If Russian agents were murdering innocent civilians to incite civil war, Irina Baranova was right that Nathan had to do something about it. He wasn't yet sure what, or how.

Nathan's seat in coach was next to the window. The middle seat beside him was empty. On the aisle was a middle-aged Finnish man with a stoic Scandinavian air. He hardly acknowledged Nathan's existence, which was just fine. Behind him sat two children with their mother. At least they weren't kicking his seat. Yet. He still had more than twelve hours to go.

Back in the cafe during breakfast, Nathan had connected to WIFI long enough to download a translation app. Translating Russian to English with an app left much to be desired, but it had given him a pretty good idea of what the GRU files said. Processing the reality that faced him was another thing altogether. From what he had gathered, Jenna's parents were involved in giving a series of lectures at Moscow State University in the early 2000s. Her father, Dr. Bill Taylor, was a political science professor at the University of California, Berkeley. Her mother, Dr. Miriam Taylor, taught sociology there. Nathan saw it from the perspective of an intelligence operative. Russian intelligence was constantly searching for potential assets in the U.S. They'd have picked out the Taylors as having potential sympathies for their cause and arranged for the university to invite them over. Next, they'd wine and dine them and make personal connections. Finally, they'd offer a way to supplement the Taylors' teaching salaries. Nathan didn't know from these documents whether Jenna's parents actually spied for the Russians, but the fact that Jenna was an asset was spelled out clearly. In light of this, Nathan wondered how Jenna was ever able to get a security clearance. Just looking at those pages left him feeling as though his soul was somehow escaping his body, as if nothing he had ever known made any sense, or even mattered anymore. He couldn't help but wonder, if she would conceal this from him, what else was she hiding? Did she actually even love him at all, or was marrying within the agency just part of the ruse? He couldn't bring himself to believe that what they'd shared wasn't real, at least on some level, and yet he needed the full truth, to process it and hold onto it, and finally understand who his wife had been and what they really meant to one another.

Jenna's handler was an agent with the code name Osprey. No identity was revealed, but the agent was said to be embedded in the CIA and referred to as her "superior." Jenna's superior at the CIA was Walter Peacock. Is that who they were referring to? Nathan would need to be very careful with what information he parted with. Already he'd sent the files to himself on an encrypted app, just before leaving the cafe. Then he'd wiped the phone's data, and the SD card, and walked them over to the edge of Helsinki harbor before throwing them as far out into the water as he could. Another phone down.

The rest of the agents in the files were part of the sleeper cell that Baranova had warned about. Nathan fully realized that he couldn't do this all on his own. He was going to need help, no doubt about that, and it had to be the FBI. Fortunately, there was one agent in that organization who he trusted more than just about anybody else on earth. As soon as he got back home, he'd make the call to his old friend Kristin Simpson. Until then, he'd do his best to get some sleep. Nathan lifted a small pillow from the seat beside him and wedged it between his head and the fuselage. He felt the vibration of the engines as they hurtled down the tarmac and then lifted off into the night.

After twelve and a half hours in the air, Nathan pried himself out of his coach seat and disembarked from the plane. It was 1:30 in the afternoon, local time. At the immigration checkpoint, he scanned his American passport and stood at an automated entry point, looking into a camera, half expecting to be flagged and held by ICE agents. After a brief pause, the two small gates in front of him swung open and Nathan walked on through. He was home again, back in the U.S. of A. Without any luggage, he walked past the baggage claim and through the "Nothing to Declare" lane, handing a customs form to an agent on the way out.

As soon as Nathan exited the security zone, he spotted a small welcome committee waiting in the terminal. Drew Spinsky wore casual attire. Standing with him were two beefy security officers in dark blue suits. They stood behind a rail, surrounded by crowds of friends and family waiting to meet their loved ones. Nathan wasn't surprised, particularly, though he wouldn't have pegged Spinsky for the job. "They've got you running the airport shuttle now, eh Drew?"

"Welcome back, Nathan. Nice buzz cut."

"Am I under arrest?" he approached the men, stopping to face them. If the two accomplices were FBI, they could pull out the cuffs. If they were CIA, they had no right to take him forcibly.

"You know that's not our ballgame."

"Who are the goons?"

"Just a little support, that's all."

"What do you want, Drew?"

"Peacock wants to see you. He thought you might be more amenable if somebody you knew brought you in."

"And if I refuse?"

"Why would you refuse?"

Nathan could simply walk away and jump into the nearest cab, but they'd catch up with him eventually. They'd go to court, and get a warrant, and search his house and his electronics. Of course, they wouldn't find anything. He'd been too careful for that, but still it was probably best if he humored them a little bit for now. "Lead the way," he said.

"That's my boy."

The three men escorted Nathan out to the curb where a third goon stood waiting by a black van, wearing the same dark suit along with sunglasses. Nathan was placed in back, in between Spinsky and one of the goons. The other two climbed in front and the vehicle headed off toward the tollway. "Peacock must want to see me pretty bad."

"Think of it as a free ride."

"To Langley? How about you guys just drop me home instead?"

"I'm just doing what I'm told, Nathan. You know how it is."

"Yeah. Sure."

"I'm sorry about Jenna. I really am."

"Thank you."

No more words were spoken as they made the rest of their way to CIA Headquarters. There wasn't much point. Drew wasn't going to give him any information, and Nathan didn't feel much like small talk. After twenty minutes, they turned in to the front gate. A guard checked their credentials and then waved them through. Pulling up to the main entrance, Nathan had a pit in his stomach as he gazed out at the building. For years he'd considered himself a part of the CIA family. This was where he'd belonged, and where he'd served with pride. Now he was an outcast. He was no longer a part of the agency, he was an adversary. At least that's what it felt like. It's why they'd sent this muscle to pick him up at the airport, as an intimidation factor. They didn't trust him, and as far as Nathan was concerned, that feeling was mutual.

Spinsky and one of the other goons accompanied Nathan inside and then all the way up to Walter Peacock's office, where his presence was announced to an assistant. After a short wait, Nathan was directed into the office. Inside, he found Peacock sitting in a chair, elbows on his desk, with his fingertips pressed together. "Nathan Grant. Have a seat, son," said Peacock.

Nathan took a chair on the opposite side of the desk. "Sir."

"What the hell is going on with you? Huh, Nathan? Why don't we just start with that, shall we?"

"Nothing is going on, sir."

Peacock shook his head and then leaned back in his chair. "Is that how you're going to play this? Really? You think I don't already know? Information is my business, in case you forgot. It was yours, once, too."

"If you already know, then why are you asking?"

"I was hoping you might provide a little context." Peacock flipped open a laptop on his desk and gazed at the screen. "Two GRU operatives show up dead in Lisbon, and guess who else happened to be visiting that fine city at the same time?" Peacock looked up at Nathan with his eyebrows raised. "Those same two operatives happened to be in Italy not too long ago."

"Could be coincidence."

Peacock spun the laptop around so that Nathan could see a photo of himself sitting on a bench in a park, next to Irina Baranova. "It seems that you made a visit to Russia as well. It's a bit odd, considering your immigration record showed you were still inside the Schengen Zone. How did you manage that?"

Nathan felt a sense of dread wash over him. Baranova had wanted her role kept secret, but now everybody seemed to know, not just the FSB, but the Americans, too. She'd put everything on the line, for him. The guilt hit Nathan hard. At the same time, an anger rose within him, that Walter Peacock would challenge him at all. This man might very well be a Russian agent himself, expediting a plot to kill untold scores of his fellow Americans. And yet, the uncertainty remained.

"What did you talk about, you and Baranova?" said Peacock. "Huh, Nathan? Why go all the way to St. Petersburg? What are you after?"

"I'm a private citizen, sir. I'm allowed to travel freely, the last I checked."

"Of course, though as far as I know, murder is still a crime."

"That's never stopped you before."

Peacock's cheeks flushed red with rage. "Your little vendetta is putting our whole organization at risk. You know the score, Nathan. We don't kill Russia's operatives and they don't kill ours. You've thrown that whole calculation out the window. They lost two of theirs, and now they're going to be gunning for payback."

Nathan didn't reply. He knew it was true. The Russians wouldn't take the loss of their people lightly, though it wasn't Nathan who'd started it. They'd killed his wife. Those two very agents. They deserved every bit of what they got in the end.

"Ever since Tallinn, the balance has been out of whack, and you're only making it worse. I've half a mind to turn you over to the Portuguese authorities."

"Why don't you?"

"Because that would be an admission that a former CIA officer was involved, and I'm not about to sully our reputation."

"I'd say your options are somewhat limited, then."

"Nathan, you need to leave these things to us. You're retired. Go out to Montana and do some fishing. Just, please, stop with the running around and killing Russian agents. Would you?"

"I'm not making any promises, sir."

"If you keep this up, I'm not going to protect you any longer. At a certain point, you're going to end up in prison, or worse."

"Are you protecting me, sir?"

Peacock continued to fume. "Just answer me one question, would you? Why St. Petersburg? Think of your loyalty to the agency. You are still loyal, right Nathan?"

"Of course. I'm loyal to my country, but at the moment I have nothing more to say."

Peacock closed his laptop, sitting a little bit sideways, uncomfortable in his chair. Clearly, he was considering that call to the FBI. "We're going to keep an eye on you, Nathan. You do realize that, don't you?"

"You've got no jurisdiction on American soil, sir."

"We've got friends who do."

"Am I free to go now?"

"You're not under arrest. Not yet."

"Who were the goons with Spinsky?"

"Just watch yourself, Nathan. We're going to get to the bottom of this eventually."

"So will I, sir." Nathan got up and walked out of the office. Whatever pride he'd once felt at being a part of the agency was gone. Instead of feeling honored to walk along these storied halls, he was hit with an overwhelming desire to get the hell out and never return. Spinsky was no longer waiting in the anteroom, nor were the goons, but as Nathan headed for the elevator, he feared running into anybody else he knew. They'd all be talking, behind his back. He didn't want to feed the rumor mill with his presence, and so he hurried along, down to the ground floor and on out. He had no phone any longer, so he asked a guard at the front gate to call him a cab, and then he waited out at the street until it showed up.

"Arlington," Nathan slid into the back seat and then gave the address. It was an apartment he'd bought five years earlier, to have a home base in the area. Working for the CIA, he'd lived in Marseille and Brussels, Buenos Aires and Budapest. As a covert operative, he was constantly on the move, but that was punctuated by intermittent assignments at Langley. He'd enjoyed having a pied-a-terre for those periods in Virginia, where he could keep his things and feel a sense of stability, though most of the time the apartment sat empty. When he'd married Jenna, he'd thought that would change. He would find a private-sector job in the District, or maybe open that furniture business he'd long dreamed of. Jenna would move out of the apartment she shared with Astrid, and Nathan and his bride would start their life together. Now that was just a cold and empty vision of what might have been.

Arriving at his apartment building, Nathan entered a door code at the street entrance and moved through the lobby. He rode the elevator up to the third floor and moved down the hallway to his unit. At the front door, he ran his finger along the jam on the top right corner of his door. It was where he'd left a tiny bit of wire sticking out, barely visible to the naked eye. He felt nothing there. It was a low-tech solution for knowing if anybody had been inside during his absence. When they'd opened the door, the wire fell out. The high-tech solution was to log in and look over the footage from his security cameras to see who it was, but he currently had no electronic devices. High-tech meant you could watch them, but it meant they could keep an eye on you, too. Nathan punched a code into a keypad above his doorknob. He heard the click of the lock, turned the knob, and moved inside. It normally felt good to be back home, in the comfort of his own place, with his clothes in the closet, his dishes in the kitchen cabinets, and his TV on the living room wall. Knowing that somebody had been there, searching the place, took a lot of the joy out of it. Everything appeared to be in order. There was nothing for them to have found, in any case. Electronics were their bread and butter, but they'd have been sadly disappointed.

For the moment, Nathan didn't want to think about any of that. He wanted to take a shower. He hadn't had one of those since St. Petersburg. He wanted to order in something decent to eat, and then he needed some sleep. In the bathroom, Nathan turned on the taps. While the water warmed up, he walked into the bedroom and opened a dresser drawer to pull out a clean pair of boxer shorts and a T-shirt. On top of the dresser was a framed photograph. He reached out to lift it up. Jenna stared back, arm-in-arm with him on a beautiful autumn day in the Shenandoah Valley, surrounded by the bright orange foliage of the season. She looked so happy, filled with an innocent joy, and yet what secrets hid behind that smile? He wanted to reach through time, to go back and ask her. He wanted to beg her to explain. That chance would never come, but he would figure it out as best he could nonetheless. Nathan put the photo down, took his clean clothes into the bathroom, stripped down and stepped into the shower, letting the warm stream wash away his dirt and grime, his exhaustion and his sorrow.

Chapter Seventeen

Contacting Kristin Simpson presented Nathan with some particular challenges. They'd known each other since they were old enough to walk. Kristin's father specialized in raising show horses, which was anything but common in the area. Most families lived on cattle or oil, or a combination of both, but the Simpsons and the Grants were friendly, which meant their kids chased each other around the kiddie pool when they were young, and grew up spending holidays together. That became complicated in high school when Nathan and Kristin briefly took an interest in each other. They went so far as to attend their high school prom as a couple, but in the end it just felt wrong. They were too much like brother and sister to make a go of anything romantic. The whole episode left them confused and conflicted, and ultimately they decided that they were better off as friends, though he was always a little uneasy in her company after that. Maybe he still carried a bit of a flame for her, though he hated to admit it. Now, Nathan needed an ally and there was hardly anybody else on earth he trusted more. Kristin was an FBI field agent, based out of Manassas. Nathan couldn't do all of this on his own, tracking down a network of murderous Russian agents. The current problem when it came to seeing Kristin on a personal level was that he didn't want her feeling sorry for him. He couldn't take the awkwardness of her pity. The prospect of facing Kristin now, with all that lay between them, was more than he wanted to bear, and yet he knew that she would do whatever she could to help him.

After stopping for a hearty breakfast at his favorite local cafe, Nathan headed for the nearest big-box electronics store, where he bought yet another phone, as well as a new laptop. Not only did he need to replace his electronics, but he'd have to sweep his apartment for bugs. Those might have been placed by the Russians or the CIA, or both. Fortunately, the electronics store sold bug detectors as well. He took his new stash and headed home. After sweeping the entire apartment, he found nothing, so he sat at the kitchen table to charge his new devices and load his software. Then he sent Kristin Simpson a text.

Hey, Kristin, it's Nathan. This is my new number. Can we talk? He didn't have to wait long for a response.

Hi Nathan. In a meeting. Call you in ten?

Sure thing, take your time.

While he waited, Nathan scrolled through the footage of his security camera. Twenty minutes were missing, deleted from the server. Whoever had come in was thorough in their preparation and execution. It had all of the hallmarks of his former employer. Next, he did a quick scan of the latest headlines. It was a lot of the usual political news. Congress was bickering, nobody could agree on anything, and protests were spreading across numerous cities coast to coast. It all provided a rich target for foreign actors intent on stoking the unrest. He was halfway through an article on a riot in Milwaukee when his phone rang.

"Hey, thanks for calling me back," Nathan answered.

"I really need to apologize for not getting in touch with you sooner. I feel terrible about that. I've been meaning to call you all week."

"That's fine, I was otherwise occupied anyway."

"I'm just so, so sorry about what happened with Jenna."

"It's not your fault."

"I heard the Russians might have been involved."

"They might have, yes."

"Is there anything I can do for you? I'm here. Anything at all, just say the word."

"I actually would like to talk to you about a few things. Not on the phone."

"OK... What works for you?"

"How about this afternoon? Let's say Roosevelt Island, six-thirty?"

"This is starting to sound a little mysterious, Nathan."

"I'll meet you in the middle of the island, in front of the statue. Would that be all right?"

"Sure, that's fine."

"Just do me a favor and leave your phone in the car? I don't want anybody listening in."

There was a pause on the other end of the line as Kristin processed this last request. "Are you in some kind of trouble, Nathan?"

He wasn't quite sure how to answer that one. "I'll explain it all when I see you."

"I look forward to it."

"See you there."

When he'd hung up, Nathan opened his secure messaging app, signed in, and downloaded the GRU files, sending them to his printer. As the machine whirred and spat out the warm pages, he lifted them in his hand one at a time. There she was again, Jenna Taylor looking back at him from the personnel files of Russian military intelligence. Maybe with some luck, Kristin could help Nathan head off whatever the rest of this remaining sleeper cell had planned.

Theodore Roosevelt Island was just off the George Washington Memorial Parkway, in the middle of the Potomac

River. Nathan parked his car in the lot and walked across the narrow pedestrian bridge onto the island proper. It was a forested spit of land roughly 90 acres in size. Checking his watch, he saw that he was a few minutes early. In his left hand he held the stack of printed files. Nathan wandered down a pathway, swallowed beneath a thick green canopy. Nobody else was in sight, which was exactly how he'd wanted it. He'd always liked this park, as a place to get away from it all and go for a short forest stroll to clear his head. In the center was a clearing, marked on the far side by a looming statue of Theodore Roosevelt, standing tall with his right arm held up in the air, his handlebar mustache hanging down on either side of his mouth. Resting on a stone bench nearby was Kristin Simpson in a Navy blue business suit over a white dress shirt. When she spotted Nathan, she rose to her feet and moved to close the distance between them, pausing to look him in the eye before wrapping him in a warm embrace.

"I'm so sorry," Kristin said.

Nathan held her tightly in return. He hadn't wanted Kristin's pity, yet this heartfelt act of empathy was like an emotional balm, soothing a small portion of the sorrow he'd carried around with him ever since that unthinkable moment on Lake Como. When Nathan let Kristin go, he took a step backwards and wiped his eyes on the back of his hand.

"Shall we walk a little?" Kristin glanced at the pages he carried, but didn't mention them.

Nathan nodded and they started off down a path that circumnavigated the island. He took some time to regain his composure. "You beat me here."

"After that mysterious phone call? How could I not? I need to know what you're on about."

"You might end up wishing I never told you."

They passed a man walking a German shepherd, and then further, a young couple hand in hand. When they were out of earshot, Nathan began to tell his story.

"I found out a few things since Jenna died, and I didn't know where else to go with it. You're the only one I trust enough."

"Are these criminal issues you're talking about or personal?"

"Both."

"I see. Your confidence is well-placed, of course, although I probably shouldn't have to tell you that if you share any information of a criminal nature, I'm obligated to report that to my superiors."

"I understand."

"I just want to make sure that if you're talking to me about personal issues, you're talking to me, but if you're making me aware of crimes that may have been committed, you're talking to the FBI."

"I appreciate your candor. It's not the FBI that I'm worried about."

"Who are you worried about?"

Nathan stopped on the path, overlooking a placid stretch of the river. His eyes scanned the printed files in his hand before he held them out.

"What is this?" Kristin started in on the top page. She saw the photo of Jenna, along with the translation of the text. As she read through the first few paragraphs, her jaw fell open. Her eyes grew wide. "Where did you get this?"

"Collecting information is what I do, Kristin, or at least it used to be. I'd rather not reveal my source. Not that it would make any difference now, but still, I made a promise."

"How reliable is this?" Kristin scanned through the rest of the page and turned to the second.

"On a scale of one to ten? I'd say it's a six. Maybe seven."

"You're telling me that you think Jenna was a Russian spy? Are you serious? And you never suspected anything?"

"Never."

Kristin flipped through more of the pages. "Who are these other people?"

Nathan waited for another pair of walkers to pass before he answered the question. "It's an entire cell of Russian agents, all undercover here stateside. That's why I contacted you. My source tells me they've got big plans. They need to be stopped."

"Nathan, I'm just a field agent. This is way above my pay grade. It needs to go all the way to the top. If what you're saying has any basis in fact, this is Presidential-level intelligence."

"I get that, but there's a problem. We need to be careful about who sees this. I think they still have someone embedded at the CIA. It might be Walter Peacock."

"Walter Peacock… Didn't I meet him at your wedding?"

Nathan nodded. "You did."

The wheels inside Kristin's head were spinning. She stood on the trail, clutching the pages in one hand and staring off into the middle distance, across the river to Georgetown on the opposite bank. "We need to lay a trap somehow. This is not at all what I was expecting. I thought you just needed a shoulder to cry on."

"I guess I needed that, too."

"Can I hang onto these?" she held up the pages.

"Discretion. That's all I ask."

"Who else knows?"

"Only my source. As far as I can guess, she's currently in Russian custody."

"Nathan, you've got to understand this is going to kick up a hornet's nest inside the bureau."

"If word leaks to the Russians, they'll do whatever they can to pull their people out. We'll lose our chance to wrap it up."

"What about Jenna's parents? You think they may have actually groomed their own daughter?!"

"I don't know." This was a question that had perplexed Nathan ever since he'd first read the file. It seemed like the only logical explanation. He pictured his former in-laws, serving coffee and scones to Jenna and Nathan on the patio of their California home. They were just a nice, well-adjusted couple who loved their daughter and wanted the best for her. Or so it had always seemed. Now everything Nathan had thought of them was put into question. What hid behind those easy-going, California smiles? Something sinister, perhaps?

"We'll need to put them under surveillance."

"Of course." Nathan wanted to fly out to California to question them himself, but there was the risk that his inquiries might tip them off.

"I need to organize a team and develop a strategy. If what you're suggesting is true, we need to act fast."

"Absolutely. The faster the better."

Kristin looked over the files a bit further. "I'm going to take these to my boss right away. He'll share this up the chain on a need-to-know basis, but don't worry, he's exceptionally discrete."

"Don't cut me out, Kristin. I need to be involved."

"Oh, you'll be involved, don't worry about that. They'll want to talk to you, ASAP. Is the phone number you called me from the best way to reach you?"

"I'm on the Signal app for anything sensitive."

"Sure. Walk me back to my car?"

"Yeah." They crossed the island, headed for the pedestrian bridge. They were both quiet as they passed through the forest and on across. When they reached the parking lot, he recognized her car, parked a few spaces down from his Jeep. Kristin paused beside it. "You can expect to hear from me in a few hours," she said. "Are you going to be all right?"

"You know me. I'm tough."

"I do know you. Tough as nails, on the outside."

"I'll be OK. Thanks for your help."

Kristin gave him one last bear hug, then climbed in her car, started the engine and headed out of the lot with one last wave. Nathan checked the time on his phone. He had one hour until dueling protests were scheduled to start, just across the river at the Lincoln Memorial. He climbed into his Jeep and started it up, pulled onto the parkway and headed toward the district.

Chapter Eighteen

The rally at the Lincoln Memorial was mostly peaceful. Nathan saw some shouting, and a little pushing and shoving on the fringes, but by and large the law enforcement presence kept the two groups separated. It was mostly civil rights protesters, gathered on the memorial steps with signs calling for racial equality, women's rights and LGBTQ freedoms; a mish-mash of liberal causes. On the other side of a row of National Park police was the right-wing response. A small group carried *Don't Tread on Me* flags, along with calls to protect the Second Amendment. Nathan sized up the two groups, scanning faces for anyone he might have seen in the GRU files. Nobody looked familiar. He headed for the monument stairs and climbed halfway up, staying to the right of the crowd. At the top, the protesters had erected a small podium and a speaker was talking into a microphone, powered by a car battery that sat on the flagstones.

"We are here to represent every man, every woman, every American, no matter their color or creed!" the speaker cried out. She was African American, and young. Nathan guessed she might have been twenty years old, with an unruly mop of hair, and wearing a green Army surplus jacket. "We don't care who you love or where you come from. It hasn't been easy, ladies and gentlemen. Our history is fraught. We've had our ups and downs through the generations, but together we strive to move forward into a more perfect union. We will take what our founding fathers supplied us with and improve upon it, every day!"

The crowd on the steps cheered, clapping hands and waving their signs in the air. The girl stepped away from the podium and was replaced by a young man, White and clean cut, wearing a brown corduroy jacket and with tortoise shell glasses on his face. "Thank you Melinda. Let's hear it for Melinda, everybody, from the Rights First America Network!" The crowd cheered again for Melinda before the young man went on. "Now it's time to take this party on the road. For those who aren't aware, this isn't just a protest, it's a march. We're marching on the White House, to go tell the President of the United States that his constituents are out here and he better not forget us! We're going to head straight up past the reflecting pool behind you and then left, to make our voices heard."

After further cheers and a bit of discussion, the leaders of the march, including Melinda and the young man, moved down the stairs through the crowd. They emerged at the bottom and led the group past the counter-protesters, who jeered from behind the police line. Nathan watched, wondering what he was even doing here. What had he expected? Did he really think he'd spot some Russian agents in the crowd? All he really knew was that he felt compelled to follow every hunch he had if it might lead him to a better understanding of what was going on. To stop this quest would be to allow a part of himself to die. This mystery was what connected him to Jenna now, and he'd follow it as far as he could. He joined the march, down the stairs and along the side of the reflecting pond toward the Washington Monument. The rest of the marchers were also mostly young, and in generally good spirits as they chanted and sang. It seemed to be a social event for them as much as anything.

After passing the World War II Memorial, the group crossed 17th St. and continued toward the towering stone edifice of the Washington Monument, then hooked left and on across

Constitution Avenue. When they entered the Ellipse, a large grassy oval, Nathan saw the White House directly ahead, past the perimeter fence and across the South Lawn. It was a familiar view. He'd played touch football here on the Ellipse on many an evening. He'd also been inside the White House itself a few times to take part in security briefings. Throughout his CIA career, Nathan had been undercover many times overseas but this was the first time he felt that he was undercover at home. Looking around at the participants, he knew there would be FBI plants among them. Some of the actual activists would have interacted with them online and maybe invited them to events, never knowing the truth about their law enforcement identities. It was all part of the game, keeping on top of any potential threats, no matter where they came from. Nathan did his best to pick the agents out. He looked for people who were old enough to have graduated from college and made it through Quantico, but young enough to still be strong and agile. This was ideally an assignment for agents between twenty-five and thirty-five. They would also be a little bit disconnected from the others, perhaps not cheering so loudly, but quietly observing. Of course, Nathan realized that he was also describing himself. Any outsider would likely peg him to be the FBI plant, if they were looking for one, and it wasn't so far off from the truth. He did spot a few other likely suspects. There was a woman, alone, quietly peering around at the others. She was in her late 20s, and while she did have a small protest sign, she wasn't waving it enthusiastically. Nathan also saw a pair of men about the same age, no signs, no chanting, just marching along on the edge of the crowd. Of course, it was all speculation. What mattered was not who the FBI plants were, but whether any Russian agents were in the mix, though this was probably the safest place to hold a rally in the entire country. Park Police shadowed their every move.

Washington, DC police sat nearby in several cruisers. On the White House grounds, Secret Service agents were carefully watching, with snipers manning the rooftop. To get away with any malevolent actions here would take some doing.

At the far side of the Ellipse, the march reached the White House grounds and spread out along the perimeter fence. The marchers still had a jubilant air about them as a subset broke out into a new chant. "Hey, hey, ho, ho! Your patriarchy has got to go!" By this time, Nathan had his eyes on the pair of men he'd picked out already, hanging near the edge of the crowd. They were certainly not your typical protesters. While everyone else seemed joyful, these two were dour. Quite obviously they were observing the scene, but to what purpose? Good guys, or bad? One of the men checked his phone to read a text, then said a few words to his partner and the pair of them left the crowd and began to walk away toward 17th Street. Something about these two was certainly off. Nathan couldn't quite put a finger on it, but instincts told him they were up to something. He let them get a short distance ahead and then he surreptitiously followed after. The men were across from the Red Cross headquarters when they reached a black van with tinted windows parked on the side of the street. The pair took a quick look around and then climbed inside.

A park bench faced the street just thirty yards down from the van. Nathan took a seat. He took out his phone and pretended to occupy himself with it. He used the camera to take a photo of the van, and then zoomed in close to snap the license plate. Most likely, these two were secret service, or perhaps FBI. Nathan was probably just watching the watchers, but still something set off his inner alarm bell. Fifty yards further up the street was a secret service guard shack. In the opposite direction, he saw a DC metropolitan police car idling in a driveway with an officer behind the wheel. Surely, nobody would try anything here. It would be a suicide mission, though Nathan knew that fact wasn't enough to rule it out.

Cars moved past on 17th street in either direction. Some of the protesters were beginning to stream by, holding their signs down low as they headed home for the day. Nathan heard the engine in the black van turn over and then watched as it pulled away from the curb and drove off. It seemed to be a false alarm after all. Nathan himself needed to get home as well, to have a shower, order in some dinner and try to sort out a game plan. It might just be time to leave the whole thing to the FBI. Stalking protests on his own wasn't likely to get him anywhere. It seemed like just a big waste of time.

In the empty parking space that the van had previously occupied, a small black Audi pulled in and screeched to a stop. A man hopped out and popped his trunk. Nathan recognized him immediately. It was Raul Gutierrez, one of the buddies he occasionally played football with. Gutierrez didn't see Nathan right away. He went to the trunk and pulled out a mesh bag full of gear; footballs, cleats, small orange cones, and flag belts. After closing the trunk, he took a step up onto the sidewalk and then noticed Nathan with a start. "Hey, hey, look at you! How about this parking spot, huh?" He pointed at his car.

"Hi Raul."

"I usually have to drive around for half an hour before I find a space."

"Your lucky day, I guess."

"What the hell did you do to your hair?"

"I thought I'd go for a new look."

"Man, no offense, but you look like a concentration camp survivor."

"Thanks, Raul."

"I'm just sayin'…" He eyed the demonstrators. "What's going on here?"

"Some protest, I think it's wrapping up."

"As long as we have room to play. What about you? Where's your gear?"

"I'm not playing today, sorry."

"Why not? What are you even doing here if you're not gonna play? Come on, man, you drive all the way over here and then let us down? You better have a good excuse!"

"You know, just a lot going on." Nathan stood from his bench. "Look, I've got to get going. I'll catch you guys next time."

"You better, I'm going to hold you to that."

"Sure thing. Have a good game" Nathan had only taken a few steps toward Constitution Avenue when he noticed a car driving slowly past. It was an ancient Dodge, from the early 1980s, with faded green paint. Inside the car was a single driver, alone behind the wheel. He sat up straight in his seat, head to the side as he watched out the window. Nathan recognized the man immediately. It was Ivan Shustov, from the Russian intelligence files. When the car had passed, Nathan saw the rear license plate flip down, revealing an opening into the trunk. The long barrel of a rifle silencer poked out.

"Get on the ground!" Nathan yelled to his friend, but Gutierrez just stared at him in confusion. "Get down, get down!" Nathan hollered again, turning to warn passersby before crouching low himself. He sensed a flash of terror in the crowd at his insistence, but nobody reacted until the bullets started flying. Screams rang out as the first victims were hit, their bodies dropping to the lawn. People ran in pandemonium in all directions, with nobody realizing where the gunfire was coming from. Gutierrez was now under the bench, with his bag of gear in front of him. The green Dodge picked up some speed and moved on, but not in any hurry. They didn't want to draw attention to themselves as they continued past the DC police cruiser and on down the block. Nathan jumped to his feet and hustled to Gutierrez. "Give me your keys."

"What?"

"Your car keys, hurry up!" Nathan had no time to lose, but his friend lay motionless, in a state of shock. Nathan leaned down and felt his friend's right pocket from the outside, then reached in to pull out a black Audi key fob. "You'll get it back!" He hustled into the car, hit the start button, and stepped on the gas, burning rubber as he pulled a U-turn. The Dodge was turning right onto Constitution as Nathan chased after. By the time he reached the corner, the green car was racing down the avenue, but now the DC police joined the chase. Lights flashed and sirens wailed as the patrol car sped behind Nathan, who hurtled up the avenue himself, weaving through late rush-hour traffic. As he gained on the Dodge, he saw a second man sit up in the passenger seat. To avoid traffic, Shustov jumped the curb and flew up the sidewalk past the Federal Reserve building before veering wildly across the avenue and into the park, tearing across the grass. Nathan weaved and darted, hopping the curb and barely avoiding a clutch of pedestrians as he gained ground.

By the time the Dodge made it to Lincoln Memorial Circle, the rear window shattered as the man in the passenger seat began shooting at Nathan. Two National Park Police cruisers joined the chase, roaring toward them from the memorial. The police fell in behind as Nathan followed the Dodge across the Arlington Memorial Bridge and into Virginia.

On the bridge, Shustov weaved into oncoming lanes, then back, and then up onto the sidewalk, all the while maintaining his breakneck speed. He scraped against another car, then bounded across the walkway and skimmed against the bridge railing, sending sparks flying and pedestrians leaping out of the way, a few of them launching themselves off the bridge, arms flailing as they hurtled toward the river below. Nathan's windshield exploded next, spraying him with bits of safety glass, but still he kept on their tail. Every bullet fired in his direction was a deadly missile that might hit him, or an innocent passerby, and yet he couldn't give up the chase. He couldn't let them get away. Glancing in his rear-view mirror, he saw chaos and mayhem. In the confusion of the moment, and the flying bullets, two cars swerved out of their lanes and crashed into each other head-on. More cars slammed into them, blocking the entire span of the bridge, with the police cruisers trapped on the other side. It was all up to Nathan now.

In Virginia, the Dodge came to an enormous traffic circle, turned right and then careened to the left across a grassy median before picking up the road again on the other side and heading south on the George Washington Parkway, toward the Pentagon and then on down to National Airport. Did they have a private plane waiting? Nathan let the Dodge gain a hundred yards on him but kept it in view, swerving back and forth just enough to keep the shooter from getting a bead on him. They'd gone another mile when the car pulled off the road at the Columbia Island Marina. In the distance, Nathan heard more sirens, converging on them from multiple directions. He took the exit and continued following at a distance as the Dodge turned left and raced through a parking lot until it reached a dead end. Nathan pulled up behind another parked car and crouched low behind his door to watch. If he'd been armed himself, he might have been able to take them out from here, but as it was, he was helpless. All he could do was witness what they were up to. The two men jumped out of the car, the passenger still carrying his rifle, and ran down to one of the docks and on out. They'd had an escape plan all along. The men jumped onto a waiting speedboat, already idling in the channel. A third man who stood waiting for them behind the wheel pushed full forward on the throttle and they took off across the water.

From behind, Nathan heard the police approaching with the wailing of the sirens. He saw them skid to a stop, three cruisers taking up positions on all sides of him. Six officers jumped out and drew their weapons, pointing them at him from behind their own doors. "Out of the car, now! Hands in the air!" After Nathan complied, they ordered him onto the ground. He lowered himself to the asphalt, his cheek resting on gravel as they pounced on him, pulled his arms behind his back and slapped on the cuffs. "You have the right to remain silent, anything you say can and will be used against you..." one of the officers read him his Miranda rights and the next thing he knew, Nathan was shoved into the back of a patrol car. Through the window, he saw more official vehicles streaming into the lot. There were uniformed motorcycle police, military police, and more Park Police, as well as unmarked cars that had to be FBI and Secret Service. It was like a law enforcement convention. Now they'd have the fun of determining jurisdiction. Nathan watched as they argued about it, while a small clutch of detectives examined the Dodge. Eventually, a white van arrived and Nathan was transferred into the back. His view was gone, but he had a pretty good idea where he was headed. After a short wait, he felt the van start up and begin moving out of the parking lot. Being in custody didn't bother him so much. He'd sort that out soon enough. What bothered him was that it seemed as though Shustov and his partner were getting away. Nathan made a fist and pounded the inside of the van in frustration. For the time being, there was not a thing he could do about it.

Chapter Nineteen

He was taken to FBI headquarters on Pennsylvania Avenue and locked into a cell. It wouldn't be long, he knew. They'd want to question him as soon as possible. It was all about gathering the right personnel to interview him. Clearly they thought he was an accomplice, if not the shooter himself. Eventually, they took him to an interview room where three agents waited inside. Nathan was handcuffed to a chair on the opposite side of a small table. On one wall was a mirror, four-feet long and three-feet high. He knew there would be a crowd of spectators on the other side, watching the interview and listening to his every word. Certainly the Secret Service would be represented. Probably the CIA as well. Maybe the Defense Department, considering he was arrested a mere quarter-mile from the Pentagon.

"Nathan Grant." One of the agents held up Nathan's driver's license and compared the photo to the real-life, flesh-in-blood man sitting before him. "Is that your real name?"

"Talk to agent Kristin Simpson out at Manassas. This is going to be a waste of time until you get her involved."

The agents were clearly not expecting this answer. "What is she going to tell us?"

"Call her and find out."

"Why did you murder those innocent civilians on the mall?" said another agent.

"Is that what you plan to charge me with?"

"Among other things."

"And you think I'm going to talk without a lawyer present? I'm not an idiot."

Now the agents looked annoyed more than anything.

"Look, I didn't murder anybody. I was trying to stop it. That's all I'm going to say for now. Get agent Simpson down here and then maybe we'll talk." After that, the third agent peppered Nathan with questions. Who were his accomplices? Where did they go? Who was he working for? Nathan sat in his chair, head tilted sideways, and stared at the man with disdain. "I have the right to remain silent. You said so yourselves." Eventually they gave up and left him in the room alone. Nathan sat that way for over an hour until the door opened once more. Two of the same agents led in agent Simpson, who was horrified when she saw Nathan in this condition.

"Get those cuffs off of him!" she cried out.

One of the agents in the room looked her over with suspicion. "We need to sort some things out first."

Kristin Simpson was visibly upset. It seemed to Nathan that she wanted to hug him again, but of course she could not. That would only raise more questions. Instead, she took an empty seat across the table. "What's going on, Nathan?"

"That depends," he replied. "Am I under arrest?"

Simpson looked to the man sitting beside her. He was in his late 50s, with short gray hair and glasses. He wore a white dress shirt with the sleeves rolled up and a blue and red tie. "Is he?" she asked.

"Look, agent Simpson, we brought you down here to get him to talk. If you know anything else yourself that could shed light on the situation, we'd love to hear it."

"I told you outside, it's on a need-to-know basis."

"You're saying I don't need to know?"

"I'm saying this is a sensitive case, director level."

"Of course it is. It's a damned terrorist attack in front of the White House! I need to know what the hell is going on!"

"I understand that, but there are certain high-ranking parties within the government who can't hear these details."

"You can't be implying this was an inside job? Is that what you're trying to tell me?"

The door opened and another agent stuck his head inside. "Clark, you've got a call. It's the director."

Clark looked at Simpson, then at Nathan, and then back to the door. "Right." He got up and left the room.

"Do you need anything to eat?" Simpson said to Nathan. "Maybe some coffee?"

"Water would be nice."

Simpson looked to one of the other men. "Can we get some water in here?"

This man left the room for a few minutes and then returned with two bottles of water, giving one to Simpson and one to Nathan. They waited for a while longer in silence until Clark finally returned. "Uncuff him."

The other agents couldn't seem to believe what they were hearing, but one hurried over with the keys and took off the handcuffs. Nathan rubbed his wrists.

"Everybody out but the suspect," said Clark.

"Suspect?" said Simpson.

"I stand corrected. Mr. Grant is no longer in custody."

"Does that mean I'm free to go?" said Nathan.

"Of course, we need to ask you some questions first."

"What about me?" said Simpson.

"Sorry."

Simpson stood and gave Nathan one more concerned look before heading out the door. When everyone but Clark was gone, a new man entered. He was tall and skinny with a thin black mustache. "So, this is the man," he said.

"Nathan Grant," said Clark, "Meet Deputy Director Fitzgerald."

"Good evening, sir."

"Is it?" The three men sat at the table. "Tell me, Mr. Grant, what do you know?"

Nathan nodded toward the mirror. "Is the CIA still in attendance?"

"No, sir, we've cleared the room of everyone outside the bureau. Believe me, they weren't happy."

"I'm sure."

"What have you got, son?"

At this point, Nathan knew he had no choice but to put his faith in them and hope for the best. He filled in the Deputy Director in on the details. He told him about the Russians, and the secret files he'd passed on to Simpson, and about Jenna, and his suspicion that a mole was still buried at the highest levels of the CIA. Fitzgerald took it all in, asking questions as they went.

"So, you just happened to head out to the mall this afternoon and you ran into this Shustov character, by chance?" said Fitzgerald.

"Not exactly chance, sir. I knew the Russians had plans to disrupt peaceful protests. I thought I'd take a look around at one."

"And then you figured it was a good idea to give chase, all by yourself?"

"In the heat of the moment, yes, I did."

"You're lucky you didn't get killed."

"Yes, I imagine that I am. By the way, could you make sure the Audi gets back to its rightful owner?"

Fitzgerald glared at him. "I'm going to let you go now, Grant, but I want your word on something. You're not a law enforcement professional. You're not even employed at the CIA any longer. You're a private citizen, understand? If you have any further information, phone it in, but otherwise we don't want your help. You got it? Leave this thing to us. Period."

"What happened to the Russians?" Nathan avoided Fitzgerald's plea.

The deputy director looked to Clark. They didn't want to share any information at all, though this was the kind of thing that would be easy enough to find out by reading any newspaper. "We found their boat in Alexandria. They got away."

"I'm sorry. How about at the protest. Any casualties?"

"Just leave the police work to us, will you?"

"Sure, good luck. I hope you get them."

Clark rose to his feet. "Come on, Grant, we'll process your release."

Nathan followed the agent out of the room. Half of an hour later, he was standing in front of the FBI building with his wallet in one pocket and his keys and phone in another. The sun had long gone down, and it was a balmy, late summer night in the nation's capital. Nathan was just a mile and a half from where he'd parked his Jeep, just off Constitution Avenue near the Lincoln Memorial. He set off on foot. A little fresh air would give him time to think. He'd only gone a few blocks before he was back to the Ellipse. By now the entire area was blocked off with barricades and national guard troops. Floodlights lit up the expansive lawn, where law enforcement personnel were still combing for evidence. Nathan had to cross the street toward the Washington Monument in order to work his way past crowds of spectators gathered on the side of the road, craning their necks to survey the scene. "Excuse me," Nathan stopped to ask an onlooker. "Was anybody killed?"

"You didn't hear?" said the middle-aged man with a bushy black beard.

"No, not yet."

"The bastards killed three people."

"What bastards?"

"Who do you think?" The man seemed annoyed at even having to answer this question. "The right-wing extremists. Just like Charlottesville. White supremacists. I hope they burn in hell."

"How do you know it was White supremacists?"

"Who the hell else would it be?" The man turned back toward the scene of the crime, hoping to see action of some kind.

"Thanks." Nathan continued on his way. So far, anyway, it seemed that the Russians were succeeding in their plot. That might change if the FBI released the information that he'd shared. One thing Nathan felt more sure of at this point than he had from the start was that Jenna had nothing to do with this chaos and terror, at least by choice. He couldn't possibly believe that she'd go along with the innocent slaughter of Americans, no matter what the Russians might have had on her. She was kind and caring, with a huge heart. Jenna was always looking out for the downtrodden and less fortunate. Whatever she *was* mixed up in, it must have been tearing her apart. She'd been carrying a nearly unimaginable burden, seemingly all alone. "Why didn't you tell me?" he said to himself once more as he continued past the reflecting pond. "I could have helped you. We could have figured it out together."

When he arrived at his Jeep, he climbed in and headed back across the river. He drove as though on auto-pilot, not actively thinking about where he was going, but following his instincts.

He wasn't particularly surprised, though, when he pulled up in front of Jenna's old apartment. It was a two-story building with four units, all facing the street. Jenna had shared apartment number one on the ground level with her friend and colleague Astrid Burns. Nathan parked along the curb and shut off his engine. The apartment lights were off. Nobody home. He replayed in his mind the times he and Jenna had spent together here; dinners and game nights, lazy Sunday mornings, her warm body beside him in bed. Before the wedding, she was all packed up and ready to move into his place as soon as they got back from Lake Como. It was a move that she wouldn't live to make, of course, and the hole that left in Nathan's heart would never be completely filled, no matter how many days on earth he still had left himself.

Nathan was about to start his engine and head for home when another car pulled up and parked just in front of him. He recognized it immediately. This was Astrid's car. He watched as she got out of the driver's side door and went around to the trunk, where she unloaded several bags of groceries. She'd stepped to the curb when she looked back and saw his dark figure, sitting behind the wheel. At first, she seemed startled. Astrid looked at the Jeep, then back to the driver. She stepped forward to the passenger window and he rolled it down.

"Nathan?" she said.

"Hi, Astrid."

"What are you doing here?"

"Trying to make sense of it all, I guess."

"I see." She stepped back and looked away momentarily as she weighed an appropriate response. "It must be unbearable," she said, turning back to him. "Would you like to come in? I can offer you a beer, or maybe something to eat."

Nathan was conflicted. Part of him wanted to drive away and never look back. All of this sentimentality was torture. Nothing was going to bring her back. He needed to accept that fact, and the sooner the better. Another part of him wanted never to forget a single moment that they'd shared. He knew those memories would fade over time, and that thought terrified him. He'd lose little bits of her, day by day. He wanted to lock in what he could. Perhaps sitting in her kitchen one last time might help. "Sure, I'll take you up on a beer."

"Great," said Astrid, though she seemed ambivalent. Nathan didn't blame her. Who wanted to spend time with a man deep in mourning? He almost changed his mind, but she nodded to one side. "Come on."

After climbing from his Jeep, Nathan came around to the curb and offered a hand. "Let me help you with those." Astrid handed him one of the grocery bags and he followed her up the front steps and into the building. As soon as they entered her apartment, Nathan was hit with a sense of emptiness. The furniture was mostly the same, but a few things were missing: Jenna's things. Her favorite chair in the living room had been replaced. Photos of hers were missing from the bookshelf, as were her scented candles and a few odds and ends from her travels. Nathan followed Astrid into the kitchen, placing his bag next to hers on a counter. Before she unloaded them, she opened the refrigerator and looked inside. "I've got a nice amber ale, or there's a bottle of chardonnay if you'd prefer that."

"Amber ale sounds great."

Astrid pulled out two bottles and set them on a counter while she found an opener. "Have a seat, make yourself comfortable. I've got some chips if you'd like."

Nathan didn't answer, but he sat down at the kitchen table and took a look around. On a little nook in the wall where a landline phone might have gone twenty years earlier, Astrid had a framed photo of herself with Jenna, arm-in-arm with the torrent of Great Falls just behind them. Somehow it soothed him that her presence was still here. She would always be remembered, and not just by him but by everyone who'd ever loved her. Astrid popped the caps off the beers and handed him one, then opened a bag of tortilla chips and placed it on the table.

Nathan swallowed some beer while he watched Astrid put her groceries away. He was tempted still to get up and walk out, to apologize for even coming, but then Astrid joined him at the table and offered a compassionate smile. "How are you doing?" she said. "I can't imagine the pain you're going through. It's hard enough for me, and I was just her friend."

"She cherished your friendship." Nathan tried to shift the conversation away from himself. How was he doing, Astrid wanted to know? If the truth came out, he might break down right here at the kitchen table.

"That's kind of you to say."

"I think a part of her never wanted to move out of this place."

"I hated that she was leaving."

"Has anyone else taken the room?"

"No. I thought I'd leave it empty for a while. You know, Jenna was one of the first people I met at the agency. She showed me the ropes. I don't know how I would have coped without her, the whole place was so intimidating those first few months."

"She was good that way. Always the calm in the middle of the storm."

Astrid stood back up to put the rest of her food in the pantry, then picked up her own beer again without taking a drink. "What will you do, now? I'm sure they'd welcome you with open arms if you wanted your job back."

Nathan took a deep, long breath. "I don't think my heart is in it anymore. I'll take some time off for a while, maybe go to Greece and rent a little cottage by the sea. Or Thailand. Jenna loved Thailand. I can learn to paint, and grow my own vegetables in a garden out the back."

"Off grid. I get it. Nobody is going to blame you if you want to just check out for a while. You've got plenty of time to figure out what your next chapter is going to be."

The sound of the doorbell echoed through the apartment, followed by a loud knocking on the front door. Nathan's eyebrows went up. "Expecting somebody?"

"Oh, that's probably just Drew."

"Spinsky?"

"Yes. That would be Drew Spinsky." Astrid was sheepish now. "Hang on!" she called out as she left the kitchen and moved to the front door.

"Hey, baby," Spinsky's voice carried into the kitchen.

"Hey, Drew, you'll never guess who just stopped by to say hi. He's in the kitchen right now."

"Who is that?" Spinsky didn't wait for an answer. Instead, he moved straight into the kitchen to see for himself. When he spotted Nathan, a range of emotions rippled across his face. First was shock, as he clearly wasn't expecting to see his old colleague here. Next was a flash of distaste, as he apparently wasn't happy about it. Third, he broke into an insincere smile in an attempt to hide the first two. "Hey, buddy, how ya doing?" Spinsky clapped him on the back. "Good to see you!"

"Thank you, Drew. Likewise."

"Join us for a beer, Drew?" said Astrid.

"Absolutely."

Astrid took another bottle from the refrigerator, popped off the cap, and handed it across.

"Are you two?..." Nathan was embarrassed to finish the sentence. He'd never known them to be an item. In fact, he'd thought they hardly knew each other.

"I'm afraid that wedding of yours got something started," Spinsky looked to Astrid and smiled, sincerely this time. She placed a hand on his back.

"I always said I'd never date inside the agency," said Astrid. "This is bound to be trouble."

"You better believe it, darlin'," Spinsky laughed.

"Well, I'm happy for you two. You make a great couple."

"Thanks, buddy." Even while Spinsky said the right words, Nathan felt a vibe. Drew didn't want him here. Maybe he was embarrassed, or perhaps he didn't want to talk about what happened to Jenna. Or maybe he didn't trust Nathan, after the little airport shuttle incident. Whatever the case, Nathan knew he was no longer welcome here now that Spinsky had arrived.

"Look, I don't want to bother you two."

"Nonsense," said Astrid. "You're not a bother. We were going to order some takeout. Why don't you join us?"

"No, I've got to get going. Thanks for the offer."

"You know you're always welcome here."

"Take care, Drew."

"Sure, man. You, too."

Astrid walked Nathan through the living room to the front door. "It was good to see you, Nathan. If you need anything at all, let me know. Even if it's just somebody to talk to."

"I appreciate that."

"I'm sorry I can't make it to the memorial."

"What memorial?" Nathan perked up.

"For Jenna? Didn't they call you?"

"I've gone through a few different phone numbers lately."

"It's the day after tomorrow, out in San Francisco. Her parents are organizing it. I'm sorry you didn't hear sooner!"

"Yeah, me, too. Look, take care of yourself. Maybe I'll see you around."

"Thanks. That would be nice."

Nathan let himself out the door and then continued down across the front walk to his Jeep. He climbed in and fired it up. As he drove home, he thought about what he might order for dinner himself, and how much a last-minute ticket to California would set him back.

Chapter Twenty

The flight from Dulles arrived at 9:40 a.m. on Sunday into San Francisco. Nathan's return was booked for 7:00 p.m. the same day. No luggage, no accommodations, just a quick turnaround. He'd spoken to Jenna's parents on the phone that previous Friday night. Of course he was welcome to come. Of course they'd tried to reach him. Jenna's mother, Miriam, seemed relieved that they'd finally managed to connect with him before it was too late. For his part, Nathan had mixed feelings about the entire thing. He felt an obligation to be there, and indeed he wanted to be, as a way to say goodbye. At the same time, he knew that Jenna's parents were suspects. They could very well be Russian agents themselves. In fact, he even considered it likely. Nathan had explained all of that to the FBI and he knew the couple would now be under tight surveillance. With the GRU files he had provided, the warrants would easily go through, their phones would be tapped and they would be followed everywhere they went. In fact, this memorial service was the perfect opportunity for FBI agents to search their home, when they knew that the Taylors wouldn't be there. How did Nathan feel, knowing all this, yet still having to smile and greet them as though none of it were going on? Of course, he wasn't going to the memorial to honor her parents, he was going for Jenna. He didn't trust Mr. and Mrs. Taylor any more than the FBI did, but he'd get through the service, spend the day in San Francisco, and head back home before the sun set.

After picking up his rental car, Nathan drove into the city. The memorial was scheduled to take place at 1 p.m. at Crissy Field, on the edge of the bay. It was always one of Jenna's favorite spots, with the Golden Gate Bridge looming to the left, the downtown skyscrapers reaching heavenward to the right, and Alcatraz Island floating just off shore. He stopped in the Marina district for an early lunch at an old 50s-style diner on Lombard Street, ate the classic cheeseburger with fries and a coke, and walked out with an hour to go before the service. It was a cool and clammy afternoon, with the typical San Francisco fog blowing in from the sea. He opted to walk, heading first to the bay and then west toward the bridge. Nathan passed the gathering point for the service. Chairs were set up on the lawn and a woman he didn't recognize was arranging flowers on a table at the front, but the mourners had yet to arrive. He continued along the pathway beside the water until he came to the end at Fort Point, where a sturdy brick fortification from the Civil War era clung to the windswept headland beneath the southern end of the bridge. Just offshore, a clutch of surfers jockeyed and scrambled for ten-foot-high waves that swept along the rocks and broke into a small cove. Nathan stood and watched them for a while, wondering what their lives must have been like, these San Francisco surfers living an existence that was so very far removed from his own. These days, there was nowhere on earth that quite felt like home to him. He'd been on the move for so long that he had no center, no place where he truly belonged.   He remembered what that was like when he was young, back in Texas with his friends and family all around, but now there was no real community that he was a part of, not even the agency that he'd given so much of his life to. He eyed a few of the surfers who were gathered by their cars in the parking lot, their black rubber suits dripping wet as they discussed their session with animated hand gestures, all while keeping an eye on their compatriots still in the water. To be a part of a community like that, one needed to stay put somewhere. Trust and friendship took time to develop, but Nathan always had itchy feet. A year in one place was enough. Too much, sometimes. That was one of the reasons he'd connected so deeply with Jenna. She was his community. She was his center. Maybe they'd have stayed in DC for a while longer, but maybe they'd have moved on. He'd liked to picture them bouncing around the world together as a self-sufficient team, perhaps heading off to her beloved Thailand for a stint, but now she was gone and he was taking everything one day at a time. He would focus on unraveling this mystery but at some point, whether he sorted it out or not, the time would come to move on, like closing a door on the past. He couldn't spend the rest of his life obsessing over all of the unknowns or it would eat him alive from the inside.

Nathan walked back toward the park, arriving again just as the guests were beginning to gather. He saw Jenna's parents, and her younger sister, Melody, standing by the table at the front and chatting with a pastor. Arranged with the flowers was a colorful urn. His heart sank as he realized that the contents inside were all that was left of her. Nathan should have handled these details himself, but he'd left the arrangements to the Taylors and now here she was, in this small container. Several people Nathan had never met stood talking in small groups, while others were already taking their seats. Nathan felt a sense of doom in the pit of his stomach at the prospect of facing them all, but there was no avoiding it. He had to go through with this, and so he straightened his posture and walked straight up to the Taylors.

"There he is," said Miriam when she'd spotted him. "I'm so glad you were able to make it."

"Me, too, Miriam." Nathan gave her a hug and kissed her on the cheek.

"We thought you'd disappeared off the face of the earth," said Bill.

"I almost did."

"Hi, Nathan," said Melody.

"Good to see you," he kissed her on the cheek as well.

"I wish it was under better circumstances." The comment hung in the air, nobody wanting to validate it with a response.

"This is Pastor Doyle, he's going to lead the service," said Bill.

"Nathan was Jenna's husband," Miriam explained.

"I'm sorry for your loss," said the pastor. "She was a beautiful soul."

"She was indeed." Nathan looked around at the outskirts of the park, knowing that the FBI must be watching their every move. He saw a man in khaki pants and a dark sweater, sitting on a bench with a book in his hands. When their eyes met, the man quickly looked away. It was only obvious if you knew to expect them. Nathan had to figure that nobody else at the service would be looking.

At the appointed time, he took a seat in the front row, next to the family. The pastor spoke first about what an inspiration he knew Jenna Taylor to be. Miriam reached out to take Nathan's hand, squeezing it tightly as if to say, you are not alone. When the pastor was finished, family and friends took turns saying a few words. Nathan went last. Standing in front of this crowd of mostly strangers, he felt as if his own spirit had somehow slipped away from his body and he was in an alternate dimension. He sensed Jenna's presence, as if she was floating high above and watching down on them. "Anybody who knew Jenna understands what a terrible loss the world has suffered at her passing." As Nathan spoke, he felt that all of those eyes upon him somehow blamed him for her death. And who could argue? The guilt haunted him every day, yet given all of the information that had come to light, he wasn't really sure. Were the assassins really after him? Or her? The blank stares told him what the attendees thought. He quickly wrapped up his comments and retook his seat.

When the service was finished, the Taylors led a small segment of the group onto a nearby wharf that reached straight out into the bay. Mr. Taylor carried the urn. He said a few last words and handed it to Nathan.

"Go ahead," said Miriam. "It's what she would have wanted."

Nathan nodded and took the receptacle in hand. The fog had lifted and it was a beautiful summer day, with sunshine glinting off the water. In his hands he held all that was left of the person he'd planned to spend the rest of his life with.

"She's still with us, right here," Mr. Taylor tapped at his chest. "She always will be. Nothing can take that away."

Nathan unscrewed the lid and then held the urn over the edge of the wharf, tipping it up to let the contents slide into the water and then drift away with the current. Melody tossed in an armful of flowers that she'd carried from the table. They all stood in silence, Miriam weeping while Bill held her in his arms. Nathan felt now as though his whole body were going to melt, straight down into the timbers at his feet. Nobody seemed to know what to say or do next. Mr. Taylor helped his wife back along the wharf toward the shore. Nathan followed, alongside Melody. "You'll come to the house, right?" she said.

"The house?"

"My parents have food arranged. Everybody is going. My mom will be very upset if you don't join us."

Nathan didn't answer right away. The only thing he wanted to do was head straight back for the airport and get on the first flight out. The service took more out of him than he'd expected, He wasn't sure he could handle any more.

"Please," said Melody. "It would mean a lot. Really."

"Of course."

"Do you need a ride?"

"No. Thanks. Can you text me the address?"

"Sure."

Nathan gave Melody his current phone number and then walked to his car. He checked her text, plugged in the house number to his navigation app, and followed the directions through the city and then onto the Bay Bridge. The Taylors lived in a stately, ivy-covered house in the Berkeley Hills. Nathan had been there once before. As he pulled up again half an hour later, he figured this would be the last time. Inside, the Taylors had catering set up on counters in the kitchen. It was buffet style, so Nathan helped himself to small finger sandwiches, fruit salad and a glass of white wine. He chatted with a few of the other guests. He was putting in his time, trying to determine how long he had to stay before he could head off in good conscience. After a good forty-five minutes, he made his way to Miriam to say goodbye. "Thanks for having me Miriam, I've got to be going now."

"So soon?" she seemed somewhat panicked. "Did you get enough to eat?"

"Yes I did, thank you so much. I'm very glad that I was able to make it out here today. It was a lovely service that did her justice."

"I appreciate your saying so. Before you go, come with me for a minute, will you?" She cocked her head to one side.

Nathan felt a little uneasy, but how could he deny her? "Sure."

Miriam led Nathan upstairs and then down a hall to Jenna's childhood bedroom. It was largely untouched. High school pendants hung on the walls, along with posters of her favorite bands. The bedspread pattern was filled with images of horses, jumping over a wooden fence. "There's something I'd like to give you." Miriam reached out to a shelf and lifted a small cardboard box. "These were her treasures. I'm sure she'd want you to have them." She held the box forward and Nathan took it in his hands.

"Thank you."

Miriam stood where she was. There was something else she wanted to say, but she couldn't seem to get it out.

"What is it, Miriam?"

"I just… I want to know what happened. I know you're not supposed to give away the details. These things are secret, but you have to understand, I need to know. A mother has a right."

Nathan understood that the house was likely full of bugs. The FBI was listening. "I'm sure somebody explained to you that a bomb was planted in our boat, but if you're asking me why, I just don't know," he told her the truth. "It's a mystery to me, too, Miriam. If there was something I could tell you, I would."

Her disappointment was palpable. Her shoulders sagged and she looked away. "I understand."

"Miriam… Maybe you can tell *me* something?"

"Anything."

"Did Jenna have any connections to Russia that you were aware of?"

"Of course, but that was many years ago."

"What can you tell me about that?"

"Is it important?"

"It might be."

Miriam couldn't understand where this conversation was headed. She didn't seem disturbed by it, in any case, just a bit surprised. If she'd actually been a spy, Nathan figured she might be a little bit panicked right about now, but if she was, it didn't show. "We took a trip there, as a family, way back. I think she was around nine years old. Bill and I, we were invited to give some lectures. Jenna, she went back again in high school and did a semester exchange. She stayed with one of the families we'd met."

"Did she keep in touch with them over the years?"

"Not that I know of. They drifted apart, you know how that goes. Does this have something to do with what happened to her, Nathan?"

"I don't know. Do you remember the name of the family?"

"They were the Volkov's I think. I can't remember the parent's names anymore. They had a son and a daughter. Tatiana and... oh, let me think. Tatiana and Lev."

"Thank you for the box, Miriam."

"You'll tell me if you learn anything more, won't you Nathan?"

"Of course." Nathan left the room, headed down the stairs and out to his rental car. With some luck, he'd be able to get onto an earlier flight.

Chapter Twenty-One

"We're picking up chatter about a protest rally in Richmond," Kristin Simpson said over an encrypted app. "We think something big might be going down."

"I thought you weren't supposed to be talking to me," Nathan answered.

"I'm not."

"So, what gives?"

"I figured you deserved to know. You'd be well within your rights to attend, as a private citizen."

"When and where?"

"Saturday at noon. They're gathering at the former site of the Robert E Lee statue. It's a big roundabout on Monument Avenue. We're expecting a big turnout of right-wing agitators, plus the usual anti-fascists on the other side. After what happened on the Ellipse, tensions are going to be especially high. We'll have plenty of agents on hand, along with a large local police presence, but it's bound to be combustible."

"Thanks for the heads up."

"Just be careful, and if you do happen to cross paths with anybody suspicious, you can call me directly."

"Right." Nathan hung up the phone and took a seat on his sofa. On the coffee table in front of him was the cardboard box that Miriam had given him. He had yet to properly go through it. Opening the lid, he looked inside. It was filled with the usual mementos of childhood. There was a medal for first place in the long jump from a fifth-grade track meet, hanging from a blue ribbon. There was a key chain in the shape of the Eiffel Tower that she'd picked up on one of her trips abroad. A cartoonish colonial figure with a large three-pointed hat was emblazoned with her high school's initials. Nathan didn't know what he was going to do with this stuff besides file it away in the back of his closet. He picked up a stack of photos and flipped through them. This, at least, was more interesting. It gave him a glimpse into Jenna's life before he'd known her, including a few shots with her friends from that long-ago trip to Paris when she was so very young and vibrant, standing arm-in-arm in a group before the Notre Dame Cathedral with a wide grin on her face. He went from one photo to another, highlighting all of the important moments of her young life. It should have been devastating to see them under the circumstances, and yet somehow they filled his heart with peace. These were the moments that she was happiest in life, and looking at them now made him grateful for the time on earth that he'd been able to share with her. None of the pictures were from Russia: no shots of Vasily Volkov or his young son Lev. When Nathan was finished, he put the photos back into the box and lifted a small plastic canister. Popping the lid, he found a roll of undeveloped film inside. It had to have been at least 10 years old, from back before the digital revolution. Why hadn't she ever taken these to be developed? Perhaps she'd just put it off as one store after another stopped offering film processing. He held the roll in hand and spun it around until he saw a date. "Best if processed before Jan. 2005." Even if he found a shop that could develop it, the film was probably decomposing by now. He put it back inside the canister and popped the lid closed before setting it aside on the table. At least he could try.

It was Saturday morning as Nathan stood at the counter in a local camera store. The attendant squinted as he looked at the roll, reading the date. "I can't make any promises, but we can see what we get."

"What are the chances you can salvage them?"

"That depends on the condition in which the roll was stored. How hot was it, how damp? If it was inside the canister the whole time, indoors, I think you'll get something usable. They might be a little washed out, with blemishes, but we can probably restore them."

"How long will it take for processing?"

The attendant glanced at his watch. "I'm a little busy this morning, but I could put them through by close of business."

"That would be fine." Nathan filled out an envelope with his name and address, dropped the canister inside, and handed it over.

"We close at 6 p.m."

"Thanks."

After leaving the store, Nathan got into his Jeep and jumped onto the beltway, toward Interstate 95 and then south to Richmond. It was a two-hour drive, which gave him some time to think. What was he expecting? That Shustov would show up again, when every law enforcement officer in the country was on the lookout for him, was highly unlikely. Nathan considered what he would do in a similar situation. What if he was abroad and his cover was blown, with local authorities hunting him down? That was a fairly easy question to answer. He'd get the hell out of that country as quickly as possible. As a foreign operative, he'd have a few fake passports, with alternate identities and appearances. Maybe one would have his photo with blond hair and a beard. Another might have him looking like an elderly man with a prosthetic nose and ears. He'd disguise himself and sneak across the border, then catch the first flight home to be debriefed at headquarters. If Shustov followed the same plan, he'd be long gone already. He'd have made his way to Montreal, perhaps, and then flown back to Moscow from there. Or maybe he'd disappeared inside the Russian embassy in DC and was hiding out. In any case, the chance of seeing him at this Richmond rally was extremely low, but that wouldn't stop Nathan from trying.

When he arrived in Richmond, Nathan drove toward the large roundabout that had until recently held the Lee statue, but the roads were closed to vehicular traffic. A crowd was already beginning to swell. He had to park more than a half-mile away. After shutting off his engine, Nathan unlocked a center console and reached inside to pull out a holstered Smith & Wesson 9mm pistol with an extra 17-round magazine. Unlike the last protest, he would be better prepared this time for any unfortunate contingencies. He climbed out of his Jeep, slid the magazine in one pocket, his phone in the other, and attached the holster belt around his waist before pulling his shirt down over it.

As Nathan walked toward his destination, the atmosphere was an odd mixture of jubilation and hostility. He was surrounded by small groups of various right-wing militias, some wearing camo, others in Hawaiian-print shirts. More than a few had assault rifles slung over their shoulders, with extra magazines of their own in their vests. Confederate flags waved in the air. It was a tinderbox, ready to go up. These people, mostly men, were gleefully looking for a fight.

One block away from the roundabout, law enforcement had the entire street shut down, to both cars and pedestrians. National guardsmen stood shoulder to shoulder behind metal barricades. It seemed that this protest would not be allowed to proceed as scheduled. Agitators stood near the front, pointing their fingers and shouting, the veins bulging in their necks. "Let us through! Let us through!" they began to chant in unison. Nathan scanned the crowd for familiar faces but saw none. In the distance, he spotted a towering stone pedestal that marked the spot where the statue had stood, in the center of the traffic circle.

From behind the groups, a local police cruiser moved slowly toward them up the street, lights flashing. The officer inside made an announcement over his PA system. "Please disperse, this is an unlawful gathering! If you do not disperse immediately, you will be subject to arrest!"

In response the crowd jeered and then closed in, surrounding the car and blocking it from moving in either direction. As they grew bolder, the participants began to rock the car back and forth. Nathan saw the lone officer inside, eyes lit up with fear. "Back away from the vehicle, that is an order!"

"Oh, it's an order," one of the protesters jeered. "What are you gonna do, start the shooting? 'Cause my gun is bigger than yours!"

"Hey, Antifa's in Meadow Park!" one of the others shouted. "They think they're gonna start something!"

"Meadow Park! Pass the word! Meadow Park! Antifa's in the park!" yelled another. All at once, the groups began streaming away, back in the opposite direction and then right onto Park Avenue. The police could keep the crowds from the monument site, apparently, but they couldn't stop the fight. Nathan would go where the action was. He followed along toward the park, knowing that if the Russians were here, or even if they weren't, the bullets might start flying at any moment. Overhead, he saw drones following along. Higher still hovered a police helicopter, with news choppers a bit further off. Whatever went down today, it would be well-documented.

As they approached the triangle of Meadow Park, Nathan saw a counter-protest gathered in wait. A crowd of multi-ethnic young men and women stood holding signs calling for peace and equality. The group was mostly unarmed though a few, dressed all in black, held pipes and sticks. If they were looking for an altercation, they were vastly outnumbered and out-gunned. Two police cruisers converged on the park just as the right-wing crowd arrived. This was going to get ugly, Nathan realized, and there was nothing he or anybody else could do to stop it.

In the center of the park, the two groups faced off in lines, waving their signs and flags, shouting in each other's faces. It wouldn't take long before violence broke out. Nathan stayed toward the back trying to keep an eye on things without being involved. The pushing and shoving at the front line had begun when a black police van pulled up and a phalanx of SWAT officers in tactical gear piled out and formed a line, holding clear plastic shields. "Attention. You are hereby ordered to clear the park. Please disperse immediately, this is your only warning!"

"Go home! Screw you!" shouted the crowd.

Up toward the front, Nathan saw a woman of similar age to him, terrified as she tried to back away. The SWAT officers didn't wait. Two of them emerged from the van with grenade launchers and immediately began firing teargas canisters and flash-bang grenades. Screams erupted and people began to flee, falling and stumbling over one another as they went. Nathan pulled his shirt up over his nose and moved back, the sting of the gas in his nostrils. A block away, he saw groups re-forming as they gasped for breath, bending over with hands on knees, some using bottles of water to wash out their eyes. "Sons of bitches!" came a shout.

To Nathan's right was a man in camo pants and a white sleeveless t-shirt. He wore a black backpack and carried an AR-

15 assault rifle. His head was shaved and he sported a bushy blond beard. The man was solo, standing back a ways and not a part of any sub-group. He seemed to be more of a spectator, like Nathan himself. Maybe he was just a loner, venturing out from his cabin in the woods to make a showing for the cause. Or, he could have been FBI or police undercover. But then he looked directly at Nathan and their eyes met for a fraction of a second that seemed to be frozen in time. Nathan recognized those eyes. Those were Russian eyes. Underneath that beard was Ivan Shustov. As soon as he'd seen Nathan, his head snapped away and he started moving off, sliding his backpack from his shoulders as he went. Nathan unsnapped his holster and pulled out his gun, though firing it in the middle of this crowd was far too risky, and so he hurried after the Russian to close the distance. When Shustov reached the far edge of the crowd, he tossed the backpack and began to run.

"Bomb!" Nathan shouted at the top of his lungs as the bag skipped past him and skidded to a stop on the pavement. "Bomb, bomb, bomb!" Nathan took off running himself, chasing after the Russian. He was halfway up the block when the bag exploded. First was the blast, and then the screams. Nathan stumbled from the shock wave, nearly falling over, but regaining his balance and continuing after his adversary. By this time, Nathan heard another blast coming from the direction of Meadow Park, then another from the traffic circle. It was a coordinated attack. Another block on and Shustov had his rifle in both hands, turning to shoot as he went. Nathan got off a few shots of his own, but the distance was too great, and he was far out-gunned. He dodged and weaved before ducking for cover behind a parked car beside a young couple, huddled together. Strapped over the man's shoulder was another AR-15 with a scope attached.

"Give me your rifle!" Nathan screamed.

The young man, frozen in fear, merely stared back at him.

Nathan holstered his pistol and then grabbed the rifle, ripping it off the man's shoulder and pulling the strap from his arm. After popping up over the car's hood, Nathan aimed up the street, but Shustov was no longer in sight. Nathan took off after him, on the hunt. He ran to the next intersection and looked right, then left. He saw a busy avenue, clogged with a mass of vehicles all trying to flee the scene. Weaving around them was Shustov, headed across the street toward a large retail center. Nathan bolted after him and was gaining as the Russian raced across the parking lot. When Shustov neared the entrance to a two-story shopping mall, Nathan worried that he'd lose the man in the maze of shops, so he stopped and took a firing stance, raising his rifle to peer through the scope. He was about to fire off some rounds when the mall doors opened and a mother with two young children hustled out. Nathan lowered his gun and Shustov disappeared inside.

When Nathan reached the mall entrance, he ran through the doors and then saw a wide corridor straight ahead, with stores on either side and a few clusters of panicked shoppers rushing for the exits while others hunkered down in place. A double set of escalators led to an upstairs level. Nathan charged up the steps, three at a time, hearing screams as he went. He was on the right track. When he reached the top, he emerged onto a walkway with an opening in the middle giving a view to the lower level. Ahead and to the right, Shustov had ducked into a hallway, half hidden behind a wall with his gun pointed back as he fired off a few more rounds. Nathan dodged into the nearest store, feeling the burn of hot lead tear at his left shoulder. Screams echoed up and down the mall as shoppers scrambled out of the way, or hit the deck and crawled toward the relative safety of the shops.

Nathan took a quick look at his arm. His shirt was torn and soaked in blood, but the wound was superficial. He raised his rifle and peeked around the doorway but he saw no sign of the Russian. Nathan charged forward once again until he came to the hallway where Shustov had just been. He saw bathroom doors to the right and a stairway to the left. Shustov would never trap himself inside the bathroom. He'd gone for the stairs. Positioning himself in front of the stairway door, Nathan pointed the rifle straight ahead and then kicked a horizontal bar on the door with his right foot. The door swung open to reveal an outdoor stairway. Below, he saw Shustov running away across the parking lot. Nathan moved forward onto a metal landing and pointed his weapon. It was just like home, shooting deer from the platform in the tree. This time, he saw Shustov through his scope. The Russian looked back over his shoulder in terror, but that didn't stop Nathan from pulling the trigger. One shot and Shustov collapsed to the ground. Nathan lowered his gun and ran after him.

When Nathan reached the man, he was still alive but just barely. Shustov gasped for breath, but all that came out was a gurgle of blood, and then no more. The edge of the man's fake beard was peeling back from just below his left ear. Nathan grabbed the flap and ripped it off the man's face. In the distance, he heard sirens. The police were on their way, but with traffic blocking all the streets, it would take them a while. He searched the sky for the police helicopter and spotted it further off, still hovering over the bomb sites. Fortunately for Nathan, they had a lot on their plate. He wasn't about to let them haul him in. Kristin might be able to help him sort this out later, but right now he still had leads to follow. Nathan dropped the fake beard, rolled the man onto his blood-soaked back and then rifled his pockets. He found a set of car keys, a wallet and a phone. He left the keys, the police could have those, but he put the wallet in one of his own pockets and then took the phone and held it in front of Shustov's face, allowing the facial recognition software to unlock it. He knew he had to hurry. That helicopter might be diverted his way at any moment. Nathan opened the phone settings and navigated to set up a new face ID. Then he held the phone in front of his own face and moved his head in a slow circle. When he tapped *Done*, he stood up and began to walk briskly away. He still carried the rifle in one hand, with his prints all over the thing, but he had no time to wipe it down. They'd connect him to the shooting in time anyway. For now, he placed the rifle into the back of a pickup truck as he went past and then continued on his way.

Nathan was able to cross through the cars on the avenue again and make his way back in the direction of his Jeep, just as the helicopter passed overhead on the way to the mall. They didn't spot him, and after the bombings, the wound on his arm didn't stand out either. He was just another in a mass of injured bystanders, as ambulances did their best to ferry the worst of them away.

Arriving at his Jeep, Nathan climbed in and sat in the driver's seat. He flipped through Shustov's wallet. The driver's license had his photo with the name David Wagner. The same name was on two credit cards. The wallet held $35 in cash. That was all. Nathan looked at the phone to unlock it. He heard the *ding* of a new message. It was the same encrypted app that Nathan often used. The sender was listed simply as *Osprey*. *Did you complete your job?* it said.

Nathan thought about whether or not to reply. He wanted to string this person along, to not let them know that Shustov was dead, and yet, what if he was required to answer in code? He'd have to take his chances. *Completed,* he wrote. *Packages delivered.*

Good. Await further instructions.

Affirmative.

Nathan next took out his own phone. In the excitement of the moment, he'd missed several calls. All of them were from Kristin Simpson. He dialed her back.

"Tell me you're OK," she picked up right away.

"I'm fine, but look, we need to talk."

"Where are you?"

"I'm still in Richmond. Can we meet at your place in a couple hours?"

"Of course, you know the address."

"Could you do me a favor and pick up some first aid supplies?"

"How bad is it?"

"Not as bad as it looks."

"Should you go to a hospital?"

"With a gun wound? No way. They'll report me."

"What happened, Nathan?"

"I'll tell you when I get there." Nathan hung up his phone, started up the Jeep, and headed off toward the interstate.

Chapter Twenty-Two

"You shot a man in the back! I'm sorry, Nathan, but you've got to surrender yourself to the local authorities." Kristin Simpson dampened a gauze pad with alcohol and then placed it on Nathan's bare shoulder as he winced in pain. "There's only so much I can do to help you here, but fleeing the scene is not advancing your case. Hold that."

Nathan held the gauze in place as she taped it down. He was sitting on a chair in her kitchen. "He shot me first. Besides, how many people died in that explosion? I had to stop him."

"I know that, and a judge is going to know that, too, but you still can't just flee the scene."

"I don't have time to get caught up in the red tape right now. We've got a direct connection to Osprey. We can catch this guy, if we play our cards right. As soon as he realizes that Shustov is dead, he'll go dark for good. We've got to act now!"

"What do you propose? That we call up Osprey and ask him to meet for coffee?"

"Come on, Kristin, don't be like this."

She shook her head, disturbed as she weighed her obligations as a federal law enforcement officer. These people were responsible for murder on a mass scale. In addition to the shootings at the White House, twenty-two more people were known to have died in the Richmond bombings so far, with many more in the hospital. "We need the kind of resources on this that only the bureau can provide."

"Having to explain ourselves is just going to slow things down. We'll miss our opportunity."

"I can't go rogue, Nathan. I'm sorry. I swore an oath and I intend to live by it. Give me Shustov's phone and I'll see what the Bureau can pull off of it."

Nathan was frustrated but not surprised. "No way, Kristin, I'm not going to give it up. Not yet. I've got a conversation going. I need to see where it leads."

"I'll have to tell them everything I know. You've got to understand that. If you want to buy yourself some time, I suggest that you don't go back to your apartment for a while."

"Thanks for the dressing." Nathan stood to go.

"Hang on." Kristin disappeared into her bedroom and came back with a folded t-shirt. "It's big on me, but for you I think it might fit."

Nathan unfolded the shirt. *University of Texas* it read across the front. "You're a woman after my own heart."

"I try."

She helped him pull it on over his head, feeding his wounded arm through the sleeve. "Good luck, Nathan. If you hear anything actionable, will you let me know?"

"Of course."

"What about the Russian's ID? You can't tell me that you still need that."

Nathan took Shustov's wallet out of his pocket and placed it on the counter. There was nothing in it that could further his cause. He let himself out of the apartment and walked out to the street. What would the Russian cell be up to now that they'd carried off such an audacious plot? A mass bombing would bring heat unlike they'd ever known. The only option that made sense at this point was exfiltration. But how? He climbed into his Jeep, fired up the engine and headed off. First things first, he needed to eat.

Over a French dip sandwich, fries and a salad at a Crystal City diner, Nathan searched online for everything he could find about David Wagner. There were scores of them online, but none looked anything like his man. Nathan felt it was a dead end. He could still text Osprey on Shustov's phone, but what could he say that wouldn't tip the man off? Anything unexpected would seem suspicious. He took the phone out of his pocket and looked it over as he drank a sip of coffee. And then he heard a *ping!* Nathan clicked on the notification. The message was from Osprey. *Departure time revised. Be advised, wheels up 22:00.*

Nathan felt like all of the air had suddenly been sucked out of the room. He could barely breathe, but this was his chance. They were fleeing the country after all, but from where? He couldn't very well write back and ask. That would be a dead giveaway, though it was best to confirm receipt of the message. *Affirmative*, he texted back. He put the phone down and ate another fry as he considered his next move. It was now 6 p.m., which meant that he had four hours until his quarry departed on what was apparently a private flight out of the country. They could be leaving from any airport with a runway long enough for a private jet that was within a six-hour drive of Richmond. How many was that? Nathan couldn't begin to guess. He'd have to try to narrow it down. It was unlikely to be a major airport. No Dulles, or National, or BWI. The security was too tight in those places, with too many cameras. In fact, it was unlikely to be anyplace that had a control tower at all. They'd want a quiet, uncontrolled airport, where they could take off without anybody noticing and fly below the radar until they were twelve miles out to sea, beyond U.S. airspace. They'd want a facility with a runway long enough to handle a small private jet, yet where there wouldn't likely be much traffic at 10 p.m.

As he continued with his dinner, Nathan scoured the web for private airports in the vicinity. There were scores of them. He quickly ruled out the three nearest Washington; Hyde Field, College Park and Potomac Airfield. These fields had security restrictions, put in place after the 9-11 terrorist attacks. Pilots needed TSA security clearances to take off or land. It was highly unlikely that any pilot with such a specialized clearance would be flying a planeload of Russian spies out of the country. This would be somebody brought in from overseas for one extremely risky job: perhaps a recently retired Russian military pilot looking for some extra cash.

Further out in Maryland, Nathan found a handful of additional airports. There was Lee Airport, Bay Bridge, Kentmore and Deale. All of them had runways of right around 2,500 feet or less. They were just too short for any aircraft attempting an international flight. The same went for the private airports in the Richmond area. Could the Russians be using a smaller, turbo-prop? Maybe they'd planned a few refueling stops on the way up the coast and into Canada? It was possible, though it didn't seem likely. Perhaps there was something Nathan was overlooking. With diplomatic passports, it was certainly possible that they could pull the whole thing off right out in the open. They could fly out of Dulles on a chartered flight, under diplomatic cover. Only, these spies weren't using diplomatic cover. Not as far as he could gather anyway. They didn't seem to be working at the Russian embassy, or a consulate, pretending to be economic officers or cultural attaches. Nathan couldn't be 100 percent sure about all of them. He picked up his phone and called Kristin.

"Get in touch with the TSA and check for any chartered flights in the area scheduled to depart at 10 p.m. tonight. Our suspects might be on board." Nathan explained himself as best he could. "I'm turning off my phone now, Kristin. I don't want anybody tracking me down. If I have anything more, I'll let you know."

After hanging up, Nathan spotted one more possibility on his map that he hadn't yet checked out. Tipton Airport was just 30 miles away. It was the site of a former United States Army Airfield. It had no tower, nor any commercial service. The single paved runway was 3,000 feet long. Was that enough for a private jet? Nathan polished off his sandwich as he did more research. A Cessna Citation Mustang needed 3,110 feet to take off at sea level. An Embraer Phenom 300 needed 3,138. Either one could manage it with the right headwind, especially if they weren't fully loaded. A Swiss-made Pilatus PC-24 only needed 2,930 feet. With a maximum altitude of 45,000 feet and a range of 2,000 nautical miles, the plane could feasibly make a round-trip from Nova Scotia, refuel there and then skip on across the Atlantic.

Nathan asked a passing server if he could borrow a pen, then jotted down directions to Tipton Airport by hand on the back of a takeout menu. He leaned back in his seat as he switched off his phone, and then Shustov's. He didn't know that the Russians would be there, but he knew that if he was in their shoes, that was exactly where he would depart from, sneaking away into the night. The only way to find out if they thought the same way was to drive on up and see.

Chapter Twenty-Three

Nathan arrived an hour early, giving him some time to scope the place out. The airport itself wasn't much. He parked in a small, empty lot near the midpoint of the field. A sign informed him that the building just in front of him housed the airport authority offices, but the windows were dark and it seemed that anybody who worked there was already gone for the day. Nathan unlocked the center console in his Jeep and pulled out his holstered Smith & Wesson, leaving the extra magazine behind. He turned on Shustov's phone to check for any updates. There were none, but he saw that the battery was down to six percent. It might shut down at any minute. He turned it back off and then plugged it into a charging cable inside the console before locking the compartment closed.

After climbing out of the Jeep, Nathan fastened the holster around his waist. He slid his own phone into one pocket, keys and his wallet in the other. The summer sun had already set, and the last light of day was fading in the western sky. To the southwest, he saw massive cumulonimbus clouds, with an occasional flash of lightning. The storm was some distance off, but a change in weather was on the way, he could feel it in the sultry summer air. Atop the building, a lighted wind sock pointed straight out as a brisk wind blew in from the northeast. Nathan walked past the office building toward the tarmac on the opposite side, where he came to a cluster of perhaps 50 small planes parked in rows under overhead lights, wingtip to wingtip on the asphalt. Just beyond the parking area was a taxiway, and further out he knew must be the runway itself, though with the runway lights turned off, all he could see was darkness.

Further down on Nathan's right was a long row of small private hangers, each one large enough for a single prop plane. To his left was a series of larger hangars, several stories high with floor-to-ceiling sliding doors on the front. Not a soul was in sight in either direction. Nathan walked toward the first hangar on the left. Out front was a sign for a helicopter rental and charter company. The sliding door was open a crack. He saw light emanating from inside and heard music. When he moved close, he peeked in to see a bright red helicopter to one side and several fixed-wing aircraft on another. Toward the back, a mechanic worked on a twin-engine plane, peering into the right engine, with the cowling removed and several parts on a blanket spread out beneath the wing. So immersed in his task was he that the man didn't notice, or perhaps care, that he was no longer alone. Nathan took a few steps inside to get a better look around. There were no signs of any passengers preparing for departure, or anybody else for that matter. He retreated out through the door and walked down to the next hangar, but this one was dark inside and locked up tight. Checking his watch, he saw that it was still forty-five minutes to departure.

It was possible that the Russians were using an entirely different airport, of course. The chances that he'd picked the correct one were actually quite low. This airport had seemed on paper like a promising possibility, but now that he was here it was beginning to feel like a complete waste of time. The place was dark, and quiet, and practically deserted, but Nathan would wait it out. In the meantime, he wandered across the tarmac amongst the parked planes, seeing what else there was to see. When he reached the taxiway, he moved on across and then over a strip of grass, where lightning bugs glowed neon yellow, bouncing through the air above the ground. When he stood in the middle of the runway itself, Nathan could make out stars shining directly overhead. Looking toward the west, he felt the breeze at his back. It all seemed relatively peaceful, the calm before the storm. Nathan took a deep breath of that moist, mid-Atlantic air. He was lost in his reveries when the runway lights flashed on. Suddenly exposed, he flinched and then scrambled off to the side, back into the relative darkness of the field. In the eastern sky, he spotted the landing lights of an approaching plane, then heard the distant buzz of an engine and watched as it came closer and closer, finally touching down with a squeak of the tires and a slight smell of burnt rubber. It was a single-engine Cessna that continued past him and then turned onto the taxiway and headed for the parking area. Nathan followed along at a distance, keeping to the shadows as the runway lights switched back off. The plane eventually pulled into a parking place between two other aircraft and the engine sputtered to a stop. A man and woman climbed out, one on each side. They tied the plane down, attaching chains from the ground to the wings, and then put chocks behind the wheels, casually chatting as they went. Lastly, the man reached into the back seat and retrieved a wicker picnic basket before locking the doors. He kissed the woman on the lips, took her by the hand, and they headed off. It was a date, and quite a romantic one by the looks of things, but nothing more.

Once again, Nathan was alone. He saw the headlights come on in the couple's car and then watched them pull out onto the road. If the Russian's were coming, he'd see them arrive just as clearly, but with less than 30 minutes to go, there was still no sign of them. He wandered back toward the car parking area and then found a step to sit on and wait. It seemed to be a wild goose chase, but he wasn't ready to make a final judgment yet. He let the minutes tick by, one after another, wondering all along if the FBI was having better luck somewhere else, or if the Russians were quietly boarding a plane at a completely different airport, perhaps outside of Nathan's estimated range. The thought of them whisking off back to Russia filled him with a boiling anger. He'd exacted his revenge on the operatives from Italy. He'd even managed to take out Shustov here in the U.S., but it wasn't enough. Nathan's yearning for vengeance was far from satisfied. He wanted the rest of this sleeper cell, and Osprey, and even Volkov. Nathan had no doubt that it was the colonel who ordered the bomb planted in their speed boat on Lake Como. Volkov must have recruited Jenna all the way back in high school. She'd lived with their family, spending time with young Lev, the man responsible for the assassination of Yuri Kuznetsov, with whom Nathan had fought for his life inside the abandoned prison in Tallinn. Colonel Volkov opened his home to Jenna once long ago, and then ordered the bomb that killed her. It was still hard for Nathan to wrap his head around it all, though he knew that the colonel likely had a hand in directing this cell on American soil as well.

From where he sat on the side of a hangar, Nathan saw the road, quiet and dark but for a few evenly-spaced street lamps. He also saw the tarmac and the parked planes. He heard cicadas, chirping in the grass. And then the runway lights flicked back on. Nathan sprang to his feet. Was another plane inbound? He ran toward the field to get a better view. Looking to the west, he saw no navigation lights approaching. He did a full 360-degree turn, searching the skies, straining his ears for the sound of a plane. At first there was nothing, but then he heard it, growing louder by the second. It was the unmistakable whine of jet engines approaching. This was it! He pulled out his phone and powered it up before calling Kristin Simpson.

"Nathan, what's up?" she answered right away.

"Tipton Airport! Maryland!"

"Tell me what you know."

"It's a little field, middle of nowhere. Three thousand foot runway. There's a private jet incoming." Nathan still couldn't see it. The plane was approaching with all navigation lights switched off, like black ink in the night, but from the roar he knew it was close.

"Have you seen any signs of the Russians?"

"Not yet. Look, Kristin, I've got to go." As Nathan hung up the phone, the plane appeared, hurtling out of the darkness from the west and slamming down hard, tires screeching. The pilot reversed thrust, throttling back up as he used the engines to slow the plane's velocity. But where were the passengers? He'd seen no cars approaching, no Russian agents skulking in the shadows. Until he did. The giant door on the darkened hangar slowly slid open. They'd been waiting inside all along. When the opening was ten-feet wide, a black SUV pulled out, lights off. It was followed close behind by a second, and they raced across the tarmac toward the plane, meeting at the runway's eastern end.

Nathan unsnapped his holster and pulled out the gun before running toward them. He was vastly outnumbered. Four people climbed out of the first vehicle, and three more from the second. In all, five men and two women stood waiting as the plane came to a stop and the door opened. A set of mechanical stairs began to unwind as a few of the men unloaded luggage from the vehicles. All Nathan had on his side were one gun and the element of surprise. But then, he couldn't just shoot them, or apprehend them all himself. His only chance was to hold them until the cavalry arrived.

"Don't move!" Nathan shouted as he drew near. A few of the passengers looked up, somewhat confused at this figure emerging out of nowhere with a gun in his hands. Others went about their business, apparently not hearing him over the noise of the idling jet engines. "I said stop where you are!" he yelled louder, pausing a good twenty feet away from the nearest man and pointing his gun from one person to another and back in rapid succession, trying to cover all seven people, plus another emerging from the doorway at the top of the stairs. This last man shouted something down in Russian as he tried to see what was going on.

The man nearest Nathan raised a hand slowly in the air. "Good evening." He was tall and thin, wore a dark suit, and spoke with a sophisticated accent. It was one that Nathan couldn't quite place. Perhaps he was the son of diplomats, born in Eastern Europe but a product of the finest British prep schools. In one hand he held a briefcase. "I suggest that you lower your weapon."

"All of you, hands up, now!"

"Do as he asks," the man said to the others.

"Drop the bags and move away from the vehicles. Let's go, I want everyone together in a group, and keep those hands in the air where I can see them!"

"Such strong commands. And where are your partners? Or are you all by yourself here at this lonely outpost?"

"Move it!"

The man nodded. He didn't seem particularly concerned, as though he knew some secret that Nathan did not. The whole group of them gathered together as the first smattering of rain began to fall, the rumble of thunder coming ever closer.

"And which agency might you be from? The FBI? Hmmm? Homeland Security? Or maybe you're just with the local Sheriff's office? Would you mind showing us your badge, if you please?"

Nathan moved closer to the nearest SUV and tried to peek inside, but with tinted windows he could see nothing. "I want everyone who's on board the plane to come join us, right now!"

"And will you shoot a group of unarmed diplomats, with diplomatic passports? That will be troublesome. I don't imagine it will go over well with your government, or the press. Do you realize what an international incident this will cause, merely holding us here at gunpoint? I suggest you release us immediately, for the sake of your career."

"Thank you for your concern." Nathan took a step forward but then the rear door of the vehicle beside him swung open with force, slamming into his outstretched hands and knocking him backwards. A large, dark figure bounded from the car and was on him in a flash, wrestling Nathan to the ground and pinning his right arm and gun to the asphalt. Nathan used his left hand to punch the man in the face, once, then twice, but before he was able to get off a third blow, the rest of the men in the group pounced on him, some kicking him in the legs, and the abdomen, and the head, while others held his limbs in place. Nathan struggled to free himself, but against so many, he had no chance.

The man with the accent pressed a foot on Nathan's wrist, then grabbed the gun and pried it from Nathan's fingers. Holding it at length, he looked it over quizzically before pointing it squarely between Nathan's eyes. "And so, once more I ask, who do you work for?"

Pinned to the ground on his back, Nathan looked up without a word as the rain began to pour down, pelting his face with oversized drops.

"Cat got your tongue, eh?"

"You're Osprey, aren't you?"

"Ah, interesting question. Clearly you're not just some airport security guard, working the night shift. Too bad you won't live long enough to give us the answer." The man turned to the brute who'd emerged from the back of the vehicle. "Search him."

The burly thug checked Nathan's pockets, pulling out the phone, his car keys, and finally his wallet. "Let's see what we have here." This man sounded American. Boston, to be more precise. He tossed the phone and keys into the car and then used the cabin lights to look over Nathan's driver's license. "It says his name is Nathan Grant. No badge."

"Nathan Grant?" said the tall man. "I can't say that name rings a bell. I will be sure to pass it along to my superiors, however." He took a quick look at his watch. "For now, it's time we bid you adieu. Let's go, everybody on board!" Those few in the group who weren't busy holding Nathan down hurried to retrieve their bags and then hustle up the stairs of the plane as the wind kicked up further and a flash of lightning illuminated the scene. The tall man handed the gun to his henchman. "Wait until we've taken off, then shoot him."

"What about the body?"

"I don't care. Dump him in the Chesapeake. Dump him in the woods. Whatever you want, but just make sure we're airborne first."

"Right."

The other men let go and followed their compatriots onto the plane as the brute kept the gun pointed between Nathan's eyes.

"Good evening to you, what's left of it," the sophisticate said to Nathan before he walked off toward the plane, up the stairway, and on inside. The stairs retracted and the door swung closed as the plane prepared for takeoff.

"Let's go, roll over and get on your knees."

Nathan slowly complied.

"Forehead on the asphalt!"

Nathan knelt forward, pressing his head against the tarmac. He heard the engines revving as the plane began to move. They were going to need every inch of runway they could get, and with this storm blowing in that meant they could take off in only one direction. The plane would need to taxi all the way to the opposite end of the runway before turning around to head into the wind. It would buy Nathan a few more minutes at best. Was the cavalry coming? Had Kristin Simpson alerted her superiors to send in some manpower? He assumed that she had, but the question was how long it would take for them to arrive. He did a bit of math in his head. The nearest FBI office was probably Annapolis, twenty miles away. The nearest sheriff's office? He had no idea. The chance that anybody would get here in the next two minutes was slim, assuming this thug had the patience to even wait that long. Nathan heard the plane moving away, the noise receding. "You don't have to do this," he said.

"Shut up."

"You know you'll be caught. That means the rest of your life in jail, if you're lucky. Is this what your momma envisioned when she raised you? A life of crime?"

"I said, shut the hell up!"

Nathan felt the barrel of the gun press against the back of his head. He closed his eyes and took a deep breath, listening to the wind, feeling the rain on his back, taking in all of the sensations of being alive for the last few moments he was able. As soon as that plane took off, a single gunshot would ring out and it would be the end of him. A cold chill ran through his entire body. He couldn't go out like this. Not without a fight. Nathan opened his eyes once more, tilting his head slowly in the direction of the plane, trying to come up with a plan of attack, and then BOOM! A lightning bolt crashed down in a massive flash, the thunder echoing like a bomb. Nathan took his chance, flipping over and grabbing the gun, directing it to one side just as the man pulled the trigger, sending a single round flying past Nathan's head. He swung his legs hard, taking the man out at the calves. The thug toppled over, landing with a thud beside Nathan as they struggled for control of the weapon. The brute was stronger, but Nathan was more agile. Four years of high school wrestling gave him just a hint of an edge. He managed to get one forearm across the man's windpipe as he slid on top, but the man used the side of the gun as a bludgeon, smacking Nathan on the side of the head and knocking him off. Prying the gun from Nathan's hands, the man clambered to his feet and was just about to shoot when Nathan caught him with a kick to the patella, buckling the man's knee with a sickening pop and sending him crashing to the ground once again. Nathan rolled on top of the man and caught him from behind in a choke-hold. His adversary managed to get a few more rounds off as he struggled to breathe, but the shots whizzed harmlessly past. Nathan held on, with his bicep cutting off all air, until the squirming stopped and the thug was out cold.

Scrambling to his feet, Nathan peered toward the far end of the runway. He couldn't see a thing aside from the parallel lights disappearing into the gloom. Somewhere down there, the jet was about to accelerate. He picked up his gun, and then fished his wallet from the thug's pocket. Once the plane took off, the Russians would be gone forever, never to face justice. There was only one way to stop them. He poked his head into the nearby SUV. The engine was running, with a key fob resting on the console beside his own keys and phone. Nathan climbed behind the wheel and slammed the door shut, then threw the vehicle into drive and hit the gas. If he could get down there to the far end in time, he might be able to block them. He pulled onto the runway and raced forward through the rain. Fumbling with the steering column, he managed to turn on the windshield wipers but he could still see very little. The runway lights marked the center line, leading him straight ahead. He heard the whine of the jet engines suddenly pick up as the pilot hit the throttle. Nathan was nearly halfway to the end when he spotted the plane, emerging from the storm and hurtling straight toward him. There was no time to react. The nose of the airplane was just off the ground when it reached the SUV, and it cleared the vehicle by a few feet, but then came the smashing sound of metal tearing into metal and Nathan had the sensation that he was floating sideways as the car spun down the wet asphalt. Around and around he went, until the vehicle skidded to a stop. Through the side window, he saw the plane lifting off the ground at an angle. At first Nathan thought they might make it, but then the right wing clipped the ground and snapped clear off. He caught a whiff of kerosene as jet fuel sprayed from the ruptured tanks. The fuselage crashed back to the ground and skidded forward as sparks lit the night and then ignited the fuel, turning the aircraft into an enormous fireball. Nathan kept his head down, covering it with his arms as a wave of heat washed over the car. Nobody was going to get out of that one alive.

Chapter Twenty-Four

"I don't know how you made it." A paramedic was examining Nathan at the scene as a pair of EMTs stood by. The storm had passed, but the smoldering wreckage of the plane still belched smoke into the night sky. Nearby rested the SUV, with the roof on the right side cleaved open like a tin can where the left rear wheel of the plane had sliced through it.

"I got lucky, I guess," Nathan answered.

"I'll say." The paramedic looked up once more toward the SUV and shook his head.

As for Nathan's condition, he was scraped up from his wrestling match. The gunshot wound in his arm from earlier in the day still ached. Otherwise, he was generally fine. Now, he sat on a stretcher as this man looked him over. Around them were three fire trucks and numerous police vehicles, lights flashing as the firemen finished spraying flame-retardant foam on the wreckage. Law enforcement officers stood by to enter what was left of the plane. Several ambulances waited nearby, though the EMT's seemed to know that aside from Nathan, they wouldn't be saving anybody else today. The thug from Boston was long gone, apparently.

"You Nathan Grant?" A man in a dark coat approached.

"Who's asking?"

"Lester Watkins, FBI."

"Ah, the FBI. Finally made it."

"Agent Simpson filled me in."

"And?"

"We have some questions for you."

"I'm sure."

"How is he?" Watkins asked the paramedic.

"Seems all right to me, but I'd get him to a hospital to check him out just in case."

"Right."

"I'm fine," said Nathan. "Really."

"Transport him down to Walter Reed," said Watkins. "Uncle Sam will foot the bill."

"Sure," said an EMT.

Watkins looked to Nathan. "You're not going to give me any problems, are you?"

"No. No problems."

"Anything else we should know about while we're here at the scene?"

"No, but I'm guessing you're going to want this." Nathan unfastened his holster and handed over the gun. "Just make sure I get it back when this is all over, will you?"

Watkins reached for the holster. "Just answer me this before you go. What the hell were you thinking, playing chicken with an airplane?"

"I was just trying to do my duty as a good American."

"Is that what you call this?" Watkins looked around in disbelief. The EMTs loaded Nathan into an ambulance. The rear doors swung shut and they headed off, back south toward the nation's capital.

A doctor re-dressed Nathan's shoulder wound, patched up a few abrasions, and generally checked him over. "I'd discharge you," he said to Nathan. "If it was up to me." Outside the door, two MP's stood guard.

"Thanks, Doc, I appreciate it." Nathan wondered if they planned to charge him with anything. They certainly had options. Like Kristin had reminded him, he'd shot Shustov in the back. On top of that, there were the deaths of an entire planeload of Russians. If they were all Russians. He couldn't be sure, but if murder was not on the table, then manslaughter was a distinct possibility. Nathan knew he could potentially be facing a very long sentence in federal prison. Perhaps the rest of his life.

When the doctor left the room, Nathan was joined by a male nurse, holding a sheet of paper in one hand. "And how are you feeling, Mr. Grant?" he asked.

"Fine."

"Are you hungry?"

"No. I could use a cup of coffee."

"Sure, we can take care of that. Cream and sugar?"

"Black, thanks." Nathan checked his watch. It was now a bit before 1 a.m. He waited for his coffee, and was carefully sipping it when the door opened again and Watkins came in, along with another man and woman wearing business attire.

"The doc says you're all right," said Watkins.

"I told you. You planning to debrief me now?"

"Nope. On your feet. You're coming with us."

"Should I be asking for a lawyer?"

"That won't be necessary."

"Where are we going?"

"Some people at the top want to talk to you."

Nathan wasn't particularly comforted by the man's assurances. He'd been running up quite the body count ever since Italy. One could argue that it went all the way back to Lev Volkov in Estonia. There were bound to be repercussions, from all sides. Nathan knew he was going to need to make a choice, though. When the U.S. government came calling, was he going to be a team player, or out on an island by himself? There was still the question of Walter Peacock, Jenna's "supervisor," who might just stab him in the back. Was that where Watkins was taking him now, back to CIA headquarters? Or was it the FBI who wanted to speak with him? Apparently, Nathan would need to wait to find that out. He rose to his feet and followed Watkins out of the room. They escorted him to a vehicle in the hospital garage and placed him in the back seat. Watkins sat beside him, with the other two up front.

After the vehicle pulled out of the parking garage, Nathan watched out the window for clues to their destination. When they turned south on Connecticut Avenue, he knew they weren't headed to Langley. That understanding was somehow comforting. They were on their way downtown, most likely to FBI headquarters. The car continued through Chevy Chase and on into the District. The streets were quiet in the wee hours of the morning and they made good time. Passing through Dupont Circle, he saw couples and clusters of revelers clearing out of bars and all-night restaurants, gathering for a last chat or cigarette on the sidewalk before heading home. The sight made Nathan long for simpler times in his own life, but then, things had never been all that simple. Perhaps when this was all over he'd move someplace that was warm year-round. He'd rent that little shack near the sea, drink coconut water out of the shell and decompress for a year, or ten. That fantasy seemed a long way away from where he sat right now.

When the car reached Farragut Square, it headed south on 17th Street, but instead of circling around the White House, it drove right on up to a security checkpoint at Pennsylvania Avenue and pulled to a stop. A uniformed Secret Service officer exited a booth and approached as the driver rolled down his window.

"George Sanchez, FBI," said the driver. "We're dropping off one Nathan Grant. He's expected."

The officer peered into the car at all four occupants. "Let's see some IDs."

Nathan took out his driver's license and handed it forward along with the others. The officer examined them, looking at each photo in turn and then shining a light in the owner's face to compare them. He took a step back and spoke a few words into a mic. Another officer came out of the booth with a German Shepard. He ran the dog around the car in a circle.

"All good," said the second officer.

A row of round metal barriers retracted into the street. "Drop your visitor at the security entrance, one hundred yards down on the right. An escort will be waiting."

"Thank you, sir." The car moved forward onto the White House grounds and then stopped to wait for another row of barriers to come down. When they were clear, Sanchez drove on through. Ahead, Nathan saw the North Portico come into view. Before they were able to reach it, Sanchez stopped beside a more substantial guard shack just beyond a second fence. Standing outside was a woman in a dark business suit.

"This is you, Grant."

Nathan opened the door and climbed out. When he swung the door shut, the car pulled a U-turn and drove back the way it had come. Nathan was left standing ten yards from the woman, with no idea at all what he was even doing there. He must have been quite a sight, scraped up, in a dirty University of Texas T-shirt, with one arm bandaged.

"Mr. Grant?" said the woman.

"That's right."

"I'm Clarissa Mitchell. I'll be escorting you."

"You got the late shift, did you?"

"Every night, that's my job. Come on, follow me."

As they approached a wrought-iron gate, Nathan heard a buzzing sound and Mitchell pushed it open. He followed her through and then into the shack, where two more uniformed Secret Service officers sat behind bullet-proof glass. Another manned a metal detector. Mitchell flashed a badge.

"ID," one of the officers behind the glass said to Nathan. He slid his license through a small opening. The guard looked it over, then punched some information into a computer and scanned the screen. He slid the ID back. "All clear."

Nathan moved toward the metal detector.

"Anything in your pockets?" said the other officer.

Reaching in, Nathan pulled out his phone and keys, then placed them in a small bowl.

"Come on through," the officer waved him on.

When they'd made it past security, Mitchell led Nathan out of the booth and up a driveway to the right. He knew from prior experience that they were headed for the West Wing. Who it was he might be meeting there, and why exactly, was a mystery. Of course, he'd just been responsible for the deaths of at least six foreign spies. No doubt they'd be wanting details.

Mitchell led Nathan past a Marine guard standing at attention by the door and on inside where they entered a narrow hallway. After knocking on a door to the right, Mitchell ducked her head in. Nathan saw a man in his 20s behind a desk. "Can you tell Ms. Jackson that Mr. Grant is here?" said Mitchell. "We'll be waiting in her office."

"Of course."

Ms. Mitchell turned across the hall and entered another room. "This way."

Nathan followed her, reading the sign on the open door as he went. National Security Adviser. He'd been here once before a few years prior, as part of a briefing, but that time he'd sat in the back and hardly said a word. This time, it seemed he would be front and center. Inside the room, they each took a chair. Nathan wanted to question Mitchell about what they were looking for, exactly, but he knew it would be a waste of time. She wasn't about to tell him anything. He didn't have to wait very long. Within a few minutes, a stocky older woman with a determined gait burst into the room. "Nathan Grant."

"Yes, ma'am."

"I've heard a lot about you. My name is Vanessa Jackson, National Security Adviser. We need to talk."

"Sure." Clearly, she didn't remember him, but that was all right. He wasn't surprised. He doubted she'd forget him after this.

"We're just waiting on a few more people. Can we get you anything? Something to drink?"

"Water would be great, thank you."

"I'll grab that." Ms. Mitchell hurried out.

"I understand you spent some time with the CIA," said Jackson.

"That's right."

"And that you have a Top Secret security clearance."

"Yes."

"That's a good thing. It will certainly assist in our conversation."

Ms. Mitchell returned with a bottle of water and handed it to Nathan. He unscrewed the cap and took a drink. "It's been a long day."

"It's not over yet."

Two more people walked into the room. One was an Army general in full dress uniform, medals glinting on his chest. The other was Walter Peacock. Nathan's heart sank at the sight of him. Jenna's supervisor. The mole himself?

"Here we are," said Ms. Jackson. "You know Mr. Peacock. This is General Davenport, Chairman of the Joint Chiefs."

Nathan rose to his feet. His instinct was to salute, though he'd been out of the service for nearly ten years.

"A pleasure to meet you, Mr. Grant."

"How are you holding up, Nathan?" said Mr. Peacock.

Ms. Mitchell slid two more chairs from the far side of the room and everyone took a seat around Ms. Jackson's desk.

"So, tell us, Mr. Grant, what do you know that we don't?" said Ms. Jackson.

"That depends on what you know."

"Assume we don't know anything. Why don't we start from there?"

Nathan looked to Peacock, afraid to give away anything that might go to the other side. Unfortunately, he wasn't in a position to hold back. "I uncovered a Russian spying operation. More than that, it was an undercover sabotage operation. My former wife was somehow involved, though I'm still unclear on the details of that." Nathan began going through it. They peppered him with questions. The session lasted for over an hour. By the end, he'd given them everything he could. Finally, a silence descended on the room as the participants let it all sink in.

"I am sorry about your wife," said Ms. Jackson. "She was a patriot."

"I'd like to think so," said Nathan.

"You can count on it." Ms. Jackson looked to Mr. Peacock.

"She was working for us, Nathan, as a double agent," said Peacock. "Jenna came to us all the way back when she was in high school, as soon as she returned from Russia. She went right down to her local FBI office and told them everything, about

Volkov and the rest. We put her to work right away, feeding them just enough bogus information to think they still had her. We knew there was an entire cell operating here, but even Jenna didn't know the identities of the others. They communicated using code names. She was trying to uncover the source."

Nathan let this information sink in. In his heart, he'd known it all along, but to hear it now was a relief unlike any other he'd ever known. She was a patriot. "I thought it was you."

"The mole?" Peacock's face showed a mixture of alarm and amusement. "No, it wasn't me. What made you think so?"

"Her supervisor. That's what the Russian files said. It was her supervisor."

"Not supervisor in that sense of the word, it was her handler. Her Russian handler. Not me."

"Then who is her handler?"

"Jenna got instructions via encrypted text message, but we never did figure out who sent them."

"Osprey."

"Yes, Osprey. We're hoping he was on that plane you managed to bring down."

"We have no confirmation," said Jackson. "Preliminary reports are that none of those on board worked for the agency."

"I'm sorry to interrupt, but we have a more time-sensitive issue to deal with," said General Davenport. "Volkov's flight is due to land in 30 minutes."

"Colonel Volkov?" said Nathan. "Don't tell me he's on his way over here?"

"No, not here," said Jackson. "We have information that he's headed to Libya, to coordinate with the Russian mercenary forces that are operating there."

"We need to get downstairs," the general said.

"Yes. I'm sorry, Mr. Grant. We've got to get going. Thank you for your assistance. Your country owes you a debt of gratitude in all of this."

"Enough gratitude to let me be in the room?"

Jackson looked to the general and then to Peacock.

"You're taking him out, aren't you?" Nathan continued. "Please, can I just be in the room?"

"I think we owe him that much," said Peacock.

"There's not much about this that he doesn't already know," the general agreed.

Jackson thought it over and then nodded. "All right, Mr. Grant. Come with us."

The entire group rose to their feet. They led Nathan down the hall to a stairway and then proceeded into the basement. Jackson escorted him past another security checkpoint and into a long, narrow conference room. Computers were lined up on the tables. Monitors covered the walls. A small crowd was already seated when the newcomers entered. Nathan recognized the Secretary of Defense, the Vice President, and the President of the United States, as well as the Director of National Intelligence and a few other familiar faces. Ms. Mitchell found Nathan a seat against the back wall as the rest of the people in the room focused on one monitor at the far end. The image was a live feed from an aircraft, circling somewhere over a desert airfield. Superimposed over the video were a set of cross-hairs, airspeed, altitude and time, local and Zulu. The local time was just shy of noon. Nathan checked his own watch. In Washington, DC, it was just shy of 5 a.m. That meant this aircraft was operating somewhere seven hours ahead. Tripoli, perhaps, or maybe Benghazi. The tension in the room was thick. Very few words were spoken. This was a group of people that were about to rain down death from above. They were about to exact their vengeance. None of them showed any signs of joy over that fact. It was more a sense of dread, or perhaps deep responsibility. Their job was to protect the lives of American citizens, and this was a dark duty that must be done. Blood had been shed on American soil. That could not go unpunished. For Nathan's part, he could hardly wait to see Colonel Vasily Volkov blown to kingdom come. Piped into the room was the occasional voice of the drone pilot as he spoke with his commander. Nathan watched along with everyone else as a jet plane landed on the runway. It was met by three large SUVs. The door to the aircraft opened and a delegation of five men came out. Nathan recognized the tall, narrow figure of Colonel Volkov. He and another man climbed into the first car, while two more got into the second, with the last man in the third. The caravan moved off.

"Do we know which car the colonel is in?" asked the President.

"Negative, sir," an adviser replied. "We believe he's in the second one. We can't be sure."

"The drone has two missiles, correct?"

"That is correct, sir."

The vehicles moved past a bombed-out terminal and headed for a roadway. "Dammit, which ones do we hit?!" said the President. "What's your confidence?"

The occupants in the room looked at each other, afraid to make the call.

"Mr. President, he's in the first car," Nathan called out. All attention shot to the back of the room.

"Who is this?" asked the President, as the cars on the screen continued down the road.

"He's one of ours," said Peacock. "Nathan Grant. He's been on this for quite some time."

"You're absolutely sure?" the President asked Nathan.

"The man killed my wife, Mr. President. I would recognize him anywhere."

This wasn't quite the answer that the President was expecting, but it was good enough. He turned to his generals. "Tell the pilot he is authorized to take out the first car."

"Affirmative, sir." An Air Force general lifted a landline phone receiver and gave the command. "You have authorization to fire, vehicle number one. I repeat, fire on vehicle number one."

Silence filled the room, the knowledge of what was about to happen hanging over them all. Down below, driving on a dusty road in Libya, Colonel Volkov had no idea. In fact, he never would know. One moment he was there, and then came a flash. The first car in the convoy exploded in a violent burst of light. When the smoke cleared, all that was left of the vehicle was a smoking hulk of wreckage.

"Mission accomplished, sir," said the officer.

The President seemed to breathe again for the first time in several minutes. "Thank you, ladies and gentlemen."

Nathan exhaled himself, a deep sigh of relief. Colonel Vasily Volkov was dead.

Chapter Twenty-Five

Nathan sat outside at a fish restaurant in Old Town Alexandria with a view of the Potomac. Across from him at the table was Kristin Simpson. She'd done him the favor of driving him back up to Tipton Airport to pick up his Jeep and now he was taking her to lunch as a way to return the favor. Nathan had the halibut with rice pilaf and a salad. Kristin had a giant bowl of cioppino with a basket of sourdough. It was a pleasant afternoon, with good company, but Nathan wasn't entirely satisfied. What nagged at him was the fact that the identity of Osprey was still a mystery. It was possible that it could have been the man he'd spoken with at Tipton Airport, just before the spy boarded the plane and was blown to kingdom come. That man had seemed to be in charge of the group, though he wasn't embedded within the CIA. None of those on board had any known connection to the agency. U.S. intelligence was fairly certain that Osprey was an insider, or at the very least connected to one. Until Nathan had some confirmation on who that insider was, he would never be fully satisfied. After lunch, Nathan would swing by FBI headquarters downtown to drop off Shustov's phone. Hopefully, they could get something out of it at this point that Nathan hadn't.

"I guess Jackson got you off the hook with the Richmond PD?" said Kristin.

"Apparently."

"That's good. It would be awkward if I had to arrest you after lunch."

"Most epic date fail ever."

Kristin laughed. "Is this a date?" They looked at each other, serious for a moment, their history weighing on them.

"Sorry, I..."

"Forget about it. That's not what you need right now."

"What do I need?"

"To grieve."

"I'll never be done with that."

"You know I'll always be here for you. Us West Texans have to stick together."

"Nobody alive knows me better than you do. For better or for worse." Nathan ate some halibut and admired the view. At a table nearby sat a family of four, with two kids, a girl and a boy. That was the future he'd expected. For now, Kristin was right, he still had a long way to go to process his loss. Nathan knew he'd never fully heal, but all he could do was get through one day at a time, to honor Jenna's memory as best he could.

"I guess they got you out of that mess at the airport, too, huh?" said Kristin.

"They called it an accident."

"Was it?"

"Well, I wasn't actually trying to run headlong into a moving airplane, if that's what you mean."

"What were you trying to do, exactly?"

"I just wanted to keep them from getting away."

"Mission accomplished, I'd say."

Suddenly Nathan wasn't feeling hungry any longer. He put his knife and fork down on his plate. Kristin ate a bit more of her fish stew, eyeing him all the while. "Maybe we ought to get going, huh?" she said.

"I don't want to rush you."

"No, I'm good." She waved for their server.

When they'd paid, Nathan walked Kristin to her car. "Thanks for the help today."

"Any time. I mean it."

"I know that, and I appreciate it." He gave her a hug. She smelled of lilac and roses, and the scent filled him with a deep sense of loneliness but he did his best to push it aside. "Let's talk soon."

"I'll hold you to that."

After turning away, Nathan was walking toward his Jeep when his phone rang. It was a number he didn't recognize, but he picked it up.

"Is this Nathan Grant?" said a voice.

"Yes, this is Nathan."

"This is Jim down at the camera shop. We've got your prints here, all ready to be picked up."

"My prints..." Nathan repeated.

"We thought maybe you'd forgotten."

"No, no, I didn't forget! How did they turn out?"

"A few age spots, but generally not too bad. We can digitize the prints and run them through some software to clean them up if you'd like."

"No, prints are fine, I'll come right by." Nathan hung up and climbed into his Jeep. These were pictures that not even Jenna had ever seen, like a portal back in time, a last little connection to her world. When he showed up at the shop, he paid and left without looking at them. He didn't want his emotions to betray him. Instead, he drove all the way home to his apartment, let himself in and tossed the envelope on the kitchen table. Next, Nathan opened a cabinet and took out a bottle of 12-year aged Scotch whisky. He poured himself a glass, added a squirt of water and took a seat. "Here's to you, babe," he held his glass aloft and then took a drink before opening the envelope and pulling out the stack of twenty-four printed photos.

The first shot was a beach scene. There was nothing special about it. He recognized the location as Ocean Beach in San Francisco. She'd taken him there once. On a bluff in the background was a square white building that he knew to be the Cliff House Restaurant. A few strangers walked along the sand in the far distance. It was the type of photo a young person might take, just learning how to use a camera. The next shot showed a windmill that again he had seen before, this time at the edge of Golden Gate Park. The third showed Jenna's mother, looking twenty years younger and standing by a car, holding one hand in the air. Things didn't really get interesting until the fourth shot. This was not San Francisco. It was not even the U.S.A. Both of Jenna's parents stood in this one, along with another couple their age, smiles all around. They were near the curb at what appeared to be an airport. A row of taxis lined up behind them had the typical signs on top, only Nathan couldn't read them. They were written in Cyrillic characters.

The rest of the photos documented the family trip to Russia, including Red Square and St. Basil's Cathedral. As the photographer, Jenna was behind the camera, not in front of it. Several more of the photos depicted the same four adults, along with another girl who appeared to be roughly nine years old. Finally, Nathan came to one with the two kids together. A young Jenna sat in a booth at a restaurant with the same girl. Both were beaming as they held spoons over giant ice-cream sundaes in elaborate glass dishes. Nathan stared at Jenna; she was so happy in that moment in time, and so innocent. Nothing better existed in the world than a glass of ice cream on a far-away adventure. He looked next at the other girl in the photo. She may have been twenty years younger, but Nathan still recognized her. It was the shape of her face, and the narrow eyes, and the dainty nose. There was no denying it. The girl at that table was Astrid Burns.

Chapter Twenty-Six

"I know I said call anytime, but I only just saw you an hour ago," said Kristin.

"Funny. Look, Kristin, I'm going to need another favor."

"Of course. What is it?"

Nathan explained the situation. When he was done, he went back out to his Jeep and unlocked the center console. Ivan Shustov's phone was still plugged in, and fully powered up. He stared at it for a good long while. There were several hours left until the end of the workday, which meant that he still had time to run it over to the FBI. Instead, Nathan took the phone back into his apartment and then waited until the clock reached 5 p.m. He slid Shustov's phone into his pocket, as well as his own, and headed out the door. Nathan drove straight to Astrid's house, parked the car and walked up to the front entrance. He wasn't sure if she'd be home quite yet, but he hoped that at least Drew Spinsky wouldn't be there. He didn't need that added complication. Nathan rang the bell but nobody answered. He sat on the front steps to wait. Half an hour later, he saw Astrid park her car on the street and head toward him along the walk with a briefcase in hand.

"Look who we have here," said Astrid. "To what do I owe the pleasure?"

"I just came by for a chat. Mind if I come in?"

"Of course not. Please!"

"How's Drew?"

"I'm sorry about the way he acted last time. Apparently he's the jealous type. There's really no excuse."

"I don't suppose I can blame him, he's got a good thing going."

"You're sweet," said Astrid, though Nathan could sense that she was only humoring him. She didn't particularly seem to want him here either. "Cup of tea? Something stronger?"

"Coffee might be nice."

"Sure. It's a little late in the day for me, but come on in."

Nathan followed her through the front entryway and then into the apartment. She placed her briefcase on a side table near the door and then led him into the kitchen.

"Have a seat." She opened a cabinet and took down a mug. "I'm going to have wine if you don't mind."

"Knock yourself out." Nathan sat down and put his own phone on the table.

"Sure you won't join me?"

"Not this time."

Astrid gave him a funny look before taking down a wine glass. Something was different, she seemed to realize, though she couldn't understand what. She poured herself a glass of wine from a bottle in the fridge and then put on a pot of coffee before joining him at the kitchen table, placing her own phone beside her glass as she sat down.

"I made it to the memorial," he said. "I wouldn't have known about it if not for you. I wanted to thank you for that."

Astrid's anxiety subsided somewhat as she gave him a smile that wasn't quite authentic. "I'm so glad. How was it?"

"Fine, I suppose, as far as those things go. I got through it."

"I'm sure her parents were glad to include you."

"They seemed to be."

"How are they?"

"Grieving, of course, but doing the best they can."

"I can't imagine how hard it must be."

"How well do you know them?"

"Jenna's parents? Not very well, I'm afraid. I only met them a few times, when they came out here to visit her. They seem like good people."

"They do. Did you know they went to Russia once, all the way back in 2003?"

"No, I did not know that. Her dad is a professor, though, right?"

"They both are."

"Maybe there was some sort of a conference going on?"

"Maybe."

"You don't think she had anything to do with all of this craziness happening right now, do you? Just because her parents went to Russia once, nearly 20 years ago?"

"I don't know. Her mom gave me a box of Jenna's things when I was out there. It raised some questions."

"What kind of questions?" Astrid stood and opened the fridge once more. She took out a small carton of creamer and put it on the table, along with a bowl of sugar and a small spoon.

"There was a roll of film, undeveloped."

"Oooo, a mystery. Are you going to have it processed?" She poured some coffee into the mug and placed it in front of Nathan, rejoining him at the table.

"I already did."

"And? How did they turn out?"

"Not too bad. A little water damage, but after almost two decades in storage they came out all right." Nathan could tell by Astrid's demeanor that she was beginning to feel nervous. She fidgeted in her seat, drinking some wine like the whole thing was all no big deal, but the forced expression on her face told him she was worried. "I suppose you might find them interesting," Nathan added. "I mean, you never knew Jenna until she was all grown up, right?"

This time, Astrid didn't answer.

"You and Jenna just met a few years ago, here in DC, didn't you?" he pressed.

"That's right." Astrid's face was losing its color, turning ashen.

"You want to see them? There's one in particular that I think you'd like." Nathan pulled the envelope of photos from his pocket. He flipped through them silently, taking his time as he let the tension rise. Finally, he came to the one of Astrid and Jenna eating ice cream. He took it out and tossed it onto the table. "What do you think of that?"

Astrid eyed the photo without moving a muscle. Nathan wasn't sure if she was going to run out of the room or grab a carving knife from a rack on the counter and attack him. Instead, she forced another smile. "I can explain."

"Can you? I'd love to hear it."

"She was trying to protect me. We both wanted to work for the agency. If they knew the truth, they never would have let us."

"And what's the truth?"

"I'm sorry to have to break this to you Nathan, but after that trip, they kept in touch with her."

"Who?"

"The Russians."

"Which Russians?"

"SVR. GRU. I don't know exactly. Intelligence services. They gave her things. They groomed her."

"Are you telling me that my wife was a Russian spy?"

"No. Never. Jenna wouldn't do that. She turned them down, but if the agency found out, she'd never have gotten a job.

We both decided we'd keep it quiet. We wouldn't even admit that we'd met before. It was the safest way. Nathan, please. This job is everything to me!"

"If they groomed Jenna, why didn't they groom you, too?"

Astrid's hue shifted a bit more toward white as she struggled to come up with an answer for this one. "I don't know. They just didn't."

"Never?"

"Never!"

"So, you're not Osprey, then?"

"What the hell does that even mean, Nathan, you're not making any sense?!" Astrid was growing somewhat hysterical.

"I called Jenna's mom, just before coming over here. She told me some interesting things. She said that you and Jenna were inseparable as kids. That was how the families became acquainted, but it wasn't the Taylors who organized the trip to Moscow. It was *your* parents."

"They had an interest in Slavic languages. What can I say?"

"It was your parents who enticed the Taylors to come along. Bill and Miriam thought it would just be a bit of a lark, but according to Miriam, your parents had a lot of interesting connections."

"I know nothing about that."

"Your parents were the ones who convinced the Taylors to send Jenna on a student exchange. Your parents who arranged for her to live with the family of a military intelligence officer. Of course, the Taylors had no idea. They thought Vasily Volkov was a history professor. Is that what your parents thought, too, Astrid? They thought the colonel was just an innocent professor?"

"This is ridiculous, Nathan. You ought to listen to yourself. It's beginning to sound like the ravings of a mad man."

"You want to know what I think? My little pet theory?"

"No. I don't. I think you should be going now."

"I think you went into the family business. I think that both of your parents were spies, and you followed right along in their footsteps. Where do they live now, Astrid?"

Astrid's eyes glassed over. "Out of the country."

"Where out of the country?"

"None of your damned business!" She shot to her feet and pointed to the door. "Get out of my house."

"Somehow you must have convinced Jenna you weren't involved. Otherwise she would have turned you in. Granted, she should have disclosed all of it, but Jenna had a big heart. She wanted to give the benefit of the doubt to an old friend. You played on that."

"Do I need to call the police?"

"Be my guest. I just want to know why. Was it worth betraying your country? Betraying your best friend? And for what? Money? Ideology? The thrill of the game? What was it, Astrid, that made it all worthwhile?"

"All you've got is a photo. That's it. A photo of two girls when they were nine years old."

"There was one thing that puzzled me all along. How did the Russians know that our honeymoon would be at Lake Como? I didn't tell Jenna. I didn't tell anyone. Whoever figured it out must have accessed my laptop, but how? I'm as careful as can be when it comes to that sort of thing. Then I realized, I used to bring my laptop over here sometimes when I'd spend the night with Jenna. How many times did I leave my bag on a chair in the living room overnight? All you had to do was fire it up and stick in a flash drive, courtesy of your Russian friends. Presto, my computer is compromised. Is that how it worked, Astrid? Is that how you did it?" Nathan reached into another pocket and pulled out a different phone. This one was Ivan Shustov's. He opened the encrypted messaging app and typed out a message. *It's all over, Astrid.* He chose *Osprey* from the contact list and then hit send. Immediately he heard the telltale *Ping* as Astrid's phone lit up on the table. "You gonna check that?" Nathan said, but Astrid only glowered at him, the anger raging within. This time Nathan picked up his own phone. "Did you get all that?" he said.

"We got it," came the voice of Kristin Simpson.

"I'll let you in." He walked through the living room and opened the apartment door. A team of FBI agents stormed through, guns drawn. They found Astrid Burns standing by the kitchen table, staring at the photo of her long-lost youth, along with her very best friend; back to the moment it all started to go wrong, the seeds of her downfall.

"FBI! Don't move!" yelled an agent. Two others grabbed her by the arms, pulled her wrists behind her back and slapped on a set of cuffs.

Kristin Simpson stood a few feet further away, watching the proceedings. "Astrid Burns, you have the right to remain silent. Anything you say can and will be used against you in a court of law..." When she'd finished reading Astrid her rights, Kristin looked to the agents. "Take her away."

They were walking down the front steps when Drew Spinsky showed up, with a bottle of whiskey in hand. "What the hell is going on here? Astrid, what's happening?"

"Kristin Simpson, FBI. We're going to have some questions for you, Mr. Spinsky."

Drew looked angrily to Nathan. "What does he have to do with this?" Instead of waiting for an answer, Drew followed along as the agents took Astrid and placed her in the back of a waiting vehicle. Another agent pushed Drew backwards as he argued for answers.

"How do you feel now?" Kristin asked Nathan while they watched the drama unfold.

"I suppose it's all wrapped up. I'd just like to know why she did it."

"You recruited foreign agents yourself for years. You must have some idea. The money, the thrill..."

"And they never seem to think they'll get caught."

"Most times they don't."

"She betrayed her best friend."

"She'll have a long time to think about that, Nathan, in federal prison." They moved down the walk, where another team of agents stood aside. "We're waiting on a search warrant. It should come through any minute."

"I left the photos on the table, along with the Russian's phone. Password is set to 9999."

"Very kind of you."

"Just trying to make things easy."

"We'll need to bring you in for witness questioning, but it can wait until we've got our ducks lined up. Expect a call tomorrow."

"Where is she going, where are you taking her?!" Drew raced back over.

"Mr. Spinsky, I'll need to take a statement," Kristin turned her attention to him. Nathan took one last look and then headed up the sidewalk toward his Jeep. After chasing those responsible for Jenna's murder all across the globe, the job was now complete. He never could have guessed that the hunt would lead him right back home, but for the first time since her death, perhaps the healing process could begin.

Chapter Twenty-Seven

For the first six months after the trial was complete, Nathan traveled the world, doing his best to adopt a carefree, itinerant lifestyle. He was lonely much of the time, and not where he'd expected his life to be at this point, but if anything, Nathan Grant was resilient. He did his best to put himself out there, meet new people and try new things. His savings were enough to power him through for a few solid years, if he was careful. With the Northern Hemisphere moving toward winter, he headed to warmer climes, first in Hawaii, where he rented a small apartment and learned how to surf. Every morning he'd wake at dawn, down some coffee and meet his instructor on the beach at Hanalei for his daily lesson. If the big winter swells were rolling in, they'd give it a miss, but on those bright, sunny mornings when he'd paddle out into the warm, blue sea and catch a wave, it was like therapy for his wounded soul. He'd smile with pride, knowing that Jenna was up in heaven looking down. "Not bad for a Texan," he liked to say.

At the end of the month, Nathan moved on. Hawaii was burning a hole in his budget, and besides, there was so much more to see. He stopped for two weeks in Tahiti, then went on to Fiji where he surfed some more. In New Caledonia, Nathan learned to scuba dive. Then it was on to Australia, and Bali, and finally Thailand. Everywhere he went, he carried Jenna with him, as a partner. He was living for both of them now and the little piece of her that occupied his heart was more than anything a reminder of joy.

When Nathan reached the island of Koh Tao, he'd been traveling long enough. It was time to settle in for a while. He rented another apartment, this time dirt cheap, and began earning his Dive Master certificate. A local outfit hired him on as an apprentice, and Nathan spent his days taking tourists on dive trips to the reefs and wrecks surrounding the island. He developed a routine and a social circle, hanging out with other dive professionals and locals in the evenings. He had his favorite restaurant, and coffee house, and nightclub, where all of the servers knew him by name. Life was not so bad. And yet... a part of him missed the thrill of his old existence. He remembered making contact with targets in hostile nations, trying to recruit assets to the American side. He remembered the sense of purpose he'd shared as a CIA operative, and an Army Ranger before that. There wasn't much purpose in taking a group of Germans on a scuba diving excursion. Sure, it was fun, but sometimes he felt he needed more. All the same, that life was behind him. He tried to move on.

One morning it was a group of Finns that he'd taken to dive the HTMS Sattakuk, a US Navy landing craft just a short distance off shore. They'd donned their gear, plunged into the sea, and then circled the wreck before swimming straight through, down long, narrow passageways once transited by eager young sailors. When they were back on the dive boat, Nathan helped the clients out of their gear, offered them snacks, and then sat back with the sun on his face for the 20-minute ride back to the beach. They were just pulling up when he heard his phone ringing in his wet bag. Nathan took it out and checked the caller. It was nobody he knew, but the number was from Washington. Or rather, Virginia. The area code read 703. He was tempted not to pick it up at all. Why pierce the reverie of a peaceful day in paradise? But then, it might just be important.

"Hello, this is Nathan Grant," he answered.

"Nathan, I hope I didn't catch you at a bad time."

"Who is this?"

"It's Graham Masterson. I'm deputy director of the National Clandestine Service."

Nathan's heart nearly seized up. Somehow he'd known that his past would catch up with him, but he hadn't expected it so soon.

"Are you there?"

"Yeah. I'm here."

"I've got a proposition for you, Nathan."

"No."

"Aren't you going to hear me out?"

"My life is fine the way it is. I'd just as soon leave it that way."

"That's a pity."

"I'm sorry to waste your time."

"Nathan, you know that you owe us. You do understand that, don't you? We had to pull a lot of strings last year with the Portuguese, not to mention the Richmond PD. Tipton Airport was quite a mess as well."

"I think you're the ones who owe me, not the other way around."

"Unfortunately, the director doesn't entirely see things that way. We're still grateful, don't get me wrong. I suppose you could say, we've also come to appreciate your talents."

Nathan hung up. For the rest of the afternoon, he was unsettled. It was his third phone in six months as he tried to keep a step ahead of any adversaries. The CIA had expended a fair amount of resources in tracking him down. He knew they wouldn't give up so easily.

That evening, when the gear was washed and put away and the empty tanks refilled with compressed air, Nathan sat on the deck of his favorite restaurant, watching the sun set over the Gulf of Thailand. He ate a vegetable green curry with rice and washed it down with a bottle of Singha beer. It was as pleasant as could be. People paid big money to come to a place like this for a week, and yet Nathan was living the dream and getting paid for it to boot. The problem was the seed of discontent that still gnawed at the back of his mind. This wasn't the life that he saw for himself. Nathan needed to feel engaged. He needed to be part of a larger struggle. That was his nature, unfortunately. He never would be satisfied unless a larger outcome was on the line. Perhaps it was an addiction, to adrenaline, or the thrill of the struggle. In some ways, it was the same dark thrill that had enticed Astrid Burns to go over to the other side. He knew it was best if he pushed those feelings down, deep inside. If only there was a support group for former special forces operatives, he'd be the first to sign up. Instead, he took a long drink of beer, finished it off and waved for another. His phone rang. This time he recognized the number. It was Masterson, calling again. Nathan didn't pick up.

When he'd finished his next beer, and the sun had gone down, Nathan paid the bill and wandered back toward the apartment he'd rented just a few blocks away. Curiosity tugged at him, but he was afraid to even find out what Masterson actually wanted. Nathan might just say yes. Sitting in a chair on his veranda, he couldn't resist checking his voicemail. There was one new message.

"Hi Nathan, this is Graham Masterson. I'm calling because I want you to know that your country needs you, right now. It's a sensitive issue which of course I can't discuss over the phone. What I can tell you is that there will be a boat waiting for you

tomorrow morning at 8 a.m. on the wharf. The name is *Free
Diver*. It will take you to Koh Samui where a plane will be
waiting. Nathan, if you don't show up, I won't call again. We
know what you went through last year, and I won't blame you if
you decide to decline. I hope you won't see this request as a
burden, but rather as an opportunity. An opportunity to serve
your country once again. Tomorrow morning, 8 a.m."

 Nathan hung up the phone and sat quietly for a while. He
went to his refrigerator and took out another beer before
returning to his seat. He popped the cap. This was paradise
indeed, though paradise would always be here. He took another
long drink. "What the hell," he said out loud. "I might as well
find out what it's all about."

The following morning, his bag was packed. He hoisted it
over his shoulder and walked a quarter-mile to the pier. There at
the end was a sleek white speedboat with the name *Free Diver*. As
Nathan walked along the planks, he passed souvenir stalls, where
vendors sold rings and bracelets, t-shirts and painted coconuts.
He stopped when he spotted a display of necklaces, lifting one
with a shell on a leather strap. "How much?" he asked. The
vendor gave a price and Nathan paid in full before opening the
clasp. He slid the shell off and tossed it into the water, then
pulled the wedding band from his finger, threading the leather
through it. Nathan put the necklace around his neck and re-
fastened the clasp before tucking the ring under his shirt where it
rested comfortably against his chest. "You always knew I'd go
back to it, didn't you?" he laughed to himself.

When Nathan climbed aboard the boat, the captain seemed to
already know who he was. Without a word, the man fired up the
engines, cast off the lines, and headed across the water. What lay
in store for Nathan was a mystery, but he wouldn't allow himself
any regrets. He was headed back into service, in one way or

another. Deep down, he knew that was exactly where he needed to be.

Printed in Great Britain
by Amazon

38198468R00142